Iron Universe Series

Iron Fist

MC D'Alton and Melanie Page

PRESS

Published by Vulpine Press in the United Kingdom in 2021

ISBN: 978-1-83919-345-3

Cover by Claire Wood

www.vulpine-press.com

MC D'alton: To my hubster and the philistines. With all my love.

Melanie Page: To my parents, Ed and Ann. My husband Craig, my kids/kids-in-law, grandkids, siblings and all the rest. I love you. If I told you how much, there wouldn't be room in this book for the novel.

Acknowledgements

To Libby, who has encouraged us all the way and to Claire Wood who has made another great cover! It's such a blessing when you know you have the BEST people in your corner.

Also in the Iron Universe:

Iron Heart

Chapter 1

Marian Finlay was careful not to betray a hint of triumph as she fanned her winning hand face-up on the baize tabletop. The men around her muttered, glowered and shook their heads. With a single glance, carefully and without haste, she picked up the short stack of bank notes from the middle of the table and scooped up the coins in her brown kid glove.

'Same time next week, gentlemen?' She pitched her voice low and deep, in keeping with the well-worn bowler on her head and the sparse ginger moustache gummed to her upper lip.

'Ye've the fiend's own luck, Finlay.'

By her right ear, someone mumbled, 'Snot-nosed clout.'

She shrugged and bade them good night. It would not do to be caught up in conversation; she was too aware of the cost of letting her guard down. She might return next week, but it would be wise to look for another tavern, or at least to lose a few hands. The money was welcome, but while the challenge had palled, Marian had no desire to be discovered.

Stepping from the stuffy back room, she glanced up at the lantern swinging from the bracket, then at the pool of light on the ground. Three feet from where she stood, the cobbles were black as

1

pitch, disappearing into the grey haze. The night had no more than a half-moon wreathed in heavy cloud. Fog swirled around her feet, but beyond the circle of light, she could barely make out familiar shapes. The sea slapped against the docks a hundred feet away.

Marian breathed out a weary, satisfied sigh. She had been particularly careful tonight to moderate the amount of whisky she drank. The big men opposite her had sucked it down like nectar while she had only sipped. Even so, the fresh sea air slammed her senses and she reeled. Slipping her hand into the pocket of her waistcoat, she pulled out a bronze watch and a tiny figure made of metal. With a dexterous thumb, she flipped the watch open.

Ten to twelve.

She grinned and stretched the kinks from her neck. She could not have taken more pride in her watch if it had been an heirloom, handed down for generations. She'd made it as a trial of skill, from the cogs and springs in the workshop; it had been the last test Old Samuels had set her before declaring she had passed her apprenticeship.

She clipped the wee metal fairy, facing backwards, to the lapel of her shirt and pushed the creature's chin with her index finger. The finely moulded wings parted, their insides each bearing a small mirror, and from the spine, a soft light glowed to show the way.

Turning from the white painted door and the lantern, she left the grubby tavern. It was a reasonable distance from the Somerton workshop and from her cramped flat, but better a walk than a barred door in her face. She hunkered down into the heavy greatcoat, grateful for its protection against the autumn night, and pocketed her watch. She slipped her right hand beneath her waistcoat, to the scabbard pressed against her belly, and traced the leather hilt with her fingers.

She decided it would be best to go home via the docks rather than through the narrow lanes in this pea soup. That route, at least, was open, so she'd be less likely to run into a wall—or the prostitutes and their johns who occasionally frequented the laneways. And if the fog lifted, the moonlight would reflect off the sea.

Marian glanced at the wee light shimmering from her collar. It helped naught this night, but it was a comfort. She'd never been fond of the dark; it was the reason she'd built her fairy night light in the first place.

She picked her way past the silent warehouses, her fingers playing over the hilt at her waist. One could never be too careful, but nevertheless, she cursed her overactive imagination and picked up her pace. She was seeing shadows where there were none. Though she was probably safe enough, she had no wish to meet up with any unwanted straggler of the night.

The fog was a comfort of sorts, Marian decided after about fifty nerve-wracked paces. After all, if she couldn't see where she was going, neither could anyone else. Still, she hated fog. Her father had always said it was a bad omen. But then, he'd also said he would be back in a week, and that had been five years ago.

The closer she got to the rhythmic suck and slap of the waves, the thicker the fog grew. There was scarcely a gleam of moonlight, either, except that which diffused through the clouds. Marian raised her hand from the hilt at her waist and, instead, held it out at shoulder height, the better to sense the rough stone walls of the warehouses.

The sound of a ship's bells carried over the water, reminding Marian that she was not the only living being in this pale grey world.

Midnight.

She had travelled three hundred yards before she heard another sound, but those she did hear chilled her in a way the October night had so far failed to do.

Voices. Arguing, then a gasp and a horrible gurgle.

Fighting down panic, Marian pressed her body against the heavy wooden door of a warehouse. It must have been her imagination, surely. But then a soft inland breeze picked up, and the fog parted like the delicate lace curtains in a well-to-do home, revealing a heavily cloaked figure, like a wall of black, standing a few feet before her. The gurgling intensified.

Marian took a few slow steps forward. What was—

Her gasp echoed in the quiet of the night; her wee fairy light had struck a hulking figure gripping a limp bleeding man by the collar.

It couldn't be! Was it?

Spring-heeled Jack!

She didn't believe in the legendary demon who terrorised the streets, but her body acted on instinct. Every muscle tensed to run, and her limbs trembled. Trying to slink into hiding, she stumbled over the warehouse doorstep and went flying, landing on her hands and knees with a bitten-off cry.

A surge of adrenaline pushed her to her feet, but before she had gone two steps, the monster turned. His black cape caught in the breeze, flapping behind him like the wings of an enormous bat. His face was like nothing she'd ever seen—a mask of pure horror, composed of cogs and metal. Her lungs emptied, seized up. Leaning forward and reaching out, he advanced towards her. She staggered backwards. Two huge gloved hands clamped around her throat. Lifted.

Even as the muscles between her shoulders spasmed, her hands came up instinctively, her fingers scrabbling against the leather-gloved hands that squeezed unrelentingly. Black and red waves crashed in her head, throwing up stars. She flailed her arms and legs and, with her last conscious thought, took aim.

Her assailant bellowed in her ear and let go.

She dropped to the cobbles and sucked in an agonising breath. The wee fairy came loose from the jolt and skittered across the floor, its light glinting off the pool of blood and the hilt of the dagger protruding from the limp body. When Marian finally managed to lift her head, she found herself looking up at the largest, most hideous man she had ever seen; if he wasn't Spring-heeled Jack, then he was even more terrible.

A stove pipe hat covered in metallic gadgets crowned a face that was not human. One hand gripped a long blade with a copper skull on its pommel, the other was covered in a thick leather gauntlet backed with silver balls. A cape, gleaming like black fish scales, hung over his back and fell to his knee. At the sight of him, Marian forced out a pitiful scream, but the monster's only response was a bone-chilling chuckle.

'It seems I have found a little *păpușă*. Shall we play? I shall be your *păpușar* and you can dance for me.'

Marian didn't understand some of the words he'd used, but there was no mistaking his intent—he meant to do her harm. She glanced to the body, lying sprawled behind the monster, then tried to scramble back when he reached for her throat once more.

She'd managed to dredge up a scream but, at the same time, grabbed at his sleeve and hauled herself up. On her feet, she took off.

A hollow ghoulish cackle rang out behind her, followed by a swish of air. Something hit her shins, tripping her, and she fell hard on the stone step. He kicked her into a supine position and dislodged her hat. She flinched when he reached out with his blade, pushed her hat back further and snagged a strand of her hair.

'Ah, little *păpușă*, you cannot be allowed to run off and call *polițiști*.' Standing over her, he put a booted foot on her sternum, just between her bound breasts, then pressed the point of the bloodied blade to the hollow in her throat.

Marian closed her eyes and screamed.

***

It was his first time in Edinburgh, but docks were the same in every city and port. God knew he'd seen enough of them. He'd scarcely disembarked on the Merseyside when an urgent message had come through. With one glance at the ship he was supposed to board swinging at anchor, he'd turned his back and had taken the first flight north.

When his dirigible descended with plenty of time before nightfall, he'd headed straight for the taverns, raising half a score of pints and glasses of whisky, letting information from loose lips flow over him. Hints of what he should look for stood out to him, flashing past like trout in a stream, and though he hadn't caught anything yet, he knew he was in the right place.

People were always willing to talk about those who didn't fit in. Sure, this was a city by the docks, and many a stranger had walked its cobbled streets, but few as large as the man he sought, and fewer still with the accent of a gypsy—as described by the flirtatious barmaid at the last tavern. The man was a mystery, probably because no one who'd ever crossed his path had lived to tell the tale.

Now, as Rollo heard the harsh, guttural sound of mangled English, his ears pricked up, even before the bloodthirsty laugh drifted to him through the fog. The voice was deep, raw and unmistakably Balkan in origin, though it came from too far away for Rollo to make out the words. He had no trouble, though, interpreting the strangled scream. Surely, he could not be lucky enough to find his quarry on the first night.

He broke into a run, and a brief gap in the fog revealed three men—one lay contorted in a pool of blood, and another was on his back, staring up at a towering figure in a heavy cloak, like an otter's glossy pelt, and massive boots. He had a sword pressed against the youth's throat—there was no more time.

Rollo turned his body and slammed, shoulder first, into the target. Unbelievably, the coat rippled, like leather bossed with metal, hard and smooth. The body beneath was hard too, with more than just muscle. Rollo twisted sideways and landed on his feet like a cat. His prey hadn't gone down either, but turned slowly, sword at the ready, his cloak undulating behind him. His mask was obviously intended to have a dual effect, but it failed to scare Rollo, nor would it afford the assassin's identity any protection once Rollo was done with him.

He dived again, not for the assailant, but for the cloak. Making sure not to touch the outer shell, he gripped the softer suede lining as he fell, pulling its wearer down with him.

The tactic had clearly been unexpected—which is why it worked. Rollo tumbled over the pile of braced logs, but his victim wasn't so lucky. He went down hard, but he was quick. Rollo barely evaded the smooth thrust of the short sword, and then the killer— for he had most certainly killed at least one of the other men—was on his feet again. He spun out, one gloved hand lifting the corner of the cape. And now Rollo could see why. It was not merely armour but also a weapon. Its edge was a serrated blade, and its scales were thin disks, each the size of a penny, overlapping like miniature protective shields.

Even as Rollo stepped back, the cloak connected with Rollo's chest, its slashing edge slicing cleanly through his waistcoat and glancing off his skin. The brute came at him again, so he tumbled sideways, landing on his feet with equal parts agility and luck.

Though Rollo had inherited the height of his Viking ancestors, this man was taller by a head. As he advanced, he switched and waved his sword from hand to hand. It was past time for Rollo to bring out his own weapon.

He pulled his stiletto free of the scabbard at his left wrist. It was small, fashioned to sit snuggly against his forearm, but it was better than nothing. He caught the onrushing sword with his own blade and thrust, then swung a little to force his opponent back. Again. Again.

The assassin was undeterred. He was scarcely human. Rollo cast a hasty glance at the cutthroat's eyes, could see he knew he had the upper hand, his monstrous mask made even more repulsive by the feral chuckle coming from beneath it.

'Three in one night. What luck!' He jabbed again. 'I will slice you to ribbons and then do the same to your friend.'

Hopefully, the surviving victim had long since gone. Rollo had been on the scene at least a minute, perhaps two, but he'd been weary when he'd arrived and couldn't fight for much longer. He needed to end this soon, or his attacker would.

With the next swing of the killer's sword, Rollo stepped into the blade, using his left arm as a shield, and took the full force of the blow. Wood snapped and crunched. Copper bolts popped free and bounced over the cobbles. He'd hidden his stiletto under his wooden arm, and now, he stabbed it upward, below the sweep of the cape, and caught the other man in the left shoulder. His blood-curdling yell pierced the air.

Pulling the blade free, Rollo reached for the assassin's mask and tried to rip it from his face. But the man pushed him away and twisted on his heel. His cape swung around, its edge like a rawhide whip laced with razors. Striking Rollo's right arm, it sliced through his coat, biting deep into his flesh, and slashed a line along his jaw.

Rollo pulled away, his face bleeding profusely, his left arm hanging limp and shattered at his side. He raised his blade to take a last stand against the monster, but the fog was empty. Taking a breath, despite the pain, he sank to his knees.

Chapter 2

Consciousness was her enemy. It hurt to stand. Her throat was crushed, and her hands, knees and chin had taken the brunt of her fall. She hadn't dreamt him then, hadn't imagined that hideous face and foul stench as he'd squeezed the breath out of her. But she'd come back to the land of the living.

For how long, though?

Sick and dizzy, she blinked and leaned against the stone wall behind her. With her hand trembling from the exertion of being vertical, she pulled her dagger from the scabbard at her waist.

When she'd come to, she'd heard the grunts and thuds of an altercation somewhere behind her. There'd been a terrific crash, as though someone had shattered a crate, and a cry of pain, or perhaps rage. Now, muffled footsteps pounded towards her, and Spring-heeled Jack ran past with his mask dangling from his right ear. Without it, the monster was not a monster at all, just a brutish man with rotting teeth, a scar that stretched across his face, and eyes that had promised her demise.

A single moan rose from the edge of the docks. The words that followed, muttered under the breath, were as salty as a barrel of herrings, but the accent was flat and rough.

Marian hesitated, then wobbled and held out her blade as she moved forward. If she were sensible, she would slink back to her rooms. But then, if she were sensible, she wouldn't have been out in the first place.

Deep breathing came from the scattered heap of logs that fed the steam crane on the edge of the dock. She picked her way through. A gap in the mist, which swirled in the sea breeze, showed the outline of a man, broader than she and taller by a hand's-breadth, she guessed. Not the massive fiend who'd nearly done for her. She nudged a log with her foot; a man looked up, and she jumped.

'I have a knife!' Her voice came out mangled.

'Well, bully for you! Is that the thanks I get for saving your hide?' The man looked her over, apparently unimpressed. 'What in the hell is a whelp like you doing out at this ungodly hour anyway? Looking for a mollisher? You'll catch your death of the pox, boy!'

His face was pale under the smattering of blood. Lush waves of fair hair fell forward over his brow and shoulders, light caught and glimmered in the prickles along his jaw, and his eyes were colourless in the darkness. But Marian's attention shifted to the pieces of broken prosthesis—a wooden arm, shattered on the ground in front of him. The cuff lay in his lap, and a torn sleeve hid his arm's stump from view.

She asked the only question that mattered. 'Is he gone?'

'I believe so. If he isn't, then we're dead, unless you've more than that penknife.'

Marian trembled inside, but she couldn't collapse. She owed this fellow something. He'd risked his life for her after all—and he thought her a man.

'Where do you live?' she asked instead.

'New York.' His voice was deadpan.

She blinked. That explained his accent. 'So where are you staying?'

He shrugged. 'I haven't booked into a hotel yet. The ones around here looked none too salubrious.'

'Well, we should go. But first we need to staunch this bleeding.' Marian pulled a white linen square from the inner pocket of her greatcoat. 'Press this to your face.'

She winced at his obvious pain, but he did as she asked and applied pressure for a minute. She ran a light hand and an eye over him, assessing the damage. Apart from the arm, nothing seemed broken. She shuddered. It could have been so much worse.

'Now, can you stand? I'll take you back to my lodgings and see to that cut.' She picked up the salvageable part of the false arm, but there were too many pieces.

'Leave it.'

The authority in his tone had her dropping the shattered prosthesis. Instead, she held out her hand to him. When he took it, she heaved, and he surged to his feet. Standing, he must have been close to six feet.

He looked around, then down at the broken bits and pieces at their feet. With apparent effort, he kicked the mechanical remains into the water. She followed his gaze to where the monster's victim still lay in a pool of blood. The gash in his throat ran from his Adam's apple to his breastbone.

Marian forced her voice past bruised vocal cords. 'What do we do about him?'

'Nothing.'

'But we ca—'

'Listen, lad. The police will find him soon enough. Believe me, its best we don't involve ourselves in this matter.'

Marian knew he was right. Besides, how would she explain herself, wandering the docks at this hour, dressed as a man?

He nodded towards the alley that would lead Marian home. 'My bag. I dropped it.'

She turned that way, and with her arm supporting him, they made their way slowly from the docks, stopping only so Marian could bend down and collect his bag and her wee night light, which she tucked safely into the breast pocket of her coat. She didn't want any trace of her presence there for the constables to find.

'What is that?' The American leaned heavily on her, his gruff voice edged in pain.

'Nothing much. Come, we have to move on.'

Blood still seeped from the gash on his face, but he didn't seem to notice. He favoured one leg and, of course, he was imbalanced with one arm around Marian's shoulder. For her part, she'd never been so glad to be wrapped in darkness, unseen and unseeable. Every sound, every footstep had her heart jumping from her chest. She hefted the bag higher and staggered a little, then slung it over her right shoulder while fisting the fabric of his waistcoat in her left hand. It was a precarious balancing act, trying to keep them both from falling with the weight of the bag continuously shifting. What on earth was in it?

'Give it here. I'll carry it.' He reached out and gripped the strap, his sour tone suggesting he was wearier than he seemed; either that or he had a problem accepting help.

Marian was not about to argue. The thing weighed more than she did.

'Hang on, let me try something.' She manoeuvred around, with some difficulty, to his good side and supported him as he took the bag's weight.

'Thank you.'

'Don't mention it.' She certainly wasn't planning to tell a soul. She wouldn't dare. And who would believe her anyway?

***

Rollo appreciated the matter-of-fact way the lad—for he wasn't a man—had dealt with the shattered prosthesis. He'd been in no mood to play twenty questions about his handicap. Though the lad had picked it up, he'd then ignored it. Perhaps his desire to get away from the docks overshadowed his curiosity. And no wonder.

As they moved along, Rollo was forced to hunch over, partly because his prop was small and weedy, but also from the pain. His face smarted like a brand. His ribs throbbed and the stump of his arm ached from the wrenching blow. He'd injured an ankle, too, tripping over logs, but it wasn't broken. The bag was heavy; even Rollo found it so, and he was no weakling. Still, he wouldn't have thought it too much for an athletic-looking lad such as this one. He glanced down; he seldom came across men with such delicate features.

They were quiet for the first hundred yards, cautious and hyper-vigilant in case anyone was lurking in the darkness. Rollo looked around. The dock was now behind them, and they'd entered a narrow laneway.

'Where are we going?'

The lad coughed and swallowed, pressed the back of his hand against his throat. 'Not far. My flat is another fifty yards, just around that corner.'

On any other occasion, it would be Rollo dragging some poor fellow to safety. He'd been injured before, as recently as the draft riots in July. He'd been one of the lucky ones, with only a wrenched knee, a dislocated shoulder, and the long gash down his back that still ached occasionally, though it was now nothing but a scar. After he'd helped carry a score of men to the medi-wagons, the oversized unicarriages where they'd heaped the wounded, he'd slunk home under his own steam. But not tonight.

The lad tucked under Rollo's arm paused in front of a dirty red door, its paint peeled and flaking. There was a narrow stair beside it, and Rollo guessed it led to a basement flat.

'Can you make it?'

'Sure.'

The steps almost did him in, and the railing was on the wrong side. He had no choice but to keep a tight grip on the lad's coat.

At last, they reached the bottom. His guide pulled a key from a pocket and shoved it into the lock, which was unlike anything Rollo had seen before. It was a whorled filigree of gleaming steel and copper, with two crescents curving above and below the keyhole. The lad slid the key in, twisted it once to the left and twice to the right. The half-moons popped up and folded back, the lock clicked open, and the lad used his free hand to force the door open.

It groaned, and Rollo knew just how it felt.

They were met by a welcome puff of warm air. The young man helped Rollo across the threshold and into the room's single easy chair, then turned the dial of the dynamic light. Soft illumination flowed out, trickling around the room like lazy honey. The flat had two rooms—a kitchen-diner to their right, with a bed in an alcove behind, and a narrow parlour. A miniscule courtyard, no more than five feet square, was visible through French doors in the rear.

The lad came to stand before the fireplace.

Rollo squinted. 'What are those?'

Half a dozen miniature metal creatures, each no more than two inches high, were displayed on the mantel. There was a beetle, a dove and another he couldn't make out. The lad dug inside his coat, pulled out two more figurines and set them beside the others.

'Is that a …?'

'Fairy and a dragon? Aye.' The lad gave no further explanation.

Rollo's attention returned to his host. In the warm light, it was clear he was oddly built. He had far too many curves, particularly in the seat of the pants, now revealed as he shed his greatcoat. His neck, too, was long and elegant. If it weren't for the moustache …

Rollo closed his eyes and sighed, then winced at the movement of his flaming jaw. The lad took a tumbler down from the kitchen dresser and poured a dram into it. Rollo couldn't think of anything he wanted less than whisky at present.

He gazed around the room. On the rough-edged mantel, beside the odd-looking metal creatures, stood a single pot plant with a bright yellow flower sprouting from its centre. Beside it stood a tiny set of porcelain shoes, such as those worn in Holland. On the table beside him was a tray on which sat a delicate teapot and sugar bowl, with a forlorn-looking rose-patterned cup and saucer keeping them company. Joining the well-used tea set was a single plate, knife, fork, and teaspoon. The single bed in the alcove bore a counterpane patterned in swirling flowers, and over the privacy screen was draped a bottle-green dress trimmed with cream lace.

'What's your name?' The words were a bark, far rougher than he'd intended.

Panic flared in the lad's eyes—his long-lashed, pea-green eyes—but it was gone almost as quickly. Rollo, though, was no longer uncertain.

Digging her composure from some unseen drawer, the girl pulled the gloves from her fingers and answered him. 'Marian Finlay.'

She turned away almost as soon as she'd said it, pulled a small box from the dresser, opened it and placed it on the table beside him. It contained lint, a roll of bandage, a pot of salve.

'You should probably get that cut looked at. It will scar.'

He shrugged. 'I've got plenty of others.'

18

She turned to the hob, poured water from the kettle into a china bowl, then placed it before him and pulled a wad of lint free.

'I can do it.' He dipped the fluffy cotton into the bowl and wiped the stinging gash. The lint came away bloody, so he did it again with a clean piece of lint.

Marian lifted her hands to her head, pulled the brown bowler hat free and started drawing long pins from the knot of her hair. A few seconds later, it swirled almost to her shoulders in a copper curtain, and Rollo forgot that he was in pain. Now that he knew, he could see the femininity of her form; she must be wearing a punishingly strict corset.

'Can I ask your name?' Her voice was cool, but Rollo could sense a tremor in it.

'Rollo Rahgstadt.'

'And you said you were from New York?' She sounded half-puzzled, half-suspicious.

'I am, but my parents were from Norway.'

She stood still for a few seconds and seemed to consider his words. The lazy light was refracted by her hair, flickering like a flame in her rioting curls and forming a rosy nimbus. There were freckles dotted across her nose.

She bent, tugged a snatch of lint free and tipped some sort of clear spirit into it, then used it to wipe her upper lip. The moustache came away, and Rollo caught his breath.

'Pity, it rather suited you.'

She grinned. 'Did I fool you?'

'For a while '

He put down the bloodied pad and rose, his hand on the arm of the chair, his weight on his good foot. She was close. He felt the warmth of her breath and caught the scent of stale tavern air that still clung to her, just as the fog had caressed the city.

His gaze met hers. 'Can I ask you something?'

A shrug. 'If you must.'

'Why do you go out at night dressed as a man? Is it work or play? Because—'

The sole of her shoe connected with his thigh, not a kick but a push, one with enough force behind it to knock him back into the chair. In one seamless movement, she slid a blade from under her waistcoat and pressed the tip against his neck. Shifting her boot to his stomach, she leaned forward, her weight against him, and pinned him down.

Her eyes were cool as malachite, her voice raspy. 'What's it to you? Perhaps I should be asking what *you* were doing at the docks, Mr Plausible Stranger.'

He gave her a pointed look. 'You mean, besides saving your life?'

She blinked, then shuddered, as if she ruthlessly thrust aside the memories that had come rushing back. Regardless, he had no intention of telling her why he was in Edinburgh. His personal motives were none of her business, and his professional reasons were classified.

He looked her up and down. 'It's not every day you see a woman dressed in such a way. Who knows, you might set a trend. But your business is your own.'

She gave a low, sultry laugh. 'Too damn right.'

'And so is mine.'

'Hmm.' She pulled the dagger back, slipped it away, then removed her foot from his belly. Bending, she picked up the pot of salve and twisted it open. It was a heady mix of aloes, lavender and peppermint. 'We should sort out your wounds or they will turn septic.'

He nodded. 'You seem to know what you're doing. Where did you say you worked?'

She handed him the jar and picked up his untouched glass. For a moment, she considered the pale golden liquid. Then, putting the glass to her lips, she drained it and flicked him a smile. 'I didn't.'

He smoothed ointment over the slash along his jaw. It stung and would no doubt hurt like Hades in the morning, but it should heal cleanly enough.

Handing over the pot of salve, he settled into the chair. 'I just wish I'd been able to stop him. Or at least get a good look at him.'

Marian was now stoking a small fire in the grate.

'Spring-heeled Jack?' She stood and faced him with eyes as sharp as the short blade of her dagger. 'His mask came loose before he ran off.'

'He's not Jack. It would be easier for us all if he were.' He leaned forward. 'Would you remember his face tomorrow?'

'It was dark.' She shrugged. 'But one could never forget that ...' She glanced away, then, after a beat, knelt down to tend the fire again.

Her self-assurance was as deep as bone. And she seemed to want nothing from him—that was quite outside his experience of women … but it was refreshing.

'Does this flat not have central heating?'

The place was small, no more than thirty feet front to back and only half as wide. In New York, most buildings were fitted with a SteamTek system.

She looked at him, perplexed, then appeared to translate the concept. 'Oh, yes. The hypocaust system runs under the floors throughout the whole building. It uses the surplus steam from the dynamic lights.' She shrugged. 'But I like my place to feel cosy.'

She stretched and tugged at the waistcoat, then yawned genteelly against the back of her hand.

'I appreciate your hospitality.' Rollo's voice was a touch formal. He was feeling mellow; the fire did give a certain ambience.

'It's the least I can do.'

She turned down the light and disappeared into the alcove, then came back with a blanket that smelled of cedar oil and dropped it across his lap.

'You are welcome to the chair tonight and some food in the morning. Don't try anything. I'm a light sleeper and keep my knife on me. Always.'

He smiled and drew the blanket higher. As she shifted the privacy screen, he heard a few bumps and muffled winces. Turning his face towards the leaping fire, he closed his eyes and, in his exhaustion, no longer saw the flames moving in their bright copper dance.

He had seen the Romanian tonight, though not his face. Still, it had been enough for Rollo to know he was the man he'd been sent to stop. Dracos was a sought-after gun for hire. It was rumoured he'd been trained even before he could walk and had never missed a target. The man was pure evil. Now, all Rollo had to do was track the beast to his lair.

But before he could do that, he had to replace the wreck of his shattered forearm. He'd planned on finding the renowned inventor and his workshop of metal smiths and mechanics, only now he'd have to go sooner rather than later. First though, he had to meet the British contact his superiors had organised. This mission would not await his convenience.

He'd been grateful that Marian had seemed inured to his infirmity. She hadn't so much as mentioned his missing arm, had scarcely even looked at the stump left behind. Neither had she shown disgust or contempt; she had been utterly matter-of-fact. The bedsprings creaked, but the alcove light burned steadily.

After five minutes, Rollo cast off the blanket and rose. He was stiff and sore, and his knee ached; he would feel like the devil tomorrow. He stood on the opposite side of the privacy screen and heard not a sound. Well, none except a slow, rhythmic breathing.

He glanced around the screen. She had changed into a thick full-length nightgown. Her legs hung over the side of the bed and her torso across it. Her knife was clasped loosely in her right hand, which was resting on her breast. Carefully, Rollo lifted the knife away and placed it on the night table. He studied her rosebud lips, puckering in sleep, then noticed the livid marks he'd missed earlier.

No wonder her voice had been husky. Her throat would be one long bruise tomorrow.

The cinnamon dusting of freckles stood out on her white skin under the bright light. Her brows were like swallow's wings, her hair gleamed like coils of the finest copper wire, and in the vee of her nightgown, the swell of her—no! He wouldn't entertain lustful thoughts of a woman to whom he owed so much. Besides, it was abundantly clear she had nothing in common with most women of his acquaintance—they would have no problem slaking his interest, though they'd ask for a handful of coins afterwards.

He pulled the counterpane over her and turned down the light, then made his way back to the chair. He would sleep for an hour or two—but then he had work to do.

Chapter 3

A hideous face leered at her. A metal mouth edged in sharp iron teeth opened wide only inches above her face. She ducked, tried to scream, but a clawed hand anchored itself around her throat and prevented her from making a sound. Marian twisted, punched and … hit the floor with a thud.

She was on her feet in a second, pushing the sweat-matted hair from her eyes and thrusting a dagger at the empty air. It took a minute before sense overcame instinctive panic, and she sagged onto the bed. Heart pounding, her vision blurred, her mouth dry as a tanner's yard.

Damn! Still, nightmares were only to be expected. She wondered if she'd cried out.

No stirring came from the armchair in the parlour; the American must be a sound sleeper. Marian paused, then peered from behind the screen. The chair was empty—no ice-blond head nodded in the chair; no feet dangled over the ottoman.

She moved into the main room where the fire still burned. He must have put more wood on it before he left. She touched the blanket she'd given him. It was folded neatly on the seat, but it held no trace of human warmth, no evidence he had been here at all. She looked around. Even the lint he'd used to wash his wound had vanished, perhaps thrown into the fireplace.

Wait!

In the flickering glow of the fire, a glimmer of white on the mantelpiece caught her eye. In one of the tiny Dutch shoes, which Dr Somerton had given her last Christmas, sat a small twist of paper. She picked it up and held it to her nose, as if it had been a real flower and not one simply fashioned from a slip of thin white cigarette paper.

Sharp blue eyes flashed in Marian's mind and her mouth turned down. A whisper of disappointment fluttered in her chest, but she squashed it ruthlessly. Men were unreliable and she didn't need or want one in her life. As for Rollo Rahgstadt, he'd left without a word. He'd saved her life and she'd done what she could for him, then he'd slipped away leaving nothing more than a flimsy token, almost as insubstantial as her dream.

She held the paper flower above the hot devouring flames for a second, but then, without quite knowing why, she set it gently in the tiny Dutch shoe once more.

***

Marian tugged at the collar of her chemisette. Her mirror mocked her. This was the highest garment she owned, but she still felt as though all and sundry would see through the fine lawn to the maroon bruises beneath.

It hurt to smile, even to hold her head up straight. The bruises beneath her eyes were almost as bold as those on her throat; she had woken screaming and gasping again in the night. Still, she needed to go to work today. Mr Somerton was the kindest of employers, but a hint of infirmity and Dr Somerton would be at her door. It was too great a risk.

The usual ten-minute walk to the workshop took fifteen this morning, given her aching muscles, but finally, she stepped through the small banded-iron door cut into the larger warehouse entrance. Her workbench, tucked behind Mr Samuels', was in the central portion of the room. The front section soared to the heavy oak beams twenty feet above, but over her head was the loft, which housed the storage area and Judith's office. Opposite her was a walled-off area, furnished like a comfortable sitting room, where their clients were fitted for their prostheses. At the back of the workshop was the forge and foundry where Cain hammered out the larger items. In winter, Marian found her situation to be comfortably warm. In summer, she dressed as lightly as modesty allowed and wished it would snow.

She could hear Judith in the loft, but the men were gathered near Samuels' workbench and had their backs to her. Cain had his arms folded across his broad chest; Will ran a nervous hand over his head. Old Samuels' gestured to his workbench again. Strewn over it was the wreckage of an old-fashioned wooden limb—a forearm with its inner mechanism lying disembowelled to one side.

'The sergeant says someone got themselves all cut up and blood-ied. But there is nay sign of a body. Of course, that close to the water, 'tis no wonder ...'

The words toppled over inside her. Had Rahgstadt gone back and moved the dead man? Or had it been ...

She couldn't think of the monster who had almost killed her. Not now.

Marian moved to get a closer look at the fragments on the bench and ice prickled in her veins.

'Detective McIntyre dragged poor Mr Somerton in here fra' his home yesterday morning, just as he was dressing for church, and all to ask him aboot this.'

Marian saw only an edge of the polished wood, snapped in half, a huddled pile of cogs and rivets, and a leather cuff. A lump of cold iron settled in her belly. She didn't need to see more; the memories were all too vivid.

She trod softly towards her own workspace, unwilling to inter-rupt the narrative and even less willing to be noticed. Samuels shook his head. His hair, always smooth like the pelt of an arctic fox, was dishevelled, and the lines on his face proclaimed a man in the winter of his years. The find had shaken him, and she would not add to his fears. He worried enough about her as it was.

It was no use, though. His eyes might be rheumy, but his ears were as sharp as ever. His anxious tone was replaced with that of a doting grandparent, rustled like old parchment.

'There ye are, lass. Judith said you were poorly. Are ye good to work today?'

The other men looked at her, taking their cues from him.

'I'm well, sir.' She was anything but, and as her words forced their way past damaged vocal cords, she winced.

He nodded though, surprising her, and waved her to her workbench where a series of cogs she needed to file smooth for an ankle assembly were waiting for her. It was a painstaking task, which was why she had set it aside last Friday night so she could work on it when she was fresh. Samuels was in charge of assembling the framework, but he was now working on the wrecked wooden forearm, inspecting it, examining each piece with slow, careful deliberation.

When Judith came downstairs at about ten, as was her custom, Marian joined her. She knew all she wished to know about the puzzle Samuels was tinkering with, but to say nothing would be to invite comment.

Marian leaned close, although she didn't need to whisper. 'What happened? Where did that come from?'

Judith shook her head at Marian's raspy voice. 'You are still unwell? Shall I ask Jimmy to take you to the South Bridge clinic? Dr Somerton will be able to give you something.'

Marian shook her head. There was nothing she wanted less. The hard-won freedom she enjoyed would be lost if they learned she had been attacked by some mysterious legend at the docks.

'No clinic. Though tea would be welcome. But, Judith, the broken forearm? Where did it come from?'

Judith threw a handful of chamomile leaves into a teapot and, bending low over the hob, poured water over them. 'Will says some of the pieces were found floating beside the docks and others beneath a pile of logs. There was an attack, apparently. The detective thinks maybe two drunk sailors got into it.' She shuddered. 'Detective McIntyre wants to know where it came from, says that with so much blood, there must be a body. If he can find the owner of that arm, he can find the body and learn what happened.'

Marian turned and looked to where Samuels was still working his way methodically through the wrecked limb. The man had almost six decades of encyclopaedic knowledge of all kinds of mechanical devices and could turn his hand from watches to automata. He numbered more than a score of well-known cogsmiths among his correspondents. The arm would yield its secrets. It would have no choice.

As Judith put sugar and honey into a beaker, Marian's stomach roiled. How long before her presence on the docks was known?

***

Just after midday, the front door swung open. For a long moment, the man who entered was nothing more than a silhouette, but something about the way he stood, the way he moved, froze Marian in her chair. She swallowed, the pain in her throat a sharp chaser to fear.

Twisting his cane around the latch, he pulled the door shut, then limped into the main area and stood in the bright pool of light coming through the multi-paned window. Though she'd noticed his looks the other night, she'd had other things on her mind. Now, however, she caught her breath.

Over his sinfully form-fitting trousers, Rollo Rahgstadt wore sturdy leather boots that hugged his calves, rose to just below the knee, and bore three brass buckles down the outside. The heels and toes were covered in a pattern of steel filigree. The tails of his coat brushed over the back edges of the boots and drew Marian's gaze higher.

His wool coat was trimmed and faced with black satin and lined with crimson. It gaped open casually to reveal a black waistcoat, thickly embroidered with a design of red interlinked cogs, over a crisp white linen shirt. His cravat was white too, and his tall black hat was wreathed in a red silk scarf, pinned at the side with a brooch made of gold-and-silver cogs as large as the palm of her hand. His thick fair hair was pulled back neatly in a leather thong.

Rollo hung the cane over his left forearm, just above the point where his sleeve was pinned tidily over his stump an inch below his elbow, and carefully removed his hat.

In the few seconds it took for Will to rise from his desk, Rollo scanned the workshop and his gaze landed on her. For the merest fraction of a second, his wooden expression lightened. His right eyebrow arched slightly, and he gave a tiny quirk of his lips. In the next moment, all hint of expression vanished, and the stiff mask of civil disinterest returned. But if Marian's talents lay in any one place, it was in reading a person's face; even the straightest bluff at the card table couldn't elude her. Rollo Rahgstadt was even more surprised to see her than she was to see him.

31

Of course, it was logical that a man such as him would eventually find his way here. At that thought, Marian felt her cheeks flare. Why hadn't she told him about the workshop the other night? Perhaps she'd expected to see him in the morning. Or perhaps it had been because the missing hand was not the first—or the second, or even the third thing she thought about when she looked at him. And maybe that was why, after one look at her, his gaze had turned to stone, locking away any expression that might have slipped out earlier.

Will ignored Rollo's missing limb. 'May I help you, sir?'

'Thank you.' Rollo set his hat down on the edge of the desk. His gaze stopped briefly on Samuels' table, then moved to Will. He pulled a sealed letter from an inner pocket of his coat. 'I was told to call on Mr Somerton. Lord Barcaple sent me.'

Will nodded. 'Certainly, sir. Mr Somerton is not in today, but we will tell him ye are here.' He lifted the speaking horn from the cradle on the desk.

A few seconds later, Judith's door squeaked open and she hurried down, then ushered Rollo towards the ground floor client area. Samuels stared at their visitor, open-mouthed. Judith went to the hob and began to make up a tray.

Samuels gestured to Will as he passed, calling him over. Marian had no difficulty hearing their hushed conversation.

'Mr Ayre, did you notice?' Samuels made a sweeping gesture encompassing the shattered fragments of the false forearm. 'This cannot be a coincidence.'

Will put a restraining hand on Samuels' arm. 'Nay. But I have sent an urgent message to Mr Somerton's own messenger and a second to the house. Do you ken the seal on the document? It's genuine. I'd stake my life on it.'

'But a letter from the Solicitor-General? Good heavens!'

Marian caught her breath and her fingers slipped off the ankle assembly she was working on. Rollo clearly wasn't here to see her, but he'd been as equally surprised to see the detritus on Samuels' table, so what business did he have with Mr Somerton? He was welcome to share his secrets with the world, but she'd be damned if she let him share hers.

Chapter 4

Rollo followed Somerton into the office at the top of the stair. The mezzanine floor ran across the middle of the building, and while the ten feet at the front was open to the rafters, the ten feet behind was vented to let the smoke and heat from the forge escape. The left-hand side appeared to be for storage, while this side housed a small, neat office that had a certain feminine touch to it. It was certainly not Somerton's. Its shelves were tidy, the table orderly. On it, a small porcelain windmill stood beside a vase, which held a single stem of lavender. The windmill, Rollo noted, was of the same make as the shoes on Marian's mantel.

He glanced over his shoulder. Through the glass panel he had a keen view of Marian at her workbench below. When he caught her squinting up at them through the narrow void of the staircase, he hid a grin. He must find a way to speak with her; she had seen Dracos and lived to tell of it. All he'd seen of the monster that night was shadow, fog and metal mask. He needed a face to put beside the cryptic description given to him via head office, and Marian had confessed to seeing at least half his face. He'd have asked Doyle, his contact, to put a man out to watch her, but then he'd reconsidered.

She'd been in disguise, so Rollo was certain she'd be safe from the murderous grasp of the Romanian, at least for the moment.

Turning from the window, Rollo studied Somerton, who stood opposite him. He was tall, though not as tall as he, with a whippet-like grace. He looked ordinary until one studied his eyes. They were odd, almost unnaturally bright, the colour a vivid hazel but flecked with copper. Both Barcaple and Doyle had spoken of this man and his sudden emergence from a shadowy half-life. He was now, apparently, a prominent ornament of the city, a famous limb-maker, and was said to be some sort of genius—one who had traded his soul for knowledge.

What rot! Besides, it was irrelevant. Rollo needed a new limb, and Beauden Somerton was the only man in Scotland who could help him. He held out the letter, but Somerton made no move to take it.

'You will want to read this,' Rollo told him.

'You are an American, Rahgstadt?'

Rollo tipped his head. 'You have a good ear.'

Somerton took the letter and glanced at the seal but did not open it. Instead, he put it on the tabletop, tucked his hands behind his back and looked Rollo in the eye.

'The remains of the prosthesis the police found floating in the water at the docks, those downstairs on my cogsmith's table … were they yours?'

A flicker of surprise ran through Rollo, but it was gone as quickly as it had come. Of course this man would make the connection, yet he could know little with any certainty. Even if Marian had spoken of her experience—and Rollo would bet against it with his last shilling—what could anyone know? He'd returned to the docks well before dawn to ensure the damned hand had gone into the sea, but he'd found nothing. Nothing except a couple of broken cogs and a leather strap.

'Arm? What arm?' Playing dumb might gain him a moment to think.

Somerton's gaze dropped, travelled the length of Rollo's left arm and back again. 'Indeed, Mr Rahgstadt.' He spoke as if he were reasoning with an idiot. 'A wooden hand and wrist, badly smashed. I was dragged away from my Sunday breakfast by a very irate detective to examine it.'

Rollo sighed and nodded to Barcaple's letter still lying on the table. 'You *will* want to read that, Somerton.'

Discreetly, he flexed his aching knee. The inflammation had subsided a little, thank heaven, but he'd been left with a purple bruise the size of a grapefruit on his thigh and a deep ache in his knee joint. He'd poulticed it with herbs in a cheesecloth bag, though he hadn't been able to do much about the slash to his face.

Somerton snapped the wax and removed the letter. A moment after he began reading, he looked up. 'You work for Pinkerton as a detective?'

'Is that surprising?' Rollo kept his expression neutral. The Pinkerton National Detective Agency made an excellent cover for his real work—the need for information, which had spawned the Culper Ring, hadn't ended with the revolution.

'How did you …? Good God!' Somerton ran one hand over his face, then shoved his fingers into his hair and tugged it. 'I cannot believe this.'

In a way, Rollo could appreciate that for Somerton the challenge was as much moral as medical. But too bad. Rollo could not afford to pander to his qualms.

He shifted and, out of the corner of his eye, glimpsed Marian and her friend staring up at him through the staircase. He would speak to Marian later. For now, she was a distraction. Reaching towards the window, he pulled the cord on the venetian blinds, causing them to slither down and hide the women from view.

'Well, Somerton,' he said, 'can you do it?'

***

Rollo and Somerton made their way down the steep stairs to the ground floor of the workshop. Marian and the other woman were there, as were two men who appeared to be in their thirties, plus a thickset man with muscles like a blacksmith, and an elderly man who had the look of a gnome about him. As Rollo walked past Marian, he kept his eyes fixed on the back of Somerton's head, though he could feel her gaze boring into him.

Somerton stopped. 'Judith, Marian, I will not need you here for the rest of the day. You will be paid, of course. Enjoy your free afternoon.'

Judith nodded, gave a little bob. 'Yes, sir.'

When Marian looked over at Rollo and paused, the gnome cleared his throat, a sound that prompted her into action. 'Yes, Mr Somerton.'

Despite the huskiness in her voice, Rollo heard her anger. She didn't like being banished. Well, he could understand that.

As the door shut behind the two women, Somerton gestured at the men. 'Rahgstadt, I would like you to meet William Ayre, my engineer and fitter, and his brother James who will assist me. Here, too, is my smith, Cain Murdoch, and my cogsmith, Mordechai Samuels.'

Rollo nodded, but the expressions on the others' faces suggested their goodwill was not to be counted on. 'Gentlemen, a pleasure.'

Somerton addressed his workers. 'Mr Rahgstadt has come to us with a letter from the highest levels of our government. We are to fashion a special prosthesis.' He let his gaze rest on each man in turn. 'You can never discuss this, gentlemen. Speak not a word of it to anyone, not even your priest.'

It was the old man who spoke next, his voice as wispy as tendrils of fog. 'This is the owner of the wooden hand the detective brought in?'

Rollo nodded. 'I am.'

Somerton pulled out the sheet of paper that had accompanied Barcaple's letter and laid it face up on his desk. 'This is the design we've been asked to work from. We'll need to adapt it, of course, but this is essentially what we've been asked to make.'

Will Ayre looked over the plans with an expert eye and said nothing, but his brother put a hand on Somerton's sleeve. 'You would never make this, sir. You've no love for weapons, and this—'

Somerton shook off Jimmy's hand. 'I will make it, for I must. It is not in my power to refuse a direct order from Her Majesty's Government.' He looked at Rollo. 'You will appreciate, sir, that my work involves helping those who have been damaged, often by war. I am not in the business of creating weapons or helping one man kill another.'

'I wish that I was not, Mr Somerton. But sometimes our enemies give us no choice.'

A shadow passed across Somerton's face, an old grief, Rollo guessed, and he nodded. 'Very well. Jimmy, please go and get the medical kit. Will, what do you think?'

Will traced the plans with a blunt fingertip. 'Aye. We will need to make changes. There is not eno' room in this design, but the basics are sound.' He looked up at Rollo. 'Did ye draw this?'

Rollo shook his head and gave thanks for Doyle's many legitimate talents. 'No. It was done by ... an engineer of sorts, but he has training as an artist. So, do you think it is viable?'

Seemingly lost in thought, Somerton stood still, his eyes closed. After a minute, they sprang open and had a glow about them that made Rollo think of a saint in a painting.

'Will,' Somerton instructed, 'fetch the prototype. I think we can adapt it.'

At the order, Will's eyes took on the same fanatical gleam. Perhaps it was contagious. He hurried over to a cupboard behind the desk, turned a key, took out a wooden box about a foot square and brought it back.

Samuels approached Rollo and pulled a measuring tape from his pocket. 'Will you be seated, sir, and let me see your arm?'

Jimmy reached for Rollo's lapels. 'Let me help ye with that, sir.'

Rollo's coat came off, then Jimmy unpinned and folded back the sleeve of his shirt. The thought of being exposed to the scrutiny of others, even dispassionate medical observers, still made his stomach squirm after all this time.

Somerton depressed the lever on the large dynamic light that sat on the desk, then bent over Rollo's arm with a magnifying glass the size of a saucer. He looked at it from every angle and made notes on a thin scratch pad.

'May I ask under what conditions you lost your arm?'

Rollo forced himself to answer, though his instinct was to shove the men aside and flee. 'Sepsis, as a result of meningitis.' He kept his voice matter-of-fact. 'I was one of more than two hundred cases that year.'

'You were a child?'

He shook his head. 'I was twenty-two and in the US Marine Corps. I joined up not long after Admiral Perry came back from Japan. Since then, I've worked for the government in other capacities.' He stared up at the window, set high in the front wall. It was so much easier not to feel.

'The surgeon did a good job.' Somerton's dispassionate tone brought back some of the sickening sense of loss, of a life turned upside down.

Rollo scowled at his uncovered stump. 'Better than dying, but not the ending I wanted. I dare say you've seen enough amputations to judge.'

Somerton nodded. 'I'm not a medical practitioner myself, but I have some knowledge of surgery. My father lectures in medicine and my wife is a doctor.'

'Your wife is a—' His voice caught the moment Somerton lifted the lid off the wooden box. 'My God! Is it made of steel?'

Somerton lifted a skeletal hand from the box and set it on a stand. Perching on a stool in front of Rollo, he shook his head. 'No. We call it star metal. A supply came to us from Germany with a selection of other metals, alloys and ores. We have an agent in Europe who is always on the lookout for new metals we can adapt and use. This one is like gregoryite, which was discovered by a British chemist. It's remarkably similar to Klaproth's titanium. It melts a little higher than iron, but it's malleable.'

'Why not use steel, or even copper?'

Somerton turned a radiant smile on him, his eyes shining like bright gold. 'Weight is a concern. This is light, much lighter than steel, and not prone to oxidisation like copper. We are still experimenting, but I think this might well be one of the hardest metals known to man.' He looked squarely at Rollo. 'You know, Rahgstadt, if we do this, you will become a living weapon. A procedure such as this has not been carried out before, but it's only a matter of time before word gets out. I know what it is to be seen as different and to carry a dangerous secret. You'll be painting a target on your back.'

Rollo studied him. The man meant well, but there wasn't an alternative.

'I know,' he said. 'But neither of us has a choice.'

Somerton met his eyes, as if to read his resolve, then turned his gaze back to the work at hand. 'I'm going to ask you to trust me.'

Will appeared at his elbow with a white cloth, on which lay five gleaming white pins and a selection of copper cords.

'What do you intend to do?' He struggled to keep the tension from his voice.

'I am going to fit these electrodes to your stump.' He turned his head. 'Jimmy, the numbing cream, please.'

Jimmy put a bowl that smelled strongly of carbolic acid in front of him. Somerton used it to clean Rollo's stump twice. Then, setting the bowl aside, Jimmy opened a small jar of brown goo and handed it to Somerton.

'This is an invention of my father's,' he explained as he wiped some of the ointment over Rollo's stump. 'He calls it topical anaesthesia. The discomfort when I fit the electrodes should only be slight.'

But as Somerton inserted the needles into various areas below his elbow, Rollo turned his head away. As promised, he felt no pain, only pressure.

'These will connect to your central nervous system.'

Rollo was no physician, but he had heard of that. Glancing down, he caught Somerton clipping the pins to the copper wires. He closed his eyes. This was a mistake. He could wait until he got home to New York and find someone there. But then, he realised, the pressure had died away; all he felt now was a distant tingle.

Somerton flicked a tiny switch beside the skeletal hand's index finger. 'Now, close your eyes and imagine you're opening and closing your hand.'

Rollo eyed Somerton dubiously, cursing the moment he'd asked Doyle about the limb-maker. And yet, some tiny fragment of hope, buried in the depths of his soul, was shouting at him to trust this apparent genius. Closing his eyes, he imagined his left hand as it had been before illness had robbed him of it. He felt the oddest tickling sensation at the front of his skull.

'Open your eyes, Mr Rahgstadt.'

'No!' His voice cracked. 'I can feel my …'

'And you can move them.'

Rollo opened his eyes to see the bony fingers on the stand—which was a foot away from him—curling and uncurling.

He forgot to breathe, could do nothing but stare. It was as though the flesh had been stripped from his arm and he could see his own bones. And they were obeying his whim! He turned the hand over, and the thumb traced an arc through the air. His heart raced; he wanted to look away, and yet, he could not. It was some kind of arcane miracle. Once he would have sold his soul to have his arm back, but now that he'd taken the first step to becoming a living weapon, the cost might well be his life.

Some time later, Rollo stepped out into the late afternoon chill. The sun hid behind the houses and fog would descend again soon.

His mind was still reeling. Beauden Somerton was certainly the genius Doyle had promised.

He looked down at his stump, pinned into his coat sleeve once more. He could still feel the pulsing current of the electrodes Somerton had connected, though the wrist and hand had not been attached yet—that would require a surgical procedure. But now, at least, Rollo knew the magic of science would give him back his hand.

He wanted to return to his hotel, pour a glass of whisky and let his new reality sink in. But first, he had to find Marian and persuade her to tell him all she remembered of the monster from the docks.

Chapter 5

Marian took one look at the body and drew back from the crowd gathered outside the tavern. She never frequented this particular establishment—it was too close to home for her to risk being recognised—but no one was looking at her now. Five feet in front of her, a young bobby drew a hessian sack over the body's gaping wound and staring eyes, leaving only the legs, clad in serviceable brown tweed, visible to the onlookers.

Blood pooled under the body and soaked into the hessian, changing the colour of the coarse fabric to brownish purple. The cloying scent of copper reached Marian's nostrils, as did other unpleasant odours inseparable from death. She was grateful she had not been the one to find the body.

Close beside her, an old woman crossed herself. 'That's the second in two days,' she declared to any who would listen. Several nodded.

A shudder ran though Marian, and the pie and ale she'd had for supper roiled in her stomach. Two days ago, she'd had a boot on her chest and a blade at her throat.

But then the woman's words registered. The second? Only she and the American had seen the body of the poor man down at the docks. His wounds had been identical to those of this victim, except that body had disappeared. Had it been recovered?

Someone else piped up. 'Nay. 'Tis the third. Constables pulled a body from under the dock at low tide.'

A ripple of horror made its way through the crowd. The docks were rough and seedy, all kinds of petty crimes were carried out there, but brutal murder was rare. Or at least it had been.

The old dame nodded. 'Poor lad that were killed last night, could have been kin to this 'un. As like as brothers, they were.'

The bobby rose. 'We'll be taking statements from all who saw aught. Especially any who were by last night.'

People in the crowd began whispering to one another. A young man arrived, black bag in hand, and knelt beside the body.

The old woman shook her head and turned to Marian. ''Tis nay by chance I'll wager that two such were killed, within half a mile of one another.' She looked Marian up and down. 'Be glad ye are a lass and not a lad with that hair.'

As Marian left the scene, an icy finger trailed the length of her spine. Two murders, less than a day apart—both victims were young men, redheads, and had been wearing brown suits. But the other man had not been. She knew that better than any. He'd worn black and a long, heavy coat. There could be no connection. But then, when she was less than fifty yards from her door, realisation hit her like a club to the skull. The killer had seen enough of her to know her hair colour and something of her face. Only he had seen a man.

Her last steps were taken blindly.

As she starced down the stair to her front door, a voice, disembodied, spoke to her. 'You look like you've seen a ghost.'

A man stepped from the shadows, his body rendered invisible by his black garments.

Marian puLed her dagger free and thrust it below his chin. Only then did she recognise him, with his pale hair falling around his face.

'What in heaven's name are you doing here! Don't you know it's rude to scare people that way?'

He looked her over slowly before pushing the knife down. 'Sorry. I didn't think knocking on a door was a crime in these parts.'

'In your case, it should be.' She wriggled past him and slipped her key into the lock. 'I apologise. It's been a trying afternoon.'

'I don't see why. An unexpected free afternoon to spend with your friend is a bonus, I would say.'

She opened the door an inch, then stood with her back to it. 'Did you leave something behind when you were here?'

He crossed his arms over his chest and his ice-blue eyes sparkled down at her. 'Are you going to invite me in?'

'It wasn't my intention, no.'

Rollo considered her. 'I need to speak to you.' His demeanour was polite, but his eyes grew a shade warmer.

'Why? You had nothing to say to me at the workshop.'

'How remiss of me.' He stepped forward, giving her no choice but to edge backwards through the door. 'Perhaps, good afternoon, Miss Finlay. I do hope you are recovered after your encounter with a murderer. How is your crushed windpipe?' He leaned against the door frame. 'Is that what you wanted me to say in front of your colleagues?'

'Not exactly.'

'Well, as you don't want me to ruin your disguise or put an end to your night-time strolls, perhaps it's as well that I didn't. And I don't suppose you revealed your knowledge of the smashed hand on your colleague's worktable? I'm sure Somerton would have been interested to hear your contribution.'

Hot blood flooded her face, and she clenched her fists.

'Now,' he continued, 'shall we have this discussion inside?'

'Of course. Do come in.' She'd sneered the words at him, but when she let him pass, she took guilty pleasure in his size and comforting strength. It was no wonder after the revelations of the last few minutes.

Her tiny gizmos let out a chorus of tweets, mewls and flutters as she shut the door.

'What are these exactly?' Rollo reached out to touch the delicate silver tissue of the gizmo fairy's wings.

'Nothing. Just some small projects I tinker with in my spare time.' She moved to cover the gizmos in cheesecloth. 'Don't touch her, please.'

Rollo lounged against the wall opposite the fireplace. She bustled into the kitchen alcove, took down a teapot and a tin box. 'Would you like tea?'

'You wouldn't happen to have coffee, would you? I've yet to acquire a taste for brewed leaves. And ... I need to know everything you saw the night you were attacked.'

She thumped two teacups onto the narrow bench. 'Coffee has never crossed my threshold and never will. And why do you want to know what happened? You were there. You saw everything.'

'I wasn't there at the beginning. And I never saw his face.' His voice grew softer then, more earnest. 'It's a matter of the highest importance, Marian. Please.'

She flicked a glance at him, by no means mollified. 'Is it the same great matter you shared with Mr Somerton? And that he shared with all the men in his employ?'

'I did not tell your employer to send you away. I only told him it was secret and dangerous.' Rollo ran his hand over his head and, closing his eyes, rubbed the back of his neck.

Marian saw, not the dismissive arrogance she had expected from him, but a tension in his brows that spoke of stress and desperation.

She caught hold of his sleeve. 'What are you involved in? Why would Beauden Somerton, a man with more honour in his little finger than most fellows I've met, not call the police on you?'

He shook his head. 'To tell you would be to put you at risk.'

Marian slipped her hand from his arm and placed the kettle on the stove plate. Then, reaching into her pocket, she pulled out one of her gizmos, a tiny replica of a dragon that had a flint for a tongue. Its tail automatically curled around her finger as she pressed its mouth to the stove plate and flicked the gas switch. A ring of blue flame danced around the kettle.

She scooped leaves into the ball-shaped infuser and dropped it into the pot. 'Am I not already in danger?'

'I don't think so. It was dark. I could barely make out the assailant. And you were dressed as a man, so your identity is well disguised. But I'm hoping you remember his face and can describe it.'

Eyes of earth, and a scar straight from the pages of a penny dreadful…

Marian shuddered and dropped into a chair. 'I think we both saw enough of each other that night … for him to have a fair idea of what I look like, too.'

Rollo dragged over the other chair and put his hand on her forearm. 'What are you not saying, Marian?'

'The murders, of course.'

He paused. 'What murders?'

She stared up at him. 'Are you telling me that a man of your profession—for you are some sort of policeman, for certain … Are you saying you haven't heard about the murders that have happened under your very nose?'

'There was a man killed yesterday,' he acknowledged, 'last night, outside a tavern, not half a mile from here.'

'Yes. And another today, not three hundred yards from this flat. While you were waiting for me, no doubt. Both were lads in their early twenties. Both had red hair and wore a brown suit.'

Silence crept into the flat like mist. In the stillness, the kettle began to hiss.

Marian rose, poured two cups of tea. Without a word, Rollo stood and reached into her cabinet for the whisky bottle she kept there. She did not attempt to stop him as he tipped a generous dram into each cup.

They sat and sipped, each occupied by unhappy thoughts. Finally, Rollo sighed. 'He's hunting down the witness to his kill, though he obviously only got a glimpse of you.'

'Yes, I'd worked out that much for myself.' Marian swirled the tea in her cup. The whisky was a clever addition; it eased the knotted nerves in her shoulders and the ache in her throat.

'Then, I'm afraid, my dear, that I'm going to have to commandeer more than just your recollections.'

Marian drained her cup and stood. 'Not without telling me who I am facing and why. I deserve that much.'

Taking her empty cup and his, she put them in the sink. Rollo turned in his chair to face her, drummed the fingers of his right hand on the tabletop and watched her with an impassive look.

'I will tell you this,' he said. 'The man you were unfortunate to meet on Saturday night is a figure of legend. He lives in the shadows of the criminal underworld and is responsible for many deaths. Not only are his murderous services for sale to the highest bidder, but he is well-known for not leaving loose ends.'

'And I'm a loose end.' Surprised by how calm she sounded, she crossed the room and put her dragon gizmo on the mantel. 'So why are you here? To stop him?'

'I cannot say.' He lifted a hand at her glare. 'I really cannot, and it wouldn't mean anything to you anyway. But you are the only person to have seen him and lived. He fears you. The trail of bodies he's leaving behind says so. But that will be his undoing.'

Marian swallowed hard. She should be curled in a ball, screaming. And she *was* frightened, but …

'What do you intend?'

'To play into his hands. To use you, or your alter ego, as bait.'

Her stomach flipped. 'Because three dead Scotsmen aren't enough for you? I must walk into the lion's den?'

He put his hand on her arm and squeezed gently. 'Because he is looking for you. People will continue to die until we stop him. And while he walks, you are not safe, Marian.'

She hated that he had a point. How she wished she had stayed home with her gizmos on Saturday night! But the memory of the young man lying on the cobbles haunted her, and she felt the warmth of Rollo's hand on hers.

She met his gaze with her own. 'No promises. Tell me your plan.'

***

Rollo was the first to disembark when the unicarriage pulled up outside the cathedral. Marian gave a hiss of surprise at their location but said nothing. His failure to answer her questions to her satisfaction meant that she'd been studiously ignoring him for the past hour.

He refrained from assisting her out of the vehicle; to do so would only draw attention.

They made their way past the cathedral, then he led Marian across the street and into Picardy Place. At the door of number eleven, he rapped the knocker twice.

Marian hung back. 'Before we go in, I want to know why we are here.'

Footsteps sounded on the other side of the door as Rollo bent to her ear. 'You've seen him. The man who lives here will be able to draw an authentic likeness. Forewarned is forearmed.'

A manservant opened the door. Without a word, Rollo handed over a card.

'Very good, sir. If you would care to wait inside, gentlemen, I will let Mr Doyle know you are here.' The servant passed through a door and returned a few moments later. 'If you would come this way, sirs.'

He led them to the main parlour, a room which faced the street and featured long sashed windows. A man of moderate height with thick nut-brown hair pulled the curtains tightly closed. He did not look best pleased.

'Rahgstadt. It was a risk coming here. I hope you took precautions.'

'Of course.'

'Hmm. And this is …?' Doyle extended a hand towards Marian.

Rollo smiled, a wicked thrill warming his voice. 'Mr Charles Doyle, may I introduce Miss Marian Finlay?'

Doyle took the shock well. He'd turned an embryonic handshake into a greeting more appropriate for a lady.

'Enchanted, Miss Finlay,' said Doyle. 'When Rahgstadt told me about you, I didn't realise …'

Rollo knew quite well to what Doyle was referring. Once he'd discovered Marian's true sex, he hadn't been able to help but notice her rounded curves either. Trousers on a lady, particularly this lady, were a serious impediment to his concentration.

53

He turned to her now. 'Marian, Mr Doyle here is my contact while I am in Scotland. He gives a thin veneer of legality to my presence.'

Doyle picked up a half-full decanter. 'May I offer you both a drink? Whisky, Rahgstadt? Some tea or a sherry, Miss Finlay?'

Rollo shook his head. 'Miss Finlay might like tea. She is enamoured of the confounded stuff. But I cannot indulge. We have ... an important errand to run tonight. Unless ...'

'Unless I can offer you coffee?' Doyle lifted a speaking tube and placed an order for tea and coffee. 'Now, how may I help you?'

'Marian saw the man we're seeking. I would like you to make a sketch from her description. It might prove useful.'

'Of course.'

Rollo felt the weight lift from his shoulders. He'd deemed it useful to have an image of the assassin, particularly if anything happened to him or Marian. He would, of course, take every precaution, but his training dictated the mission come first.

They made small talk until the maid delivered a lavish tea tray. Eager to be gone, Rollo was in a ferment, but he understood that Doyle was attempting to set Marian at ease with his tales and recollections. At last, he went to a bureau on the far side of the room and withdrew a sketchbook of thick artist's paper and a handful of drawing charcoals.

'Tell me what you saw that night, my dear. Was his face long, broad, thin?'

Rollo watched from a corner of the room, sipping a second cup of coffee and aiming to be as unobtrusive as possible, but as Marian took a long shuddering breath and began describing what she'd seen, it was hard to keep his place. Listening to her story, he felt the urge to go to her and enfold her in his arms. Because although he'd come to her aid that night and had fought off the assassin, he'd given no thought to the fear she'd suffered. He only wished he could go back to that moment and wrap his arms around her, instead of berating the young man he'd thought her to be. But it was too late now; first impressions mattered. It didn't help, either, that she knew he was keeping secrets from her. Even if he wanted something more from her, it was impossible. And soon, one way or another, their association would end. Which was for the best.

On the other side of the room, Marian watched Doyle draw, made suggestions for alterations. Her cheeks grew paler until, at last, she nodded. 'Yes, that's the monster I saw.'

She moved to where the tea tray still sat and waved away Doyle's offer of a medicinal tot. Rollo crossed the room and took from Doyle's hand a charcoal sketch that was enough to put fear into the most hardened heart.

Dracos's face, which had been hidden behind an iron-and-copper mask, stared back at him. A broad brow, dipping slightly at the temples, bulged over high cheekbones. From there, his face tapered to a sharp, stubbled jaw. His lips were thin under a slightly bent aquiline nose, while his ears were high and stood out from the head. He had a gold hoop thrust through one ear. Dangling from the hoop was a small anchor with a rope twisted around it. He wore a broadbrimmed hat encircled with a leather strap on which was attached a single lens and a silver skull. But his eyes were what chilled

Rollo's marrow. They were not black as he'd supposed, in a face seen only in the dark, but were light and narrow. They had no soul.

'You've outdone yourself, Doyle.' It was an amazingly detailed image, almost as good as a daguerreotype. 'Will you keep it here for the time being? Make a couple of copies?'

Before Doyle could reply, the door opened and a little boy of perhaps four or five ran in, paused when he saw Rollo and Marian, then ran to Doyle and wrapped both arms around his leg.

'Arty! You should be in bed.' Doyle shook his head. 'Sorry, Rahgstadt.' He bent down. 'Arthur, where are your manners? Please, greet our guests.'

The child extended his hand to Rollo. 'Good evening, sir.'

He detached himself from his father's leg and crossed the room to where Marian sat on the chaise, sipping her tea. He peered at her for a moment or three, then held out his hand politely. 'Good evening. Why are you dressed like a boy, please?'

Rollo had to laugh, but Doyle let out a groan and crossed the room.

Marian held up a hand. 'Please, he is just observant. I'd like to talk to him.'

Over the next two or three minutes, Rollo went over the plan with Doyle, but he could not help sneaking glances at Marian entertaining little Arthur. At one point, she took off her hat to show him her hair, tightly pinned to her head. Doyle cleared his throat, bringing Rollo's attention back to the matter at hand.

'If I do not contact you by noon tomorrow,' said Rollo, 'use this drawing and what we've already learned as you see fit. The detective overseeing the murders along the docks is a man called McIntyre.'

'Yes.' Doyle furrowed his brow. 'I believe that Palmerstone still intends to come to Edinburgh en route to Balmoral. He will be here the day after tomorrow.'

'Bring pressure to bear, Doyle. They don't call him Dracos the Destroyer for nothing.' He turned. 'Marian, we must go.'

She nodded and rose. With her hat firmly back in place, she bent to the child. 'Farewell, Master Doyle.'

She took her hand from her pocket and opened it, revealing the tiny fairy she kept on her mantelpiece. Placing the wee thing on the child's upturned palm, she gently pushed the creature's chin up. A click sounded, and the wings parted, opening at ninety degrees. A soft glow came from the creature's spine and reflected off the mirrored inner surfaces of the wings, as bright as a miniature moon.

'Please accept this, Arthur. It will help keep those pesky goblins away at night.'

The child's eyes were as brilliant as the tiny torch. 'Thank you. Look, Papa!'

'Indeed.' Doyle Senior appraised Marian as if with new eyes. 'Farewell, Rahgstadt, Miss Finlay. Be safe.'

Chapter 6

A thick fog had risen off the water and now enveloped the dock, the lanes and the Silver Goose Tavern. Marian felt as though someone had tied a thick blindfold over her eyes, then had spun her around. She could not make out landmarks, nor see more than three feet ahead.

She knew, somewhere deep in the sensible part of her mind, she should be terrified, or at least weak at the knees. But instead, she felt a rush of exhilaration, a sense of daring. She straightened her bowler hat and smoothed an index finger and thumb over her neatly gummed moustache. Even though she had suffered at that monster's hands, knowing Rollo was waiting, here in the suffocating fog, and was ready to spring the trap, meant her fear had turned into pure excitement.

Swaggering up to the bar, she ordered whisky. She'd played here before—it was one of several bars she favoured with her custom, although most were closer to the docks—but it was already the third bar she'd visited tonight. Moreover, this was her third whisky, though she'd taken just a few sips from the previous two. Unfortunately, there had been no sign of their prey in either of those taverns.

But it seemed her luck had turned. He was here, sitting in a corner of the room, just out of reach of the firelight. She leaned one elbow on the bar and looked around, then took her mirror messenger from her inner pocket and scrawled one word. After slipping it away, she took her whisky and leaned casually over a table at play.

'This seat taken?'

She sensed movement on the far side of the room, felt eyes boring into her.

One of the players looked up, a hardened type with a thin cheroot dangling from his lips. He nudged his companion.

'I do enjoy teaching young shavers a new trick or two.'

On any other night, the banter would have put her on her mettle. When she met a man who thought he could fleece her, she delighted in taking him down a peg or two. But tonight, this man's comment rolled off her like rain on oilcloth—she had bigger fish to fry.

They played one hand while Dracos watched her, and she picked up a tidy sum. Rollo came in then and made his way to the bar. He stood with his back to the post, his missing arm hidden by the folds of his cloak. She caught a glimpse of him only once; for the most part, she kept her eyes firmly on the cards. Then a faint whiff of cologne with a hint of musk and pine swirled in the air beside her, and her quarry took the seat opposite.

Marian's heart seized as a rush of memories assaulted her. The dark of night. His hands around her throat. All the horror rushed back. She picked up her glass, still half-full, and downed the contents in one gulp.

She forced herself to stay at the table, not to overturn it and flee screaming into the night. It was not only the sight of him—though his thin lips parted to reveal the rotten teeth that had woken her in a cold sweat these past two nights—there was also a definite stench, of stale sweat and … copper.

He was large. She thought perhaps her memory was exaggerated, but he was even more massive than Cain who worked the forge. Under brindled week-old stubble, his skin was pasty, and he kept his left arm close to his body, seeming to move it only when necessary. She remembered now the blood on Rollo's dagger. So, he had wounded this fiend!

'Gut efening.'

When his mangled English struck another chord, one laced with painful memories and cruel intentions, she met his gaze.

He smiled, oh so slowly, then gesturing for the player on his right to deal him in, flipped a shilling onto the table. 'Do you play heer ovten?'

Ignoring his words and pale grey eyes, clear and empty as water, she fanned her hand in front of her and considered probabilities.

'This lad bain't much of a talker,' one of the players offered, clearly still seething after having lost money on the last hand.

The monster nodded sagely. 'Perhaps the cat has taken his tongue?'

Marian gave him a look that could freeze the North Sea. 'Not interested in chit chat, is all.'

At the sound of the rasp in her throat, his face took on a smug look, and her heart plummeted. It seemed that if he had been uncertain of her identity before, he was uncertain no longer. Her instincts hissed at her; her fingers itched to throw down her cards and pull out her hidden weapons. But something told her she would be dead if she did. She guessed he would prefer to kill her elsewhere, but she doubted he'd hesitate to do it now if she ran.

With her free hand, she tugged once on the brim of her hat, signalling to Rollo, then she straightened and pushed her stake to the centre of the table. The other players either grinned or cursed and laid down their hands, but the man opposite only smiled.

Losing the hand gave her the excuse she needed to quit the game, and moments later, she stepped into the crisp night air. The alleyway wasn't completely deserted; a doxy and her client were transacting business not fifteen yards away. Marian heard nothing though—nothing except the blood crashing in her ears and the hammer clanging on the anvil of her heart.

Gaps in the fog allowed Marian to see where she was going, and shoving a hand into her trouser pocket, she grasped the tiny single-shot pistol tightly. She let the other hover at her waist, where the hilt of her dagger was already loosed for action.

Rollo had drilled her in the path she was to take from each of the taverns. This was one of the easier routes, as the alley emptied onto the main dock. But heavy footsteps echoing behind her gave her a jolt, as if she'd been shocked by the electrodes of a dynamo. She took a sharp left onto Pound Lane, then a right and, forcing herself not to run, another right. Sweat dampened her brow as she stepped from the lamplit street into a dank lane that led back to the docks.

The muscles in her throat constricted, but she pushed back the horrid memories threatening to choke her. This time she was armed and ready. This time Rollo was hidden, waiting to strike. Her mind was confident, but her heart …

The sounds of lapping water and a distant steam engine told Marian her destination was at hand. The vice squeezing her heart eased just the tiniest amount as she stepped from the alley—and a hand gripped her shoulder.

Nails bit into her flesh as she spun; Rollo had shown her what to do. Her dagger came cleanly from its sheath, and she had the pistol in her hand. She looked up triumphantly to face … Rollo Raghstadt!

***

The next morning, Rollo turned into the lane on which the Somerton workshop stood, and when he lifted his gaze, a flicker of pleasure warmed him. Marian had just turned into the street too, at the opposite end, and was walking past the large unicarriage parked beyond the workshop. As the distance closed between them, he could read the languor of her stride.

'Good morning, Marian.' He tipped his hat to her. 'You didn't sleep well.'

It was not a question. The soft bruises surrounding her eyes were evidence, not that he needed it. He knew she hadn't slept because he had not slept either. Once he'd delivered her safely to her flat last night after their sorry attempt to bait the assassin, Rollo had stood in a dark pocket on the street and watched her door. Dracos had clearly guessed their purpose, and Rollo would have been taking a risk if he'd left. He had to assume they may have been followed, that he may have led the brute straight to Marian's door. Thank goodness there had been no disastrous ramifications to his plan. Now, after he'd answered the limb-maker's mirror messenger summons, he would ponder his next move.

Marian leaned against the workshop door and glanced up at him. When she spoke, her voice was soft, and though they stood only inches apart, he had to lean down to hear her.

'You don't look very chipper yourself. Did you get any sleep at all?'

'An hour or so.' He brushed back a tendril of hair that had escaped her bun, and it curled around his gloved finger, as soft and playful as a ginger kitten.

She turned her cheek into his hand. Surprise and some other nameless emotion flooded his exhausted mind, and he stood transfixed, losing himself in the depths of green that stared up at him.

Lowering his hand, he offered his arm to her. 'Perhaps we should go in. Ladies first.'

Despite her obvious weariness, she smiled at him. 'I'm surprised you'd describe me as a lady after all that's—'

Her gaze darted over his shoulder, and wild roses bloomed in her cheeks. Rollo turned to see Beauden Somerton standing a few steps away, intently regarding their linked arms.

'Good morning, Mr Rahgstadt.' Somerton spoke coolly, his words sharp and edged with suspicion. 'Good morning, Marian. You are not required today. I will have Judith let you know when you are to return.'

Her glorious cheeks changed to the colour of whey, and she pulled an ancient mirror messenger from her plain black reticule. 'But Mr Samuels instructed me to come in, sir.'

Somerton put his head through the door. 'Samuels.'

The old man appeared a few seconds later.

'I thought it was understood I did not want to involve the women in this business.'

'Aye, sir, and I would not.' The old man wiped his brow with a large handkerchief, his eyes sunken and rheumy. 'Except I cannot do what needs to be done in the time you wish. My eyes are no' so keen, nor my fingers so nimble as hers.'

Pressing his long pale fingers to his temple, Somerton closed his eyes and sighed. 'Very well. If it must be.' He glanced at Marian and Rollo. 'In any case, it seems as though Marian is more involved in these events than one might have thought.'

Rollo met Somerton's bronze gaze. Though he would soon be gone, Marian must continue working with these men, and he did not want to ruin her standing with them or cause them to view her with suspicion. Somerton seemed like a fair-minded man, but he was unlikely to take a dispassionate view of her nocturnal adventures.

'It is not due to any wrong done by Miss Finlay,' he said, deciding to give a version of the truth that didn't divulge Marian's secrets.

'On the contrary, I was fortunate that she came across me when she did, or I would have been in far worse shape after my confrontation.'

'I see. Well, no matter. We need to be off. My wife awaits you. I take it you are prepared for her to perform the procedure today. Time is of the essence, after all.' He looked from Marian to Rollo. 'Jimmy, put the box in the unicarriage, if you would.'

'Aye.' Jimmy walked past with a sizeable wooden box.

'Samuels, the exoskeleton and the … accessories need to be completed today. This is our only project. And strict secrecy is needed. Rahgstadt, please accompany me.' Somerton walked up the lane and got into the unicarriage.

Marian put a light hand on Rollo's arm as they followed. 'Thank you, but I don't need you to lie for me.'

'It was no lie. If you had not been there, my wound would have gone unattended. And I wouldn't have made it to safety without your assistance. There was no need for me to mention any other details.'

Her eyes softened, turning from bright green to soft moss as she allowed one finger to stray lightly over his hand. 'You will be in the finest care in the land with the Somertons, but I will keep you in my prayers, none the less.'

She went into the brightly lit workshop, where the old cogsmith was standing at his desk, scowling, with a large magnifying glass in his hand.

Rollo met the old man's vexed gaze and knew it for what it was; Marian seemed to bring out a gentleman's protective streak. He nodded in acknowledgement, then turned towards the unicarriage and his appointment with the good lady doctor.

Chapter 7

Rollo settled into the unicarriage, and as they moved off, he could feel Somerton's eyes upon him, appraising him. Several moments of uncomfortable silence passed.

'How deep have you dragged my employee into your world?' His emphasis made it clear that Marian was by no means friendless or unprotected.

Rollo heard the suggestion that he was insinuating himself where he had no right to go. He should not react; he needed this man's assistance. Besides, Marian had never given him any rights over her … and yet, the need to stake a claim gnawed at him.

'You speak as though you have some claim on Miss Finlay?'

'Miss Finlay is her own person, but she has no kin. Only Samuels who is an unofficial guardian. She's had a sad life and a troubled one. We will not stand by and see her harmed. Not in any way.'

The underlying meaning of the words cut deeply, especially given the events of the previous night, and some minutes passed before he could reply with equanimity.

'Rest assured, sir, she will come to no harm at my hands.'

Something in Somerton's eyes eased, but the steel in his voice was no less. 'I'm glad of it. So, may I ask again, Rahgstadt, how deeply involved in your games is Miss Finlay?'

Rollo directed his iciest stare across the swaying unicarriage, but to no avail. Turning to the window instead, he watched trees and houses, people and parks flash past as he sifted through his memory, recalling the dealings that had led to this moment, and sought small nuggets of truth he could offer Somerton without betraying Marian or his mission.

'Deep enough for her to be considered a much-needed player in the events currently unfolding.'

Somerton's heated glare and the determined set of his lips made it evident Rollo's answer would not suffice.

'Each one of you have sorely underestimated Miss Finlay,' he continued. 'She is extremely intelligent and a keen observer. She happened upon me wounded and took it upon herself to offer me aid and comfort. She clearly realised I was no threat because she took me home and nursed me. I left before dawn the next morning only to run into her at your workshop. Believe me, my surprise was as great as hers.'

'What was she doing, to come across you injured?'

Rollo gave a careful shrug. 'I don't believe I asked. Her business is her own after all, and I was only too glad of her aid.'

Somerton appeared to be weighing his words, as if trying to decide whether or not they were true—which of course they were. Some men can hear a lie, and Rollo was not about to risk alienating him.

'And how does helping a stranger in need drag her in too deep?'

'It doesn't, but more than that, I cannot divulge.'

Somerton merely nodded, but Rollo was not fool enough to think the interrogation was over.

A mile and a half later, he turned his head. 'Where are we going? This is not the way to the hospital, or the free clinic at the South Bridge where your wife works.'

Somerton arched a quizzical brow, but there was a hint of respect in his eyes. 'I suppose I should not be surprised. Learning about my family's comings and goings is child's play to someone who trades in secrets. But it's something of a relief to know there are truths of which you're not aware. My father and my wife maintain a work-shop and operating room in our home.'

Rollo sank into the leather seat. 'A secret surgery?'

'Of course. It's not a dungeon of torture. Very few know of it, though it has been used occasionally, mostly for emergencies.'

Rollo resisted the urge to tug at his collar. As they grew ever closer to the crucial moment, he could not help remembering. He'd been lucky, all those years ago in New York, to have been treated by a competent surgeon. But the agony, the stench of his own rotting flesh, the grinding crack of the bone saw … he would never be free of the memories. The doctor had given him as much laudanum as he could stand, but it had only imbued his few lucid moments with all the hallmarks of a nightmare.

Just when he thought he might leap from the unicarriage, they turned off the main thoroughfare into a side street, then made their way through a tall gate. With a gush of steam, the carriage stopped, and a moment later, Jimmy opened the door, revealing a courtyard paved in grey stone. The house beyond had a brass and oak door and a few slim windows. Underneath were sheltered planters holding a few lavender bushes and autumn flowers. The roses were already in their winter hibernation, and the neatly trimmed creeper was bare of leaves.

Somerton turned a key in the door and led Rollo into the foyer. The walls were a vivid turquoise on which hung a dozen pictures, a mixture of artworks and portraits in silver frames. One painting, of recent date judging by the fashion, depicted a dark-haired woman holding two toddlers. High in the wall was a glorious example of a leadlighter's art—a woman held an infant in one arm and a heart in the other. A staircase with a silver balustrade led up, but Somerton did not turn that way. Instead, he opened an unremarkable door, revealing a narrow stair.

He stepped back and gestured. 'After you.'

Behind them, Jimmy entered, carrying the box, and shut the front door. With all hope of escape gone, Rollo passed through the door and moved down the stairs with the enthusiasm of a man descending into Hades.

At the foot of the stairs, Rollo entered the small surgery Somerton had mentioned. It was as wide as the house and had two windows set high in the front wall. A bed sat on a plinth in the centre of the room, and a workbench, divided into sections, lined the wall. The ceiling and walls were of beaten copper, and dynamic lights were positioned at regular intervals. A dynamo, hidden somewhere in the walls, hummed.

A woman, wearing a long white coat over a plain crimson gown, stepped away from the storage cupboards at the rear of the room. Perhaps his own age, or a little younger, she wore her dark hair coiled around her head in neat braids. From her neck hung a strange device—two narrow copper pipes, curved almost to the shape of a heart, with a leather tube clamped to it. At the end hung a gleaming copper bell the size of an egg cup.

She came forward with her hand outstretched. 'Good morning, Mr Rahgstadt. I'm Dr Galena Somerton.'

Rollo extended his hand, and an icy vice clutched at his gut. He'd known Dr Somerton was both a woman and young, but having the reality standing three feet away was quite a different thing. He'd be damned if he'd let a chit of a girl maul him about. Still, he managed to utter a polite, 'Doctor.'

She turned to Somerton. 'Thank you for bringing Mr Rahgstadt here, my dear. I need to ask him a few questions. If you wish to go up, the boys are about to have their morning nap.'

She grasped her husband's hand, and Rollo was taken aback by the obvious love in her eyes. And not only in *her* eyes. He caught a glimpse of Somerton's face and deliberately turned away to study his surroundings.

From behind him came whispers, murmurs and soft sounds that had no name. He fixed his eyes on the odd machines set on a far bench. Pipes ran from each but went nowhere. A skeleton hung from a thin cord, suspended from a hook. When the sounds ceased, he turned around. Somerton gave him a final look, then crossed the room and disappeared up the stairway. The door snicked shut.

71

Dr Somerton took a seat, smoothed her skirts and gestured to the chair opposite her. 'Shall we begin, Mr Rahgstadt? I have a great many questions, and I believe time is of the essence.'

**

Rollo didn't trust easily. He'd lost too many friends who'd put their faith in the wrong people, had trusted in ideas or fate. Half the terror he'd experienced on the battlefield had not been caused by the enemy but had been a direct result of relying on men from his own side. Independence, isolation—they were far less chilling than having to trust.

Now, Dr Somerton and the two who'd arrived to assist her moved as though they were accustomed to each other's actions and needs, and they seemed to have little use for conversation. It was as if they each knew what the others were thinking. The man, Douglas Warwick, had shaken Rollo's hand firmly before explaining what they hoped to achieve. Rollo listened as best he could, though he was conscious of Dr Somerton and the other female doctor preparing instruments and a weird copper apparatus. He now had a greater understanding of how his muscles were attached and where the nerves ran, but he eyed their preparations with a churning stomach. He had never met a female surgeon; that he was about to put his life in the hands of two was as incomprehensible as what they were planning to do.

He removed his jacket and shirt, wincing as he bared his stump to the cold light of day, then sat on the surgical bed. Beside him, the other female doctor, Olive Warwick, checked the connections that ran from the leather face mask to the long pipe and the metal canister. She set the three gauges, each labelled differently, and made careful notes, then rubbed her hand unconsciously over the prominent curve of her stomach. He would drift off to sleep, she said; he would feel no pain and have no memory of the surgery. He remembered all too well the carnage after Bull Run, the screams from the surgeon's tent. Unconsciousness was a boon.

Dr Somerton crossed the room and, lifting a draped cover from a nearby trolley, took a silver circlet and slid it on her head like a crown. At the front was a disk as large as his palm; it was highly polished and had a small glass globe in the centre.

'I know it's a lot to take in, Mr Rahgstadt, but I hope to put your mind at ease. Beauden used star metal to fashion the arm, which is incredibly light and strong. Although it may take a while for you to become familiar with its skeletal structure, you'll soon forget it's not flesh and bone.'

She folded back the linen cloth to display elegant metal bones. It was similar and yet dissimilar to the forearm and hand hanging from the skeleton in the corner. Made of dull silver metal, the fine bones of the forearm were parallel and flat, each less than a quarter inch thick. They met at the hinged wrist. Its palm consisted of two flat sheets and was pierced with a shape reminiscent of a *fleur de lis*. The fingers were made up of short thin rods that had not only hinges but were also cut away, making them extremely dexterous.

He couldn't take his eyes off it. Trepidation and excitement rushed through him when he recalled how he'd felt his missing hand, how he'd made the fingers of Somerton's glove bend and flex with nothing more than the power of his mind.

He forced himself to speak when Warwick came to stand beside Dr Somerton—anything to bite back the hope currently bursting through him like fireworks. 'Why are there holes in it? Won't that weaken it?'

Dr Somerton shook her head. 'No, Mr Rahgstadt. The holes are anchor points for other elements Beauden and Will plan to add later, though I believe they're something of a secret.'

'Yes, ma'am. I hope you won't say anything once this is over.'

'Yes, yes, Mr Rahgstadt.' Warwick's voice held a laughing disdain. 'We've all signed your terrifyingly official document and will be locked in a dungeon for the rest of our days if we dare speak a word. We are aware. But we are doctors, you know. We are accustomed to patient confidentiality.'

Rollo met Warwick's eye, but despite the flippant remark, he could detect no antagonism. He turned to Dr Somerton. 'Perhaps, ma'am, I should ask you to call me Rollo. Rahgstadt is a handle and a half.'

She smiled at him, making him think her a very pretty lady. Her hair was black as pitch, and she had shapely curves under a plain gown. The other lady doctor was an ashy blonde who reminded him of his sister, which was unsettling. But Marte only thought she knew everything; this lady really did. She pointed to a thin metal disk that had four tiny needles protruding from its side, like tiny hooks designed to anchor in his flesh.

Warwick picked up the disk in a gloved hand. 'I can hardly believe, Galena, that you have created an electrode system to connect bone, muscle and nerves.'

'I have not, Douglas, but Beauden wanted to avoid working the copper wiring into the muscle and bone from the outside. This will act as a neural conductor.'

'That's genius!'

She flushed. 'He does not take the credit. That goes to Dr Ortiz, a Catalan professor who has written of his researches. Truly, he is the genius, though the technique is still experimental.'

'How does it work?' Olive Warwick inspected the disk carefully but did not touch it.

Rollo leaned forward. He felt like a child listening to talk of magic and the enchanters who made it.

'The disk acts as a conduit. It will ensure that Rollo's thoughts are transmitted to the fine copper wiring, just as your own hand responds to the nerve impulses from your brain. It will operate the hand and all its features.'

'Its features?' Warwick turned his head a fraction, giving Rollo a window into his thoughts.

'Just concern yourself with the here and now, Douglas. The rest is up to Beauden and Will.'

Warwick shot a heated glance at Dr Somerton, though he said nothing.

Dr Somerton gestured from the disk to the skeletal hand. 'The technique is called *ossintagrationem*. We'll connect the bone and nerves to the plate and the plate to the disk, allowing the seamless transition of thoughts. The neural and muscular binding should give the patient intuitive control of the hand.'

Warwick shook his head, as though in disbelief. 'Have you tested it, or has Dr Ortiz?'

'Only on dogs and cats. Not yet on a human.' Dr Somerton smiled at Rollo, but his stomach clenched despite her attempt at reassurance. 'This opportunity came upon us quite suddenly.'

Rollo no longer wanted to hear the intricacies of what they were going to do to him, so he turned his eyes to the trolley and the large brown bottle and primed syringes that lay on top. He still wasn't comfortable giving up control to strangers, but he wanted the job done, to know if maybe, just maybe, he could regain some part of what he had lost. His mission made it urgent, but it was his own desire spurring him forward now.

'It is time, Rollo,' Dr Somerton said softly. 'Douglas will help you prepare while we scrub up.'

As Rollo slipped into a sterile smock and allowed Warwick to position his body just so, he tried to draw his customary armour of cynicism around him. But it was lost. As he felt the prick of the needle in the crease of his arm, all he had was hope.

Chapter 8

Marian leapt out of her chair. 'So you think I'm a strumpet then, is that it?'

'I did na say that, lass. I only asked—'

'Aye,' she spat, 'how well I know that Rahgstadt fellow. You're not my brother, Will! Judith might let you get away with your pushy overbearing ways, but you have no say over me!'

'I only asked how you came to know him.' He leaned over the bench towards her. 'It's no crime to watch over a lass. You've no need to spit and snarl like a wee ginger kitten.'

'Maybe I was dancing in a burlesque show and he took a fancy to me.'

Will pursed his lips and clenched his fists. 'Och, you would never. But you don't know him, or his business. He isn't fit company.'

'No, I don't know his business, and you are forbidden to tell me because I am a mere female.' But she didn't need Will to confirm what she already knew—Rollo Rahgstadt had spy written all over him. 'Do you think I can't see what he is for myself? Are you accusing me of impropriety or stupidity?'

'You took him to your flat, lass.'

'He. Was. Wounded.'

'What were you doing out, in any case?'

'I was in a gambling hell, playing cards for money.'

'Marian—'

'Go away, Will. I have work to do, and so do you.'

'Mr Somerton will want to know.'

She slapped a leather work glove at his chest. He moved off, grumbling, and looked back once, but she ignored him.

Damn Will Ayre! How dare he chide her for her behaviour, or for her interest in Rollo! Mr Samuels had taken a grandfatherly turn and had presumed to lecture her instead of treating her like a promising pupil, but while she'd managed to hold her tongue with him, Will had asked for everything he got.

Truthfully, she wasn't sure how she felt about Rollo Rahgstadt. Perhaps she wasn't utterly indifferent to him, though she would never admit it—and certainly not to Will! Only now, she had to contend with his baleful looks. She kept her head down and continued to ignore him.

Perched on the stool at her workbench, she busied herself with fitting the ratchet to the spine of what would become a tiny hidden crossbow.

She should be enthralled in the work—it was so much more interesting than adding tension to metal wrists and elbows, which had been her most recent task. She should be thrilled, too, to be included in this assignment, so secret that she was forbidden to tell even Judith. She *should* feel that way ... but she didn't.

She set down the fine soldering torch and unclamped the vice, then turned the frame to check the welds. It had to be strong; its torque would be considerable. Mr Somerton had made calculations for a miniature bolt to hit its target at twenty yards. She turned the screw again and checked the tension. She'd have to test it.

But she failed to keep her thoughts on her work, and her fingers still clenched with residual anger. How dare they all but accuse her of being a hussy! Except the truth weighed her down—everything she'd hidden from them, the secrets she'd kept before and after meeting Rollo, the other life she led. They would be appalled.

When it was all business and dark shadows, she'd managed to ignore the way she felt, putting it down to nervousness—but it wasn't nerves that now caused her heart to stutter. She'd reacted to Rollo's presence as a flower does to rain. She recalled the soft stroking of his hand on hers this morning; the merest touch and she'd melted. All the other men she knew were open books—anyone could read them. Rollo Rahgstadt, on the other hand, was full of secrets, written in code in invisible ink. She burned to know his secrets and the man who was locked and chained inside the spy.

With a shake of her head, she refocused her attention on the tiny bolt mechanism. She had to get it right. One day, Rollo's life might depend upon her work, though she would never know. He was not a man for home and hearth, and truth be told, she was not a woman who wanted a man like that. Her freedom was her most precious possession—the ability to do as she pleased, to tinker with her gadgets—and no man was worth giving it up. So what if her senses tingled and her body thrummed when he was around? It had been exciting, though, to be part of his adventures. She could not imagine sharing such experiences with anyone but him.

She banished the thought. Best not dwell on what could not be. It only led to disappointment. Soon, Rollo, with his iron fist and world of shadows, would be gone, and she would still be here, working on false limbs by day and playing at falsehood by night.

Nestling the small crossbow into the shell of the arm Samuels had handed her, she checked the alignment. Perfect. It would hide safely inside the leather-and-metal vambrace designed by Mr Somerton once it was fitted over the metal skeleton.

Next, she pulled out a spool of fine copper wire, ready to attach the parts to the metal plate at the juncture of arm and prosthesis. As conductors of Rollo's thoughts, the threads would tell the crossbow when to fire. She measured the first strand of wire and checked it against the diagram. Measure twice, cut once.

An eternity later, she finished the final thread, stood back and studied the completed phenomenon. It was fantastical. And yet, it was not the first amazing, impossible thing she had seen within these walls. She saw ordinary miracles every week, but the most exciting day had been when Mr Somerton had walked through the door with a new gold heart beating in his chest—and it had been forged right here in this workshop!

The door slammed back, revealing Jimmy, his eyes searching frantically as he ran into the room. When his gaze locked on her, her heart dropped to her belly.

'Marian. Come now!'

She set her tools down on the bench, her arm like treacle, and put one foot to the floor. He was at her side already, with cold hard determination in his eyes. Jimmy, who always had a smile for her.

He seized her arm. 'Hurry, lass!'

Will rushed over, and Samuels creaked to his feet. By the expressions on their faces, they were as mystified as she.

'Jimmy? What—'

'They have asked for you at the house. Urgently!'

She pulled the heavy leather apron over her head as Jimmy danced beside her like a duck on a griddle. He hauled her out to the Somerton unicarriage and handed her up so briskly she stumbled. After slamming the door, he let out the damper; they were racing down the Leith Road within seconds.

Alone in the jolting vehicle, Marian hung on to the straps and wondered what had happened. The only thing that made sense was that her secret was out. Mr Somerton would not take kindly to her going about town in a man's garb and fleecing gamesters; never mind that they had little skill and inflated egos. He might well summon her, and she would be lucky not to lose her place.

Once in the Somerton courtyard, Marian was poleaxed by the sight of Dr Somerton beckoning from the open doorway of the house, a smeared white pinafore over her crimson skirts, her hair wrapped in white linen like a laundry maid on wash day.

'Miss Finlay, thank goodness!' She didn't touch Marian but ushered her towards a door. 'Please, come down.' She darted down a steep set of stairs, and Marian followed, pausing only on the landing where the steps turned at ninety degrees.

Marian heard her name and garbled words, some in English, some in a foreign tongue. Despite the hoarseness and reediness of the voice, she recognised it—and her barred heart cracked wide open. He sounded so desperate, so desolate. She paid no heed to her surroundings. Her gaze was fixed on the figure of Rollo, strapped to a long metal table where he was thrashing and moaning her name.

She rushed to his side. 'What's the matter? What happened to him?'

Rollo was unclothed to the waist and his arm bandaged afresh. She touched his forehead lightly. He was cool, not fevered as she'd imagined.

Standing opposite Marian, Dr Somerton explained. 'He had a bad reaction to the medication we used to help him sleep through the surgery. We are working to counter it, but when he started calling for you, we thought it best to fetch you.'

Marian put her hands to Rollo's face and leaned in. 'Rollo, I'm here. Don't worry. You are safe, and all is well. Rollo? Can you hear me?'

She whispered the words over and over. Slowly, very slowly, his thrashing eased. As she ran her hands over his brow and cheeks and whispered to him, Dr Somerton and the others worked opposite her—and she didn't care one iota.

***

What devilry was this! What in hell had they done to him?

Rollo gasped for air and held both arms up to his face. His hands weren't of flesh; instead, he had two skeletal metal horrors fixed where his arms should be. They glimmered in the harsh red light, gore dripping from his serrated fingers.

He rose and, looking down through the hands and the grey fog of his mind, saw spreading pools of blood on the floor. There lay Marian—limp, lifeless, and horribly, brutally gashed. He knelt at her side but dared not touch her. If he did, his hands would cut her to ribbons. Had he done this with his monstrous limbs? In a frenzy of panic, he ripped at the silver atrocities bound to his arms. Only he could not touch them, could not be free of them. He swore, first in English, begging for forgiveness, then in the language of his childhood.

'Marian, *Gud tilgi meg.*'

But it seemed that God wasn't listening in Norwegian either.

Rollo raged, turning to the Italian and Swedish of the New York docks. Fighting against the devils that bore him backwards, he lashed out as invisible chains wrapped around his arms and ankles. He was bound, shackled to some invisible wall, with a leather gag strapped fast around his face. The air was sickly with some sweet stench, like the scent of lightning-struck earth. The grey fog deepened to a livid black, and he shivered from the sudden chill. His left arm throbbed, burned. He lay panting, gasping for air under a sodden blanket. He fought until he was exhausted. Then, out of the roiling fog, he heard a voice.

'Rollo, I'm here. It's me. Don't be afraid.'

The voice came closer, grew sharper. The words were spoken into his right ear, so close he could almost feel the speaker's sweet warm breath.

The air seemed fresher, so he took a lungful. Light danced at a distance, promising warmth and safety, but his feet, fingertips and ears went up in flames, and he could not put them out.

Another voice spoke, this one male. 'Be calm, Rollo. You are safe.'

'Rollo, stop fighting it. I'm here and all is well.'

The light rushed at him, and he ducked to avoid it, only he could not move. He winced and waited for it to hit him, but instead, cool air filled his lungs.

He opened his eyes. Above him, beautiful as the moon, was a pale face with huge green eyes, shadowed like craters and red-rimmed from crying. A fiery curtain framed it in unruly satin curls.

'Marian.' His voice was not his own, harsh and strained. He reached for her but— 'Why can't I move?'

'You are in the Somerton house.'

'I remember.'

Dr Somerton's face appeared in his peripheral vision. 'You reacted badly to the sedation, Mr Rahgstadt. We had to restrain you for your own protection. We were halfway through the operation, and you were about to harm yourself.'

She moved, unbuckled a leather strap, and he felt the weight on his injured arm ease. With all his strength, he raised it and assessed the bandaged stump.

'You weren't able to complete the surgery?' All that for nothing?

84

His heart shrivelled.

Dr Somerton shook her head. 'We completed the surgery. As I said, we were already halfway done, so we increased the dosage of the anaesthesia, changed the balance. You were sedated once more, but you started hallucinating as the effect wore off.'

He remembered the hallucinations. They had seemed so real. He had never been more relieved in his life than when he'd heard Marian's voice and had seen her beautiful face hovering over him. He had thought her dead—at his hand! It was a vision that would haunt his sleep for months.

He looked up at her again; her pale, radiant beauty made her appear like an angel in a stained-glass window. She touched his cheek, and he turned into her hand. 'How do you come to be here?'

Marian exchanged a glance with Dr Somerton, who stepped forward.

'You called for her in your delirium, Rollo. It is as well that my husband knew of your … admiration for Miss Finlay. We were able to put two and two together.' She paused. 'Now, I will give you something for the pain so you can sleep until the residual effects have worn off.'

'May I have some water first?'

'Of course.' The doctor stepped away, and Rollo took the second of privacy to speak with Marian.

'Thank you for coming.' He couldn't articulate how much having her close had eased his fears. He didn't dare admit she was his weakness.

'Of course I came.' She spoke fiercely.

The doctor came back and, holding his head, offered him a mouthful of water from an invalid cup. When he was done, she placed a wide-mouthed tube over his heart and put her ear to the other end. Finally, she picked up a silver syringe.

'No!'

Dr Somerton looked down at him, her expression stern. 'We know that some medicines do not sit easy with you, but this is simply for the pain. It will not have the same effect as the anaesthesia.'

'I will stay with you.' Marian laid one hand on his shoulder, and without thinking, he covered it with his good hand. 'I won't leave, Rollo, but you need to rest. Trust the doctor.'

He closed his eyes and again felt the prick of the needle. This time he was conscious of peace, of warm, bright joy at the core of his being. Heaven only knew the feeling had no place in the life of a man such as him. Nor did the emotion that filled him when Marian gazed into his eyes. Love was blissful terror, he decided, as sleep claimed him once again.

Chapter 9

As Marian stood in the basement workshop, sunlight streamed through the high windows and glinted on the copper sheathing, turning the whole room golden. After Rollo had been moved upstairs to a bed last evening, she'd maintained a vigil by his side until the housekeeper had relieved her, then she'd gone to rest in a spare bedchamber. When she'd come downstairs this morning, Dr Somerton had offered her the opportunity to see the prosthesis fitted. It was an honour Marian had not expected, but it was clear that the lady doctor could diagnose matters of the heart without the aid of her stethoscope.

The metal skeleton lay cushioned in the velvet-lined box on the workbench. Marian ran a light finger over it. It was a work of pure genius and had the ability to change Rollo's life for the better. Yet the capacity for chaos was there too; she thought of the work she'd been doing on the tiny crossbow. She shuddered but refused to consider she was helping to make a man, a good honourable man, into a living weapon.

She closed her eyes and imagined Rollo with this new appendage. Though he walked in the shadows, he was not the sort to be easily swayed by power. She knew because she spent her evenings watching men, winning more hands than she lost because she could read not only the cards but the men holding them. Rollo, like King Arthur, would only wield his sword for good and wouldn't be blinded by its power.

She turned at the sound of the door opening.

'Good morning, Marian. I hope you slept well.'

'I did, thank you, Dr Somerton.' Marian fought the urge to curtsey to her employer's wife.

'I'm so glad you're here to see this. It's a big day for Rollo and my husband.'

Dr Somerton's eyes shimmered with something to which Marian found she could connect. Perhaps it was a hint of excitement tinged with fear or even awe at this great leap for their men. However, Rollo was not and never could be her anything.

As Dr Somerton checked over the metal prosthesis and tools lined up on the linen-covered tray, Marian retreated into her thoughts. Another few days and Rollo Rahgstadt would move on with his mission. And she would be glad. Perhaps then, her stomach would not flutter every time his name was mentioned. Perhaps then, her dreams would not swirl around a tousled Viking man with blue eyes that pierced her soul.

Footsteps sounded on the stair and the dull burr of male voices drifted through the open door. Marian's heart sank when Rollo emerged looking exhausted; his skin was pale as milk, and the dark crescents beneath his eyes were like coal smudges. His good arm was thrown over Jimmy, who kept him upright, while his bandaged arm was secured to his chest with a sling. Though she'd sat by his side half the night, she had for some reason imagined he would be magically restored to good health today.

'This chair, please, Jimmy.' Dr Somerton picked up Rollo's wrist and held it between thumb and forefinger for several seconds. 'You still look the worse for wear, but I think the residual drugs will be out of your system by tomorrow.'

She and Jimmy crossed the room to the cupboards, but Marian could not avert her eyes from Rollo. No matter that he could not stand on his own, he was a hero in her eyes. What courage he had to take experimental technology into his body!

As she looked at him, he turned his head and their eyes met, his as blue and sharp as in her dreams. He considered her for a long moment, then his lips turned up, only slightly, but it warmed her to the soles of her feet. She moved towards him without conscious thought as Mr Somerton clattered into the room.

'Well, Rahgstadt, are you ready?'

***

Rollo turned reluctantly. He'd dreamed again last night, and the mere memory of it sickened him. He'd looked upon Marian's mangled corpse, had seen his long silver claws dripping with her blood. But this procedure had to be done, and once he'd dealt with the assassin, he would be free to go.

Unclamping his jaws, he summoned some enthusiasm. 'Of course.'

Jimmy moved to Rollo's side and set the tray of instruments and the box containing the new limb on a trolley. Marian stepped away, but he could still sense her presence at his shoulder. As the doctor unwound the bandage from his stump, Somerton leaned into the box and lifted the prosthetic arm with all the delicacy of a father gathering a sleeping newborn from its cradle.

Rollo was grateful for the distraction. He did not want to see the results of the previous day's surgery; his stomach roiled at the thought alone. A light touch on his right shoulder and the gentle hand resting there soothed him. The last of the bandage came free, revealing not the fleshy stump he'd expected but a thick silver band.

Somerton pushed the trolley under Rollo's arm. 'Rest your elbow here, please. It's quite sterile.'

Holding the metal arm in both hands, Somerton brought it into contact with the flat metal plate on the end of Rollo's stump. As contact was made, Rollo felt the sensation of pins and needles in his missing hand and the slightest movement in the wrist, as if it had spasmed.

'*Faen!*' Rollo couldn't believe his eyes.

Somerton, still manipulating the arm, smiled and looked up at his wife. 'See? It's as though it's seeking the connection to complete the circuitry.'

When a click sounded, Somerton extended a hand towards Jimmy, who slapped a screwdriver into his palm. With it, Somerton made deft turns at half a dozen points along the band, securing the arm in place.

When Somerton stepped back, Rollo lifted his arm, brought the hand level with his face and turned it this way and that. 'My God, it's incredible! I don't know what to say.'

'It is some of my finest work.' Somerton spoke softly, deep satisfaction laced with humility.

'You are a genius!'

Somerton reached for his wife's hand and interlaced his fingers with hers. Though they said nothing to each other, an indefinable sense of completion and relief emanated from them. They each offered Rollo a nod and a smile, then turned aside, leaving him sitting awestruck while they put away the tools of their trade.

Marian pressed her hand over his. 'Congratulations. This is a wonderful moment for you.'

Turning his head, he glanced up at her. She'd saved his life on the docks and, yesterday, his sanity. He would not forget that. His mission was paramount, but so was her safety, and he'd bring nothing but danger into her life. He had to keep his distance.

'Thank you, Marian.'

After a few moments, Dr Somerton pulled a chair from the workbench and sat opposite Rollo. 'Now, Mr Rahgstadt, it will take some time for your nervous system to become familiar with the appendage. Come, let us try some exercises. Hold your arm out straight and see if you can bend the wrist.' She put out her own arm and bent her hand down at a slight angle.

Rollo stretched out his arm, but the wrist remained obstinately straight.

He hadn't thought that would happen. The hand had moved of its own accord when Somerton had attached it just minutes ago. Rollo focused on the wrist joint and willed it to bend. As minutes ticked by, sweat prickled on his neck.

Marian dropped to a crouch at his side and rested her hand on his good arm. 'You are trying too hard. Don't force it.'

'I won't.' Concentrating on getting his breathing under control, in the same way he would when a mission was critical, he stretched his right arm out beside his left.

Marian spoke softly into his ear. 'When a child takes his first steps, he does not tell his legs to obey him, he lets instinct guide his path.'

At first, nothing happened, but then, as though in a ballet, both Rollo's hands tilted up and down. He laid his right arm down again, leaving only the prothesis extended, then he tilted his left wrist and watched his hand move, haltingly at first, then as he raised the right again, both hands moved in slow synchronicity. His heart was full of wonder.

Marian touched his shoulder. 'That's amazing.'

He turned and met her gaze and was drawn into a place where there were no shadows and where rejection itself was banished.

A sudden shuffle of Jimmy's feet and a 'Congratulations!' from Dr Somerton brought them back to reality. An exuberant Somerton whooped, then pulled his wife into his arms and kissed her.

Rollo stared at Marian and raised his arm. 'I … it's … just look.' Then taking her hand in his good one, he curled his fingers around hers. 'Thank you, Marian.'

As she smiled at him, her eyes glistened. 'It was my pleasure.'

Chapter 10

Rollo sat opposite Marian in the great bay window of the Somerton's solarium and turned his face to the weak winter sunshine. The alcove was filled with a massive series of windows made from wrought iron and glass and was adjacent to the principal family parlour—an elegant room, two stories high with scarlet walls that were lined with bookshelves. The professor, Somerton's father, had his desk there. Another large portion of the room was given over to a nest of chesterfields under a cupola, suspended by a chain as thick as a human wrist. The opposite corner of the room held a child's rocking horse of bronze and leather, as well as a waist-high castle made of blocks. Two miniature unicarriages and a mechanical menagerie sat at its base.

It had been an eventful morning. Rollo stretched out the miraculous hand again and marvelled at its strength and beauty. This had been the most incredible week of his life. Was it really only this time last Wednesday when he'd received the message that had sent him racing from Ireland to Scotland? It had been a mere five days since he'd arrived in Edinburgh, two days since he'd learned such technology was possible, and only two hours since he'd moved the fingers of his new hand for the first time.

When his unsuccessful attempts had caused his heart to plummet, Marian had been the one to encourage, prompt and guide him. And during last two hours, she'd been focused on helping him use the device effectively. Now, it responded more than ninety percent of the time, albeit slowly. As Rollo worked, Marian seemed to be mentally cataloguing the items they'd need to add to the vambrace, which was, even now, being built in Somerton's workshop. She was unique, Rollo thought—but was it her intelligence or her undeniable gamine beauty that so ensnared him? He was curious to know more about her.

'How long have you worked for Somerton?'

She gave him a wary glance. 'About five years.'

At that, he looked her over critically. 'You would have been a kid.'

She shook her head and looked away. 'I was sixteen and lucky to get the opportunity. It's rare for a girl to be offered such a position.'

'Somerton must have seen exceptional promise in you.'

She laughed; a cold, dry chuckle. 'If only that were the case.' She looked him in the eye. 'I'd lost my mam a couple of years earlier, then my dad disappeared. I was a bedraggled little stray, and Mr Somerton felt sorry for me. Except, he wasn't the man you see today. He was ill, dying. I can't explain why, and you wouldn't believe me if I did. But his own ill health meant there was little he could do for me, so he made a place for me in his workshop.'

Clearly, there was a lot she wasn't saying, but Rollo let some questions slide. He wasn't interested in Somerton; he wanted to know more about her.

'Did you ever find out what happened to your father?'

She shook her head. 'He might have been killed, but I think he was shanghaied.'

He frowned, considering. 'It's an issue back in the States, and in Liverpool, but I've never heard of it happening here.'

She shrugged. 'Dad was pretty handy at maintaining ships. He would have been an asset, so it's as likely as anything, I guess.'

He noticed she was fiddling with one of her gizmos, a snake of sorts, lithe and jointed, which wound and unwound itself around her ring finger. Though she spoke calmly, her hands were anything but, so he changed the subject.

'How did Somerton find you?'

She gave a brilliant smile. 'I was a Shabbos goy for Mr Samuels, like Mam had been. You know what that is?'

'Of course. You went to his house on the Sabbath to light the fire and so on.'

She nodded. 'After Dad disappeared, I couldn't pay the rent, so Mr Samuels arranged my little flat through a friend and took me to see Mr Somerton. Then he offered to train me.'

Shame tugged at him. Unlike the old man, instead of rescuing the damsel he'd found in danger, he'd encouraged her to step right up to the abyss. He should have never permitted her to get involved with his mission. His was a treacherous world; she was an innocent and alone. Well, he could make amends now. Though to send her away would take more strength than he possessed.

The door opened then, and Somerton stepped into the room, but he wasn't alone, nor did he seem in an agreeable frame of mind.

The unease in Rollo's chest quadrupled when he noted that one of the two men with Somerton was Charles Doyle. The other was a tall man, squarely built with fine hands and an unobtrusive manner. His wool suit was buttoned asymmetrically and embellished with leather detail and bright bronze buttons. His thick moustache disguised his mouth, but there was a keen intelligence in his grey eyes.

'I apologise for the intrusion.' Somerton threw Rollo and Marian a glance that was more wrath than regret, but he crossed to the buffet near the chesterfields and poured whisky into four crystal glasses.

Rollo stood and held out a hand for Marian. She took it and rose, as wary as he. She released his hand and clenched her fists in her gown.

'Marian, may I introduce you to Mr Charles Doyle, who is with the Royal Surveyors Office. Miss Finlay.'

Marian's tone was mild. 'I have had the pleasure of meeting Mr Doyle before, sir.'

Somerton's eyes gave a flash of incredulity before his expression grew grimmer. 'Have you indeed?' He passed her a small glass of sherry and his gaze turned to Rollo. 'I see. And Rahgstadt, you have met Mr McIntyre of Her Majesty's Inspectorate of Constabulary?'

'I have not.' He shot Doyle a glance, but he was imperturbably sipping his whisky. 'I take it this is not a social call.'

'There are a few matters that cannot wait.' Doyle looked around at the other gentlemen and Marian, weighing his words. 'Since I spoke to you last, Rahgstadt, we have received some intelligence from an informer.'

'I should leave.' Marian put down her untouched glass.

The detective shook his head, and Doyle turned to her. 'No, Miss Finlay, I am afraid your help is required.'

'I cannot see why.' Somerton spoke from the fringe of the group, and he glared at Rollo. 'Just how deeply have you entangled Miss Finlay in this sordid business?'

'Don't answer that, Rahgstadt.' Doyle spoke with authority. 'And before you go any further, Somerton, you should know that Miss Finlay has now become a very necessary part of this endeavour.'

'Damn it! Out with it, Doyle!' Rollo was in no mood to draw this out.

'It seems our assassin has left Edinburgh.'

'He's gone?' It didn't make sense. Prime Minister Palmerstone was due to make a speech at Trinity House tomorrow and wasn't supposed to leave until—

'Holy hell!' He slammed his iron fist down on the buffet, dinting the wood and causing everyone in the room to jump.

Doyle and the detective stared, but when Doyle spoke his voice was mild. 'We are no longer sure he meant to strike at Lord Palmerstone here in Edinburgh.'

Rollo put his hand to his head and pressed his temple. 'No. He was only here to get his orders. He would have left already except he was concerned about a possible witness to one of his crimes.'

'Yes.' The detective stepped forward. 'The poor lads who were murdered out by the docks. And now, for some unfathomable reason, he has dismissed you as a threat. He is off and going about his bloody business. Well, we must set the hounds on him.'

Doyle tapped his glass contemplatively and glanced at Rollo. 'I have informed Detective McIntyre of the sketch I drew at your behest.'

Rollo tried to control his snarl. 'Was that necessary?' He wasn't accustomed to inviting the constabulary into his murky world.

'It was rather. With you out of commission when this information came to light, I needed his assistance. Don't forget he discovered the arm you were careless enough to leave at the docks. Without him and his men, we would not have received the information we now possess in such a timely fashion.'

Rollo took the detective's measure. He had the breadth of shoulders and the calmness that many associated with a slow intellect. But there was nothing slow about the cogs that whirled behind those inscrutable eyes.

Doyle gestured. 'Please tell our American colleague, Detective McIntyre, what is the Prime Minister's next destination?'

'He has been invited to join the hunting at Balmoral, sir.' The detective spoke placidly, as though he had not just announced the greatest disaster since the death of the Prince Consort.

Rollo put his glass down carefully, only glad that his hand wasn't shaking. 'I must leave at once.'

The dram of whisky he'd consumed on top of the pain medication, not to mention the shock he'd received, sent his world spinning. She might not be his queen, but his life wouldn't be worth living if his quarry succeeded in killing the Queen of England. And even if the Queen was safe, there were the royal dukes to consider. The list of potential targets grew like Jack's beanstalk.

Doyle nodded. 'Yes, I am afraid you must. We have people in Scotland who are loyal and capable, but none with your, *ahem* ... particular talents.'

Marian touched his arm, her hand coming to rest in the crook of his elbow, and she spoke into the silence. 'We will be ready to leave first thing in the morning, Mr Doyle.'

Her words were simple, her voice unshakeable.

Rollo was grateful ... and appalled.

***

'Marian, be reasonable.' Mr Somerton turned his troubled copper eyes on her. 'You cannot involve yourself with these men more than you have already. Espionage? Assassination? Good grief! It's not the sort of thing gentlemen should expect of any decent girl.'

It was his mention of expectations that made up Marian's mind, even more than talk of decency. She was certain Rollo and Mr Doyle wouldn't expect anything of her, but she'd be damned if she'd let this opportunity pass her by. She straightened her spine and lifted her chin, but Mr Somerton didn't give her a chance to speak.

'In any case, Rahgstadt will not be in any state to travel for a week. He has undergone revolutionary treatment and needs to be monitored while he adjusts to the new prosthesis.'

'Sir—'

'No, Marian.' Mr Somerton's voice softened. 'I know you care for the man, but I have to think of your safety.' He turned, placed his glass on the sideboard with a distinct thud. 'Marian Finlay is my employee and, in a sense, my responsibility. I will not permit her to be drawn any deeper into this imbroglio.'

'I am inclined to agree, Somerton. She shouldn't be involved.' Rollo pulled away from her side, distancing himself from her physically and metaphorically. She felt a distinct chill. 'I appreciate all that Miss Finlay has done, but she has served her purpose and must return to her normal pursuits.' He glanced at Mr Somerton. 'As for the hand, I'm afraid I cannot remain here for you to see how your handiwork performs. I thank you and your wife for all you have done. You are both geniuses and more gracious than I can say. But once the vambrace has been fitted, I'll take my leave.'

Marian felt a jolt as the bottom fell out of her world. So she had served her purpose, had she? She was a means to an end, was she? Well, to hell with them! She was done with men making decisions for her, telling her what she could or couldn't do. She was up to her neck in this, and she would see it through, come hell or high water.

But as she opened her mouth to speak, she caught Charles Doyle's eye. He appeared to be amused. Before she could do more than draw breath, he shook his head at her and stepped smoothly into the conversation.

'Somerton, the Crown thanks you for all you've done to this point. But I'm afraid'—he glanced sideways and ran an appraising eye over Marian—'when duty to queen and country call, there is no reason short of death to prevent any subject from doing his, or indeed her, duty.'

'You do not need Marian.' Rollo stepped forward. 'Let her go home.'

Mr Doyle shook his head, and Marian was aware of a subtle change in him. In his home, he'd been helpful, affable. Here, he held an air of command.

'I need not remind you, Rahgstadt, that while you are in this country, you are in our jurisdiction. So far, we have extended you courtesy and assistance. That can change. Miss Finlay's assistance is essential, and I will have it.'

Rollo seethed. 'God damn you to hell, Doyle.'

'Quite possibly.' Mr Doyle smiled and winked at Marian, though the other men didn't seem to notice. 'Somerton, I see the first part of Rahgstadt's procedure has worked well. Are the vambrace and armaments ready?'

Mr Somerton flicked his gaze to Rollo and back to Mr Doyle in an instant. 'You know about them?'

'My dear fellow, I designed them. I'm assuming the work is well in hand?'

Mr Somerton glanced from Doyle to Marian, clearly uncertain of his ground and debating if he should take the fight further. He was not trying to lord it over her, Marian knew. He was only concerned for her.

He sighed and his shoulders sagged. 'Marian?'

'Almost, sir. The cog assembly is complete. I was setting the tension when Jimmy came to ... collect me yesterday.'

'How long, Miss Finlay?' Mr Doyle looked at her intently.

She considered. 'It should be finished by now, sir. I'm sure Will has assembled the final pieces. Perhaps this afternoon?'

Mr Somerton addressed her next. 'Are you willing to give them the help they require? I would not have you forced into anything.'

Willing? She strove to keep the excitement from her tone. 'I am a loyal subject, sir. I wish to help.' Her attempts at composure must have failed, because his mouth turned down.

'Yes, I can see you do. Well, remember, you will always have a place with us.' He put one hand on her shoulder briefly. 'Come home safely, Marian. Gentlemen, you can see yourselves out.' And he left without another word.

Chapter 11

As the door shut behind Somerton, Rollo glanced down at his metal hand and was not surprised to see the claw-like fingers curling into a fist. In his business, anger was a weapon, but right now, his was on a hair-trigger. Doyle's arrogance grated on him, and Marian's pain at his rejection showed in the flash of colour in her cheek, the briskness of her tone. He regretted his words; she deserved better. But though her presence this last day had been a soothing balm, he owed her safety. And now he'd failed at securing that for her, too, thanks to Doyle.

'Start talking, Doyle. I want to know everything. Let's start with what you know, and what you think you know, about Dracos Rebeniuc.'

'McIntyre?'

At Doyle's nod, the detective stepped forward. 'Mr Rahgstadt, Mr Doyle approached me after you indicated you'd lost the suspect on Monday night. Locating him became our highest priority. Once we had the image you provided and knowledge of where he'd been seen, we were able to trace him to his accommodation. Unfortunately, he'd left already and had killed the landlady. Her son recognised the picture, confirming we were on the right track. We then traced him to the Waverley train station, but he has not been seen since.'

'So he has left Edinburgh—'

The detective held up a hand. 'We know he has purchased clothing. We have a note with the word *Ballater* on it and the remains of a map. The section of Aberdeenshire is torn out.'

'But if he is intent on killing your queen, why come to Edinburgh at all? And if his target is Palmerstone, why Balmoral and not here?' Rollo pulled his hand through his hair in frustration and caught Marian watching him intently, her sea-green eyes shadowed.

'We don't know, damn it!' Obviously, Doyle's superiors were breathing down his neck. 'We have sent enquiries to the royal household, asking which guests are already present or expected, but we still don't know enough to guess Dracos's immediate plans, to say nothing of his ultimate intention.'

Nodding, Rollo turned away. 'You need motive, and more information, to give you a better picture.'

'Yes.' Doyle put his glass down, all business now. 'And that brings us to the reason for our visit. We need you to go after the man. McIntyre will send men, resources, anything you need. But they haven't seen him. You have.'

Rollo crossed his arms. The offer of men and resources was generous. He hated to accept it, but he was not at his best and God help them all if he failed. Still, he resisted. 'You do realise I don't actually work for the British Crown.'

'As of now you do. Your ambassador took very little persuading.'

'I don't come cheap. And what of Marian?' Rollo nodded in her direction.

She had been following the conversation like a spectator at a game of tennis. Now, she furrowed her brow and ran her fingers over the rim of her sherry glass.

Doyle glanced at her before turning back to him. 'Miss Finlay, unlike you, is a subject of the Crown and has seen the villain. It was her description I used for the likeness, after all. She can also assist you in using your new appendage and mastering its weapons.'

'I can manage.'

'And, finally'—Doyle's voice got harder—'it was your idea. You were willing to use her as a stalking horse before. Why not again?'

'You bastard!' Tossing aside his crystal tumbler, Rollo yanked on Doyle's brass-studded lapels with his good hand and, with his long metal fingers, clutched at his neck.

Marian called out, but in the next moment, Rollo's left arm was clenched in the detective's iron grip. Pain shot through him, his flesh still sore and tender from the recent surgery. He shoved Doyle away.

A grimace etched the corners of Doyle's mouth. 'And you're worried the thing doesn't work?'

'Let's get this over with. You want me to find Rebeniuc and kill him?'

'Not unless you must.' Doyle rubbed his throat. 'We need to know, as a matter of some urgency, who is behind this and why. How else are we to avoid another assassin following after him?'

Rollo sighed, put a hand to his brow and injected as much vitriol into his words as he could muster. 'And what role do you envisage for Marian? Is she just there to prompt my memory and teach me to feed myself?'

'Not at all,' said Doyle, then turned to Marian and extended a hand to her. After a second's hesitation, she took it, and Doyle pulled her forward. 'Mr Titus, meet Mrs Titus. As members of the hunting party, you will make a formidable team. Two is a far better weapon than one.'

Marian gasped at Doyle's words, and her eyes widened a fraction. But though she quickly schooled her features, her face now wiped of expression, Rollo could see the cogs turning.

He faced Doyle, a ripple of tiredness washing over him. 'You think you're clever? Very well. Is there anything I don't know about the political situation? Britain has been making threatening gestures at Russia …'

'Not precisely.'

'Near enough. If the Russians weren't concerned about your intentions, their navy wouldn't be anchored in New York Harbor. And don't forget the interest Britain and France have taken in the Southern cause.'

'I don't make policy, Rahgstadt. I do know that not all the Russian dukes were sanguine about the move to the States. There's a view that if there is to be a second war in the Crimea, Russia would be wise to dictate the terms.'

'Just a minute.' Marian spoke up, her voice confident and clear as a bell. 'This is all speculation until you know who the target might be. Yes, it could be the Queen or the Prime Minister, but it could be another party entirely. You must suspect a reason for Dracos being here, surely.'

Rollo considered. 'It could be any number of things. To create instability. To give a pretext for war. Perhaps even to force a position where Britain would be compelled to declare war. Assassinate a significant Briton and the people would bay for blood.'

Marian seemed to assimilate the information in the blink of an eye. The lightning fast processes of her mind and her uncanny ability to read people and situations were gifts.

Her head came up. 'Gentlemen, I will do anything I can to help you stop a war. Count me in.'

'Rahgstadt?'

Rollo looked from Marian to Doyle. 'Do you know what I am doing in England?'

'I imagine it has to do with the two ironclads being built for the Confederacy at Birkenhead.'

'My task was to ensure they didn't sail.' He met the man's eyes and held them, implacable. 'I want your word.'

'You have it.' Doyle shook Rollo's hand, then reached forward and shook Marian's. 'So, Rahgstadt? What will you do to prevent the world from being dragged into a great war?'

Rollo glanced at Marian; there was so much at stake. 'Whatever it takes.'

***

Marian sat in the unicarriage, stroking her fawn leather gloves and admiring the bronze chains studded at the wrists. She caught up the woollen skirt of her new carriage dress. The sage green was the ideal complement to her eyes, and the burnished leather corset set it off to perfection. Mrs Doyle had exquisite taste in fashion and had insisted Marian be outfitted with clothes that were both practical and tasteful. It would not do for Rollo's wife to draw attention to him because of poor tailoring.

They'd embarked on the trip to Balmoral, and when the unicarriage lurched as it steamed towards Holyrood Palace, she was thrown against Rollo yet again. His close proximity was unnerving. She was accustomed to him but was also acutely aware of him and his every movement.

She straightened. 'Do you do this often?'

'Hunt assassins?' His voice was soft; his weariness edged with melancholy.

'Well, no. I mean, pretend to be someone you're not.' She fiddled with her pocket watch, which she had secured to a loop on her leather corselet. Besides her wee gizmos, it was the only object she'd brought with her that was hers, a talisman in an unreal world. 'If you had told me this time last week that I would soon be on my way to meet the Queen, I would have laughed in your face.'

She studied him as he considered her question. Maybe Mr Somerton had been right and she'd rushed headlong into a situation for which she was unprepared. Was this her life now? A fiction wrapped in lies and deceit? But then, what had she been doing before, dressing as a man to win money from gullible gamblers? It had been a game, she admitted, a challenge. But now?

Craving a distraction, she slipped her hand into the pocket of her skirt and pulled out her bird gizmo. She perched it on her gloved index finger, licked her lips and whistled a few notes to the mechanical creature, then flicked a lever in the bird's breast and put the beak to her ear to listen. Her voice came back as a tinny echo.

She smiled sadly. Her gizmo was cleverly made and could accomplish its intended purpose, but it wasn't real; no one would mistake it for a real bird. And sitting here in these beautiful clothes, she realised she was as artificial as her tiny creations. Would anyone believe she was who she pretended to be?

Beside her, Rollo shrugged. 'I've pretended to be someone I'm not more often than I can remember.'

She met his gaze, took in his shuttered face, devoid of expression, and felt compelled to ask, 'Even with me? You know, the night we met?'

She thought she saw the hint of a smile, but she might have imagined it.

'No. You're one of the few people I've let … who I've been honest with.'

A wealth of meaning was woven through his words. The air fizzed and his eyes lured her, drawing her deeper. Turning her head, she lowered her gaze to her gizmo but was soon distracted by Rollo's hands, folded neatly in his lap. Both were clad in fine black leather gloves. She could not tell one from the other. Certainly, no one would suspect that under one of the gloves was a sheath made of hammered iron plates, each one scarcely thicker than a calling card, nor that they overlaid a star-metal skeleton.

Yesterday, once she and Rollo had taken a courteous leave of the Somertons, they had found Mr Doyle waiting outside in a nondescript unicarriage. As soon as they were seated inside with him, he'd handed Rollo a leather-bound folio with papers, maps and blueprints.

'You are Rollo and Marian Titus.' He'd nodded to Rollo. 'You are the son of a Pennsylvanian oil baron. You and your Scottish wife are here to provide the energy council of Great Britain with an indication of when and how oil can be transported from the United States to London, Belfast and Edinburgh. These identities will allow for movement and give your presence legitimacy.'

'Who at Balmoral knows the truth?'

Mr Doyle had gestured at the folio. 'It's all there, but the background notes don't leave my house. Burn them once you've studied them. We've given you a letter of introduction and a few personal effects that will support your covers. Keep those, of course.'

'Funds?'

'Some, but you won't need much, since you'll be guests of Her Majesty.'

Rollo had laughed at the euphemism. 'My old teacher always swore I'd wind up in prison.'

'Let's try to avoid that. I've included several hundred pounds, in notes and coin. Little sums to encourage confidences.'

'When do we leave?'

'Tomorrow morning at nine. You will arrive at Balmoral shortly after lunch.' Mr Doyle had looked at Marian as she'd fiddled with her gloves. 'Don't be troubled, Miss Finlay. We will organise suitable garments and some small instructions. But if you take your cues from Raghstadt, you won't go wrong.'

He'd been as good as his word. Besides the carriage dress she now wore, she had two glorious evening gowns and three day dresses packed in an elegant trunk, along with a dainty box Dr Somerton had given her. Marian was sure she wouldn't need the herb lozenges—after all, she and Rollo weren't actually married—but the doctor had been so concerned, Marian hadn't the heart to refuse.

Now, the unicarriage jolted over a bump, jerking Marian back to the present. She tucked her tiny mechanical bird back into her pocket and looked up at her faux husband. Rollo had scarcely said a word since they'd set off this morning.

The unicarriage slowed and gave a wide berth to other vehicles on the road before sliding down a narrow, cobbled lane. A plaque labelled with *The Abbey* flashed past the window.

Soon, they came to a steaming, shuddering halt at a large, grey edifice behind the palace complex. Other unicarriages disgorged sombre-suited gentlemen and elegantly garbed ladies. The butterflies were back in Marian's belly, this time chased by a herd of elephants. Could she do this? Could she convince people of rank and stature that she was one of them, the wife of a wealthy American oil man?

Rollo turned his Icelandic blues on her and her heart misbehaved.

'Ready, Mrs Titus?' His American accent seemed more prominent, more noticeable. He stood taller, more formal, and moved as if the sea would part before him.

It was an adventure, Marian reminded herself. And with Rollo at her side, she had a good chance of pulling off the deception. With that thought, her confidence rose.

'Quite ready, Mr Titus.' Her voice caught on the strange last name, but Rollo held out his arm and she took it.

It would take some time to get used to such familiarity. Jimmy, Cain, Will—they all treated her kindly and with their own innate courtesy, but they'd never thought to treat her as a lady. She wasn't used to being helped out of carriages or offered the support of a man's hand beneath her elbow. She stifled a pang for her old freedom of movement and, suddenly, no longer envied the wealthier women she'd seen from time to time. But this was merely a means to an end. She'd have to remember every pointer Doyle's patient wife had given her last night. How to behave in company had never been a concern of hers, let alone all the folderol that would occur should she be introduced to Victoria Regina.

They strolled away from the unicarriage, and Marian did her best to pretend indifference to the porter loading their trunks onto a small trolley.

Rollo patted her arm. 'Doyle said we wouldn't be the only guests travelling at Her Majesty's convenience.' He gestured to the scenery.

The station was tiny, though very pretty, with floral borders flanking the granite stairs that led to the platform. Wooden balustrades sat atop a delicate brass barrier. Benches, perfectly appointed for ladies to sit, graced the wide platform.

And then, she saw the train.

Chapter 12

Rollo couldn't help but smile. He'd seen engineering marvels before, but nothing as sumptuous as this. And Marian was simply stunned, her gasp drowned by the shriek of steam emitting from the long boiler.

Queen Victoria's private locomotive was the sleekest, most glorious, most … superlatives failed him. It was incredible. Both the long boiler and the smoke box in front were made of copper, smooth as silk and banded with steel. The steam dome was also banded, but in the metal was a crown, inlaid in gold lines with the royal monogram. Along the side of the boiler, thick polished steel pipes ran down and disappeared into the wheels, six of which were facing him, each with wide spokes and joined in pairs by pistons. Mounted at the front was the valve case in vibrant copper, set off by bright steel. Three whistles of various heights rose from the driver's cab, their tiny mouths billowing steam. The Queen's monogram was everywhere—on the heaped coal car and each of the royal blue carriages that trailed behind the engine. It had even been embroidered on the uniform of the conductor who hurried up to greet them.

'Mr and Mrs Rollo Titus?'

Rollo nodded.

'Indeed, if ye will come this way, sir, ma'am.' He set off down the platform.

Rollo whispered in Marian's ear. 'Come, my dear, mustn't keep Her Majesty waiting.'

He wasn't surprised when she gave a guilty start; she'd been staring at the engineering, as awestruck as a child peering through the window of a sweet shop.

The swirls of steam in the air brought out the delicate scent of jasmine from Marian's person, which he was trying hard to resist. Heaven knew he'd noticed her beauty before, even hidden under the dull workwear and leather safety apron she'd worn in Somerton's workshop. Now dressed in soft, flattering colours, her bonfire hair and milky skin rising from silk and lace, she was utterly distracting. The next few days of enforced proximity and the charade of marriage were going to test every ounce of restraint he'd ever imagined he possessed.

He took her by the elbow as the conductor led them along the platform to the third car and opened the second compartment for them. Up close, the carriages were even more magnificent than the engine. Thickly gilded wood ran along the roof of the train and the tops of each door, while gilded cherubs sat between each compartment.

The conductor bowed them in. 'We expect to leave in approximately ten minutes, sir.'

'Very good.' Rollo considered for a moment. 'There is a leather valise with my luggage. Would you be so good as to have it brought here?'

'Of course, Mr Titus.' The man withdrew.

Marian sank onto the lush blue seat. Opposite her was another seat, along with hooks and shelves for coats and hats. The floors were covered in an Axminster carpet in vivid reds and gold.

The porter delivered the black leather case and left, and Rollo breathed a sigh of relief to have it back in his hands. When he turned the brass handles on the doors to both the platform and passage, Marian took off her hat and gloves, unlooped the cog clasps on her coat and slipped out of it. She was exquisite, he thought and at once resisted. His unruly desires would be his undoing, and hers.

Instead, he knelt before the valise. 'Shall we take another look at the vambrace then?' It was a better option than the only other thing he could think to do during a four-hour train journey.

Twisting the cogs that locked the valise shut, he opened it, reached in and pulled out the wooden box. He set it between them on the plush seat as a steam whistle pierced the air and the train lurched forward.

'Certainly.' She flashed him a bright smile. 'Give me your hand, please?'

He smirked at her. 'I thought you would never ask.'

She rolled her eyes and grinned. 'Fool.' Then, taking his left hand in hers, she pulled the short glove free and folded back his coat sleeve. 'You can wear the armour beneath your clothing and simply explain it away as part of the prosthesis.'

Rollo lifted his hand and turned it, amazed all over again. Its outer shell had been fitted into place last night by a truculent Will

Ayre, who had been none too happy to learn Marian was involved in murderous goings-on.

He flexed the fingers, curling them slowly, in and out, then one at a time. Shaking his hand, he reached down and removed the glove from his right hand. 'I doubt I shall ever get used to this marvel.'

Marian lifted the vambrace free of the box and placed it on her lap. 'Bolts, please.'

He handed her the needle-sharp miniature bolts, and she loaded thirty into the vambrace.

She smiled and ran a finger over the metal. 'This crossbow is the best thing I have ever made. Beautiful but deadly.'

'Rather like you.'

She looked adorably confused for a moment, then laughed softly and shook her head.

When she pressed the shell of the vambrace, it clicked into place and she lifted her hands away. 'That's it. You will soon be able to do it for yourself.'

'I appreciate your confidence.' He turned the shell this way and that, marvelling at the recessed hinges, the snug fit. 'But why isn't it the same colour as the bones of the hand?'

She crooked her head to the side. 'The hand's skeletal structure is made of star metal, which Mr Somerton purchased from Germany, but only in a small amount because the hand was an experiment on his part. When Will went to make the outer shell of the vambrace, there wasn't enough star metal left, so Cain added some copper to the crucible. That's what's given it this lovely pink look.

It's also why the outer casing of the hand is made of plain iron. It's heavier, of course, but the amounts are smaller, and it's all we had available.'

'You'll get no argument from me.' He lifted his hand, flexing the joints and watching the thin plates slide over one another like those on a knight's gauntlet. Then he turned his arm and examined the vambrace. It came to a sharp point on the dorsal view of the hand and ended in a correlating point on the anterior side of the lower arm. Discreetly built into the structure was the small but powerful crossbow Marian had made, now loaded and ready to fire up to thirty darts. She'd succeeded in making the weapon a seamless part of his body.

'This is incredible work, Marian.'

'Thank you.' She gave no coy blush but was, instead, pragmatic about her work. 'Cain made over two hundred darts in all. The spares are in the base of the box, as is the mould. It's why it's so heavy.'

'I'd noticed. And there's no need to reload?'

'No.' She pressed the catch, opening the top again. 'These cogs make up the self-loading mechanism. And these are the winding gears, operated from the wrist.'

'And the upper part of the vambrace? Why leather?'

'A metal-studded leather shield over metal,' she corrected. 'Within it are scabbards for two knives, a stiletto and a throwing knife.'

'You've thought of everything.'

She shrugged. 'Doyle designed it. We only made it. Now, come sit beside me. Remember, while the safety is on, the fist is safe. The firing mechanism cannot be engaged.'

'Marian.' He waited until she looked up.

'Yes?'

Though common sense screamed at him to stop, he leaned forward and brushed his lips against her cheek. 'Thank you.'

Now, she blushed. 'You're very welcome.'

***

They meandered past open woodlands at thirty miles an hour. The trees were half-bare, and drifts of gold and russet leaves swirled away from the train, but Rollo was scarcely conscious of the scenery. Instead, he pointed his fist towards the open window, inhaled and took aim. The crossbow rose from the top of the vambrace and the string grew taut. He flexed his wrist downwards, winding the mechanism, and pressed his fingers into his palm. Finally, he imagined the tiny bolt hurtling down the barrel.

Nothing happened.

'Ugh. I'll never get this thing to work. Are you sure all the parts are screwed in properly?' He threw an uncharitable glance at Marian, who was making notes in a slender notebook.

'You're trying too hard.' She didn't look up, but he didn't need to see her face to know she didn't care for his attitude.

'You could check it again.'

'I've checked it, Rollo. And unless you want me to get my tools out of the luggage car and take it apart, you're going to have to trust me. The mechanism works.'

'Damn!' He thrust his right hand up to his temple and tugged at his hair. 'How long will it take for me to master it then? We are no more than an hour from Balmoral, and I still can't use it.'

Marian sighed and shut her book. 'It has been less than a day. I know it's difficult, but your body has to learn new skills and relearn old ones. Come, practise the control exercises with me again.' She stretched her left hand in front of her, the gold wedding band gleaming against her pale skin.

'I don't need to practise. The hand is responding well to my control.' He shook his head, knowing he was behaving like a child, but time was no longer his friend, and neither was the damn vambrace!

Without a word, she turned the saucer-sized captain's wheel on the door, and the window slid shut, blocking out the frigid air. The cabin began to warm again instantly, so it wasn't that which made her close her eyes and shiver.

Compassion prickled at him. He reset the safety on the vambrace and moved across the carriage to sit beside her.

'What's the matter, Marian? You don't need to be nervous about reaching Balmoral. You'll be wonderful.'

When she glanced at him, he could read the tension in her brow. She tugged at her lip with her teeth, and her eyes, normally starlit gems, were instead dry moss.

He frowned. 'Or is it something else?'

121

'Making your hand work will be for naught if we can't find him.' Her tone was petulant, like that of a fractious child. 'It's not like he'll be hunting in the open. And we don't even know for certain who his target is ... unless you found something in the papers Doyle gave you.'

He shook his head, and she seemed to deflate a little more.

Her sudden change of mood and the anxiety on her beautiful face woke a tenderness within him, something with which he'd had little experience. This vulnerability, so unlike the strength to which he was accustomed, tugged at his heart. A tear sparkled on her cheek, and he wiped it away. Giving in to the temptation, he cupped her cheek.

She nestled closer, and he gave a silent sigh of relief. Her warmth seeped into him through his heavy woollen coat and he allowed himself to luxuriate in the feel of her rose-petal skin against his hand. When she closed her eyes, he took the chance to study the soft spray of freckles that spanned her nose and cheeks. Her pink lips beckoned to him. He wanted to take her tiny pointed chin between thumb and forefinger and—

He checked himself. The kiss on her cheek had been a mistake. He'd simply meant to thank her for what she'd done for him, so he'd kissed her as he would have kissed his sister. But she wasn't his sister.

He forced himself to pull his hand away, and a blade of regret slid between his ribs.

She looked up at him, and for a moment, he wondered whether she was reading his thoughts. But if she had, she said nothing, just smiled sadly.

'Tears, Mrs Titus? That's not like you.'

'I'm sorry. I haven't been sleeping well lately.'

He was surprised she was sleeping at all, but he pressed her hand gently. 'We will find him. We know what he looks like, how he operates. We can work out how he thinks. And once we are at Balmoral, we can gather more information about who the target might be. Who knows, maybe we can force him to come to us?'

'Yes, but if we can't?'

'We will. Because we don't have a choice.' Instantly, he regretted his abrupt tone.

Marian nodded once, then turned her face away.

Sick dread roiled through Rollo. What if she was right? Before they could defeat Dracos, they had to figure out his plan. If they couldn't, the intended target would die. Who could say what pandemonium such an act would cause? There were untold lives at stake … and then there was Marian. Stubborn, loyal, courageous Marian Finlay, who'd been in the wrong place at the wrong time, had stumbled into a world of danger … and into his heart.

It was one thing to risk his life in the service of others—this wasn't the first time, and God willing, it would not be the last—but he was no longer sure he could put Marian at risk. He closed his eyes and mentally damned Charles Doyle. She was a distraction he could not afford.

Chapter 13

Marian cupped her cheek where Rollo's hand had rested all too briefly. She didn't want to be attracted to him, but her body refused to listen. His recent kiss had made her yearn for more.

This damned situation! She had to pretend they were lovers—that they were *in love*—yet could not fall into that snare. But his kiss, his touch, had been mere polite gratitude. They did not warrant this pathetic need, this hunger that roiled inside her like mistimed cogs in a grandfather clock. And logic told her it was dangerous to feel too much for him. He walked in shadows, wore half-truths closer and more comfortably than he did the coat on his back. She knew he did so to avoid betrayal and the very real threats his occupation courted. But the part of her that was all woman, eager for love and hungry for his kiss, refused to acknowledge any such hindrance. Her mind and her heart were at war; she could only hope to keep her folly hidden from him, the handsome spy who sat opposite her, seemingly lost in a world of worry.

Marian closed her notebook, some sixth sense telling her the train was slowing. Perhaps it was just as well. Her mind refused to absorb any more of Mrs Doyle's maxims.

'Are we there?'

Outside the window, a large grey pyramid of stone slid into view. The train hissed like a tired dragon.

'Ah, no. I think this might be Prince Albert's Cairn. Apparently, the train always stops here to observe a minute's silence.'

He spun the wheel, turning down the window, and they sat in silence. A dove-grey cloud drifted across the lazy autumn sun. Even the twitter of birds seemed to hush, as if to pay tribute to the Queen's love and loss. From somewhere in the distance, another sound wafted through the window in the wake of damp, earthy scents.

'Is that music?'

Rollo touched Marian on the shoulder, pulling her lightly back into the carriage. 'I believe so. Perhaps gypsies? And ladies do not poke their heads out of train carriages.' He then popped his own head out and looked up and down.

The train jolted into motion, sending hot clouds of smoke billowing from the wheels.

Marian considered. Gypsies. She'd never met any, but she'd read about them. Their lives sounded intriguing. Mysterious. Free.

Minutes later, the tip of the great grey tower of Balmoral peeped from beyond the crown of tall pines. The royal ensign fluttered on the breeze; Her Majesty was in residence.

When the train pulled into the Queen's private station on the north end of the castle, Marian froze in her seat. This was it. The time had come for her to take her place in the game of lies and daggers. A quiver shuddered through her body. What if she ran into the assassin again, but this time Rollo wasn't there to save her?

Another thought followed hard on the heels of the first. She turned and put her hand over Rollo's. 'Where would he hide? Is he disguised as we are?'

'I don't expect a man of his stature could blend in easily, and I very much doubt he would hide in plain sight as we are doing.'

She looked back the way they had come. 'Would he attempt to blend in with the gypsies?'

He shrugged, placid as a lake. 'It's a possibility. We must keep our eyes and ears open for anything out of the ordinary.'

She flounced; she couldn't help it. 'And just what part of this situation is ordinary?'

The hint of a dimple appeared in his cheek and hidden laughter warmed his voice. 'It will work, Marian. You know what to do.'

A reply rose to her lips, but she choked it back. His gaze was on the liveried men who were unloading the luggage. Not one of them was tall enough to be the monster, but the mission was all that mattered to him now. His eyes held a diamond sharpness; the soft blue gaze she'd noted at the Somertons' home after the operation had vanished. His soul was masked from the world; others would see nothing but what he wanted them to see.

With conscious effort, Marian pulled her new personality around her and extended one gloved hand to her husband.

***

Rollo leaned close. 'Don't forget, everyone is suspect. Divulge as little as possible.'

He'd spoken curtly, but although he didn't like to cause Marian pain, he could not afford to have her inexperience betray them. She was clearly overwhelmed with their circumstances; her eyes were soft and lambent, and her hand often strayed to her lips or cheek. She looked at him dourly but said nothing.

Rollo offered his hand as she gathered her skirts and stepped into the waiting unicarriage. It was one of several emblazoned with the royal crest, ready to receive those who had travelled from London and Edinburgh. Among those disembarking was an elegant redhead, beautifully gowned. Rollo identified her with a frisson of concern. He also spotted several liveried servants and plainly garbed retainers, plus a small boy. Several other couples stood on the platform, along with one rotund gentleman of advanced years and high forehead. He also looked uncommonly familiar. Crates were being unloaded from the baggage car, most of which were stamped with the hallmark of Fortnum and Mason. But Rollo could see no outlandishly tall, masked black-caped assassins.

'Do you think Dracos will have spies in the royal household, or in the entourage of the other guests? After all, we do.'

'Yes.' His response was abrupt by necessity. They needed to have this conversation later.

'Was there anything in the note Doyle gave you this morning?'

'Yes and no.' Yes, there had been. But no, he hadn't expected that *she*—that *they*—would be on the same train. He'd hoped for a chance to gather more information on their fellow guests before being pitched into close companionship.

He glanced at Marian. Though she was a little pale, her nervousness had not dulled the intelligence in her eyes, so it seemed only fair that he should divulge the information Doyle's note had contained.

'Perhaps I should've mentioned there was a last-minute addition to the guest list.'

He looked towards the first unicarriage in the line, just ahead of their own. The Queen's representative was bowing and scraping before the redheaded lady. Her low musical voice carried as she spoke in perfect, unaccented English. The child stood beside his nanny. Rollo processed the information about their entourage and filed it away to discuss with the contact Doyle had promised him.

He spoke softly so only Marian could hear. 'I'm worried, certainly, though I don't think she's a threat if that's what you're asking. Glance to your left. The lady with the red hair and the ostrich feather in her hat. Our fellow guest, Her Imperial Majesty The Empress Eugénie of France.'

'Oh my!' Marian gazed across the platform and then back to him without any discernible reaction. 'And the child?'

'The Prince Imperial.'

Marian's eyes grew wide. 'I thought her an English lady.'

He shook his head. 'Her grandfather was Scottish, and she passed part of her education here.'

Rollo noted Marian's abstracted frown, evidence of furious thought on her part. 'Are we to add the Empress to our list of potential logical targets?'

Well, she was a quick study, he would give her that. For all that she knew no world but Edinburgh, she had a ready grasp of the dangers into which they had willingly stepped.

He nodded. 'And consider members of her entourage as possible conduits of information.'

'Ah.'

The damper hissed and the unicarriage jolted forward. They, and the Imperial party, started for the castle.

***

Marian decided the Queen's drawing room at Balmoral was an un-settling mixture of grandeur and simplicity. Though its furnishings were not so very different from those at the Somertons' residence, the size and sheer number of rooms was overwhelming. Almost as panic-inducing were the knots of people, more than a score and all beautifully attired, gathering around the room. Against the wall, close to her ear, a handsome clock with polished cogs on display behind a glass front, struck the hour.

Rollo must have noted she was dragging her feet. He leaned close in an affectionate, husbandly way. 'Be calm, Marian. Remem-ber, this is all utterly familiar to you. You are not nonplussed by a large home filled with art and furniture.'

'But all these people—'

'Are just people. Her Majesty seldom has guests here. Many of these are members of the local aristocracy, aside from a few digni-taries.'

Marian wasn't so sure. Her eyes were going to pop out of her head at the setting, but she took a deep breath and relaxed her shoulders, slowed her gait. It would not be impolite to take an interest in the furnishings, she decided. They passed filigree encrusted tables and a dynamic candelabra in wrought silver, heavy with images of fruit. Rich fabrics adorned long windows and the mantelpiece was covered with tiny porcelain ornaments. The walls bore landscapes and images of children while an enormous image of the late Prince Consort hung in pride of place.

Marian viewed the other guests more cautiously. She did not want to be caught staring. Subdued laughter came from one group near the window. A tall, slim man bowed courteously to two ladies and withdrew.

At the door, Marian and Rollo were greeted by a short merry-faced woman.

'Mr Titus.' She extended her hand and Rollo saluted it with perfect gravity, as though he were born to court. 'Mrs Titus. Welcome to Balmoral. I am Lady Claire Lindow, one of Her Majesty's ladies-in-waiting. I hope you had a pleasant journey.'

Lady Lindow poured both Marian and Rollo a cup of tea and offered tiny sandwiches. 'I am the comptroller of the royal household. Please do let me know if there is anything you need.' She looked warmly over Rollo's shoulder. 'Mr and Mrs Buchan, are you acquainted with Mr Titus and his wife?'

Marian turned to see a man in his middle years, accompanied by an elegantly slender woman. Although her face was mostly unlined, there were thick streaks of grey in her chestnut coiffure. The man reached out and took Rollo's hand in a firm shake.

'Titus. Dear fellow. I don't think I have seen you for five years or more. It was at Easter one year, do you recall?'

If Rollo was surprised, he gave nothing away. 'Of course, Mr Buchan. I recall a feast of large red eggs. It was a memorable visit.'

As Lady Lindow took her leave, duty done, Marian realised the enigmatic conversation explained Mr Buchan's presence. The sportive gentleman was Rollo's contact.

Rollo introduced her to the couple, but they had not achieved more than bare civility before there was a stir at the door. A stolid man dressed in a kilt, with a tartan sash pinned to his shoulder, tapped a long staff on the floor. The boom brought the murmuring crowd to silence.

'Her Majesty The Queen and Her Imperial Majesty The Empress Eugénie.'

Along with every other lady in the room, Marian curtsied, eyes downcast. But not before she had seen the plump, dour face of the Queen and the regal loveliness of the Empress. The two royal ladies walked the length of the room, offering a word here, a greeting there. The Queen passed by Marian, then lingered briefly in front of Rollo before taking her seat in a strategically positioned high-backed chair.

At some predetermined sign, the interrupted conversations resumed, though they were now more subdued. All around the room, people sat in groups around low tables. There were about two dozen people, not including the maids who were carrying out plates of delicacies. Mrs Buchan escorted Marian to a pair of chairs.

'This is a beautiful room.' Marian was careful to keep her voice conversational.

'Isn't it? This was Her Majesty's favourite parlour, where she and the late Prince Consort were wont to entertain.'

Unsurprisingly, the room had a homely feel in the soft furnishings, the plethora of ornaments, and in the chairs that flanked the fireplace. Marian could imagine Her Majesty sitting there, her children playing at her feet. The room reminded her of the Somertons' family parlour. Suddenly, it was a little less intimidating.

'What do you know about the Empress?' Lady Buchan questioned.

What was there to say? Marian knew precious little that wasn't in the public domain, and neither did she know if Mrs Buchan could be trusted. A knot formed in her stomach.

'Only that she is Spanish and that the Emperor was ensnared by her beauty. She would not be his mistress, so he made her his wife.'

Mrs Buchan inclined her head. 'She is a force to be reckoned with. The Emperor often seeks her advice. He left her as regent of France a few years ago.'

Marian watched the Empress Eugénie hold court and thought she did so with a light hand. She appeared interested in her companions but not familiar and kept a kindly distance from the other ladies. One nodded, curtsied and left her side.

'Ah, here comes Emily Palmerstone.' Mrs Buchan's tone held just a hint of disdain. She and Marian rose, and Mrs Buchan smiled when the Prime Minister's wife stopped in front of them. 'Dear Lady Palmerstone, I'd like to introduce you to Mrs Titus, the—'

'Yes, my husband mentioned there would be an American couple among the guests.'

Marian detected an undertone of condescension in Her Ladyship's politeness. 'I'm afraid only my husband is American, Lady Palmerstone.' She offered the woman a smile and a greatly abbreviated curtsey. Even that went against the grain.

Lady Palmerstone's watery grey eyes widened at Marian's accent. 'You are a Scot.'

Marian inclined her head. 'I am, indeed.'

With a grimace and a nod, Lady Palmerstone left, accepting a seat and a cup of tea from Lady Claire.

'I thought you should meet her, though take care when you speak with her. She has a somewhat exalted opinion of herself.' Mrs Buchan turned and offered Marian her arm, then smiled. 'Come. Let's have some of the tiny scones with a slice of strawberry. They are quite delicious.'

Within a few minutes, they were seated with Rollo, Mr Buchan, and Lord and Lady Avondale. A maid poured tea into a delicate china cup. It was the best Marian had ever tasted, and she sipped as she watched the others. His Lordship was, it seemed, a local landowner and would not be a guest in Balmoral itself, although he would join the hunting party.

Mrs Buchan scanned the refreshments. 'Now, tomorrow is the first hunt, and by the sounds of it, there'll be three or four hunting trips this weekend. The first, tomorrow morning at the crack of dawn, will be for the men only.' She took her plate and held the gilded tongs over the scones. 'Would you care for some?'

'Just one, please.' Marian thought the scones looked delicious, as did the tiny tartlets and the slivers of fruit cake, but her stomach was in a Gordian knot. 'Will we not be attending the hunt?'

Mrs Buchan smiled at her. 'We ladies will only attend when Her Majesty does, which will be tomorrow afternoon when we ride out to the grouse field. I take it you ride?'

'Not well.' Or ever. Oh, why had she not considered this? 'Please, excuse me.'

Marian rose and made her way towards the corridor where she knew the ladies' retiring room was located. Her corset was tight, but it was not that which had her breathless. Why had she thought she could do this? Yes, she had been willing to act as bait for the monster of the docks, but that had not required half the courage of taking tea in the presence of royalty.

Slowly, the breath returned to her lungs. She considered re-joining her party, but something compelled her to wait, to spend a moment observing. After all, when would there be a time to consider who might be a target ... and who might be an enemy in disguise?

Chapter 14

A gentleman stood in a corner of the room, staring up at the painting of the Royal Albert Bridge. Marian recognised him from the train. He was not much taller than she and had dark, friendly eyes, an open face, long sideburns and a pair of bronze goggles pushed up onto his thinning hair. He was solidly built, wore a waistcoat that was snug at the belly, and held an unlit cigar, distinctly chewed, in his left hand. He held out his right.

'You are a fellow train traveller, ma'am?' He seemed as jolly as Saint Nicholas, and his hand was warm and firm.

Marian smiled in spite of herself. 'I am, sir. Do you recognise me?'

He beamed. 'I always make it a point to recognise beautiful ladies.'

'Sir, you flatter me.'

'Well, of course. I'm hoping you will do me the honour of conversing with me. I believe you are Mrs Titus, am I right? And is that your husband talking to our distinguished Prime Minister?'

He was right. Rollo, at just that moment, had risen to shake hands with Palmerstone.

'You are very observant, sir.' Surely that would be an excellent quality in a spy. Why had he sought her out?

'An occupational hazard, my dear. My name is Brunel. I happened to notice the ornament you wear.'

Marian felt dizzy. Isambard Brunel was Britain's most ingenious engineer. The bridge in the painting, which had been named after the late Prince Consort, was this man's design. And he was inquiring about her gizmo? It was as though God himself had deigned to notice her.

'My beetle, sir?' She unhooked it from the breast of her gown and laid it in his hand.

He turned it over, minutely observing it for a moment. 'Indeed. Quite intriguing. May I ask where you acquired it?'

Her heart leapt. Being recognised by her idol made her incautious; the words were out before she'd given them thought. 'I made it, sir.'

Brunel's eyes stretched as wide as a unicarriage wheel. 'You don't say! Does it have a function?'

It was a pleasure to share her ideas with a man who was capable of understanding them. He continued to study it and seemed particularly fascinated with the joints of the wings and carapace, and the internal cog work, too. She showed him the tiny compact tools layered within.

'Well, Mrs Titus, your husband is a lucky man indeed.' He gave her a particularly beatific smile as he handed it back. 'And it is a pleasure to converse with such a beautiful and talented engineer. Where did you study?'

Now Marian demurred. 'I did not attend university, sir. I have recently had the privilege of working with someone who is a genius in his own right and has no qualms about teaching me.'

Brunel's eyes twinkled. 'Who is this genius, may I ask?'

'Mr Beauden Somerton of the—'

'Ah, of the Somerton Metal Artisans Company? Of course. I would not object to working with Somerton myself, though I tend to build things on a larger scale. And you have not yet been to America, I hear?'

'No, sir.' A ripple of worry ran through Marian. Had she invalidated her cover by mentioning Somerton? 'My husband has a great deal of business to manage, both here and on the continent. I will be fortunate to see my new family and home within a twelvemonth.'

'Never mind, my dear.' Brunel patted her hand, giving her the impression of an avuncular walrus. 'It is but a few weeks across the pond. Several of my ships are on that route. And, from here, I will be going to Glasgow where I have several experimental models. If time permits, you would be welcome to visit the ship works. I believe you would find it as interesting as I have found your own work.'

Rollo appeared at her side. 'Pardon the intrusion, but I must reclaim my wife. We have been invited to speak with Her Majesty.'

'Of course.' Scrupulously polite, Brunel bowed over her hand. 'Perhaps, Mrs Titus, if you have an interest, I would like to show you some of the design blueprints I have with me. I plan to install a combination single screw and paddle wheel on one of my ships.' Though Brunel addressed her, he looked at Rollo, and Marian felt the sudden weight of being her husband's property.

137

She flicked a glance at Rollo before replying. 'It would be a pleasure, sir.'

Halfway across the room, Rollo lowered his mouth to her ear. 'Why did Brunel want to show you a blueprint?'

'Because I told him I built this beetle.' Her fingers brushed over the tiny object.

Rollo's lips tightened. 'You do realise that according to our cover you are not an engineer.'

She met his eyes without hesitation. 'I am now.'

***

'What's the news from below stairs, Moody?'

Rollo handed the constable his copper-embroidered waistcoat and pulled the cravat from his throat. Ah, but that felt good. Just as a woman must feel when the laces of her corset were released.

They were in the small, windowless dressing-room that adjoined the bedroom, where, even now, Marian's maid, borrowed from Mrs Doyle, was preparing her for bed. McIntyre, in a fit of genius, had managed to find Moody, a constable who had spent a year in service before joining the ranks. The servants would know a true valet, would sniff out a false one in hours, so he had undertaken to provide.

'There are no new staff ta'en on here, sir. And all the ones who have come with guests have been in their positions above a twelvemonth.'

'I see.' It wasn't exactly a dead end—in fact, it was the information he'd expected—but it was disappointing all the same.

Removing his cuffs, he pulled the drawstring on his shirt and dragged the garment over his head. When he sat, Moody crouched and pulled off one boot, then the other.

'Nothing else, I take it?' Rollo hoped for anything. Even a crumb of information was better than what he had currently.

Moody shrugged. 'Word has it, they gypsies 'ave come up to camp near the castle. Her Majesty permits it so long as they only take rabbits, not the deer. That gillie of Her Majesty, Brown, has no time for them. Says they cause trouble, make him uneasy.'

Rollo nodded, then paused, deep in thought. He pulled his mirror messenger from his pocket, checked the silver paper and wrote a short, neat message with his black wax stylus. When he closed the lid, the message was sent with a flash and a puff of smoke. He tapped the charred paper charge into the fireplace.

As Moody tidied away the clothes, Rollo changed into a nightshirt and contemplated the evening. It had been uneventful, for which he should be grateful. Her Majesty had been a generous hostess, though her black-draped presence was a sobering one. The Empress on the other hand was elegant and charming enough for both. Of the men arrayed around the table, the most logical choice of victim for an assassin's bullet was Palmerstone. Assassinations were conducted for political gain, and while Avondale was tedious, he wasn't worth importing a killer. His Royal Highness The Prince of Wales would have made an excellent target, but he was in London, and in any case, he had sufficient royal brothers to succeed him.

Rollo had managed to make contact with Brown, the Queen's servant, and had spoken to Palmerstone at some length. But though the Prime Minister knew of the assassin, he was only cramming his head deeper into the sand. According to him, nothing had happened; therefore, nothing would.

Folly.

Palmerstone had been less than courteous to Rollo, but perhaps it was simply the stress of knowing, or at least suspecting, that someone wanted him dead. It had to be bad for the digestion. Lady Palmerstone, too, had watched Marian with less than perfect amity.

At the thought of Marian, Rollo smiled to himself.

She'd handled herself well at the card table this evening. He knew her to be a superlative card player—she could read the other players as she would a child's primer—so it must have taken all her willpower to fluff her hands so convincingly.

He had enjoyed watching her, learning the little clues to her thoughts. Only someone who knew her would notice the tiny tremor of her lower lip, or the way she fisted her fingers around her thumbs when the stress began to weigh on her.

But then there was the situation with Brunel …

That was worth a heartfelt sigh. It seemed that like called to like; Marian had managed to attract the only engineer in the room within minutes. And when Rollo had offered her the mildest of rebukes for exposing their story to scrutiny, she'd told him she was only following Doyle's advice.

'The best cover,' she'd said, looking over her shoulder at him, 'is a mere sprinkling of illusion over the truth.'

Minx.

But the spark of creativity in her had been a beacon. When they'd taken tea in the drawing room after dinner, the Empress had noticed Marian's beetle gizmo with its delicate gold carapace and had asked about it. Marian had pulled it off her gown for the second time that evening and had demonstrated some of its features. With any luck, the interest shown by ranking members of the party would result in closer access to them. Surely someone would have a clue in their heads about why the assassin was here.

After dismissing Moody, Rollo dialled down the dynamic light in the dressing room and turned the bedroom door handle.

'Out!' Marian clutched a gown to her body and dashed behind the privacy screen.

'I beg your pardon!' Though he'd only caught a glimpse of a long, white flank, it was enough to enliven his night. 'I had thought you would be dressed by now.'

A rustling sound indicated she was wriggling about behind the screen. Averting his gaze, he focused instead on the line of gizmos arrayed along the mantelpiece and recognised the dragon she'd used to create fire. The turtle dove emitted a short burst of sound. The beetle she had worn on her gown was a clever multipurpose tool, like the one he wore on his belt but more compact. He took in the gizmos' precise industrial beauty and felt a sense of chagrin that he had been so dismissive of a woman's ability. Meeting Marian and the lady doctors in Edinburgh had given him a whole new perspective. Not to mention that in this very castle were two women with phenomenal political power. Nevertheless, he dismissed such philosophical musings and turned his mind to happier things.

The room held only one bed. He should be a gentleman—after all, they were not married nor likely to be. Even still, he'd been unable to curb his desire for his faux wife. More than once, he'd caught himself watching her mouth, and at one point, his gaze had played over the swell of her décolletage and slender neck. He'd even felt a tinge of jealousy when she'd laughed and smiled at Brunel earlier, though the man was a good thirty years his senior and in bad health. Fortunately, their room also held a sofa. As pleasant as it would be to sleep beside Marian, he would be foolish to torment himself so.

Laughing inwardly, he reached for one of her gizmos, then stopped. His hand, extended toward the mantelpiece, was not flesh but cold hard iron. He had iron in his belly, too.

No. The nightmare of his anaesthetised dreams rose up again and his face grew clammy. He did not want to be near her, to risk touching her with this.

Though none of the other guests had said anything, he'd seen the flare in their eyes at the sight of his gloved hand. Moody had been charged with spreading the cover story in the servants' hall, as if in the strictest of confidences, about his master's scarred limb and how it had been disfigured in a fire.

Rollo brought the hand up to his face and, feeling the unyielding metal against his skin, spun away from the mantel, sickened.

At the sound of movement behind him, he turned—and sucked in a lungful of air. Marian wore a nightdress made of embroidered lawn, almost sheer. Its length fell from a pleated panel above the breast and ended in a wide ruffle at her feet. If Botticelli had clothed Venus in a nightgown on that shell, she would have resembled Marian, with her glorious wildfire hair tumbling over her shoulders. She had washed the stage paint and powder from her throat, so now the residual bruises could be seen in faint yellows and greens.

Slipping into the bed, she pulled the deep blue velvet cover up, wriggled towards the foot, then leaned forward. 'What are you doing?'

Thinking about putting your nightgown on the floor where it belongs.

'I was just looking at your gizmos.' A little distance would be a good thing right now. 'We should sleep. Tomorrow will be busy.' He took a pillow from the bed and bent to take a blanket from the box at its foot.

'What on earth are you doing?'

'I should sleep on the sofa.'

'Oh no.' She shook her head vigorously. 'I sat there earlier. It's harder than Castle Rock. And anyway, there is more than enough space in the bed.'

'You don't want me to see you in your nightclothes, but you don't object to sharing a bed?'

Her cheeks flushed the same shade as freshly cut strawberries. 'I know. It's nonsensical. But I trust you.'

Trust. That word was an arrow to his heart. Trust always came with strings. Or at least it always had for him. Would this time be different?

'Besides,' she grabbed the bolster that ran under both pillows, a thick sausage as wide as the bed, 'I can put this between us. And I always sleep with my dagger.'

Rollo looked at the lumpy sofa with its hard cushions and too-short base. In the end, it was not the sofa that lost but desire that won. He would keep his distance; the bolster would see to that. As would her dagger.

The thought made him smile. Let her barricade the bed. The pleasure of sleeping with her would be compensation enough for lack of more carnal aspirations.

'In that case,' he slipped between the cool linen sheets, 'I will risk it. I only hope my virtue will be safe with you.'

She narrowed her eyes. 'Safer than you will be, sir, if you say another word.'

He chuckled. 'Goodnight, wife. Sleep well.'

Chapter 15

The soft ting of his mirror messenger, which sat on the bedside table, brought Rollo awake and alert. Apart from the glow of embers in the fireplace and the rim of light under the cover of his device, a residual effect of the photographic flash, the room was a dull grey. He was not groggy—years of living on the edge of danger had left him with the ability to wake ready for anything—but he had not slept so peacefully, or so deeply, in years.

And yet he could not move.

The bolster was shoved ignominiously to the foot of the bed, and his right shoulder was pinned down by a fiery head. A sweet floral scent tickled his senses. He turned, as much as he could, and rolled slowly onto his right side, attempting to pull his arm out from under her. She murmured and snuggled closer, a lock of hair falling across her face. She looked like a ginger kitten.

He moved to brush the strand of hair away, then froze. Slowly, not trusting he wouldn't hurt her, he moved his iron hand away.

After managing to extricate himself, he snatched up his messenger, stole into the dressing room and, closing the door behind him, read the terse message.

Damn! Quickly, he lifted the speaking tube and summoned Moody, then pulled off his nightshirt.

'Sir?'

Rollo buttoned the nondescript tweed trousers, which Moody had left out the night before, over his linen drawers. 'I'm going with Mr Brown to reconnoitre the gypsy camp. Please let my wife know where I have gone when she wakes.' He pulled the box that held the vambrace from its secure location. 'And help me with this, please.'

'Yes, sir.'

Rollo checked the crossbow, making sure the magazine was full, then laid his left arm in the bottom half. Moody closed it, secured the clasps and tightened the leather strap.

Lifting his arm, Rollo tested the added weight. Slowly, he raised his hand and pointed his index finger at the small silver horse figurine sitting on the dressing table. Taking a deep breath, he curled his middle finger inwards until it touched his palm, and the miniature crossbow rose from the vambrace with a whirr of cogs.

He eyed his target, then clenched his fist and flexed his wrist down sharply. A slender bolt, two inches long, slammed into the picture frame a hand's-breadth above the figurine.

'God damn it all to hell! Will I ever—' Rollo shook his head and pinched his brows together. It didn't matter. He'd only been fitted with the arm a few days ago. Time. He was getting closer.

Moody sucked in a gasp of air. 'Good Lord above, sir!' He stared wide-eyed at the crossbow and had a death grip on the handle of the carry case.

'Surprised you, did I, Moody? I've only been using it for a day. Still getting the knack.'

Moody shook his head. 'Well, sir, you are a quick study then. That were a good shot. Wound the beggar, for sure.'

'Thank you, only don't mention it outside these walls. Not even to your colleagues. We had to bend a few rules.'

'Och, aye, sir. The detective had me swear on a Bible before he would let me come wi' ye.'

Moody handed him a clean shirt. Rollo pulled it over his head, then adjusted the cuff of the shortened left sleeve so it sat under the rim of the vambrace. Mrs Doyle's seamstress had done an excellent job.

After slipping on a vest and heavy frieze coat, Rollo followed Moody down the servants' stair and into the stable courtyard. It was still dark and the birds weren't yet stirring, but the moon was low. He caught a faint whiff of—

'Titus.' A brusque voice spoke from the shadows and a stolid figure built to match moved from the lee of the stable wall.

Moody spun on his heel, but Rollo was not taken unawares.

Brown tapped his pipe and the fragrant cherry tobacco tipped onto the gravel. He ground it out with his heel, then put the pipe in his pocket. 'Weel, are we away?'

Rollo gestured into the darkness. 'Do we require lanterns?'

'Nay.' Brown's voice was placid as milk, his face expressionless. 'The moon will light oor way.'

'Very well.' Rollo turned to Moody. 'If we're not back in good time after dawn, let McIntyre know.'

At Moody's answering nod, Rollo put the bulk of the castle behind them and set off in Brown's wake. They left the gravelled forecourt, then passed onto manicured lawn and the dark woods beyond. Though the light was swallowed by the trees, there was just enough to make out their next few steps.

Brown, it seemed, would know these woods blindfolded. He skirted around the rockier parts, following a slim trail. Sometimes they went single file, but eventually, they broke into a wider ride, and Rollo was able to do more than merely follow.

'I ken ye be looking fer some fiend in human form?' Brown stumped along with his eyes downcast as he followed the path.

'That's right. He killed four people in Edinburgh.' His comment was met with silence, except for the swish of their feet over dewy grass, but Rollo felt a moment of keen scrutiny.

'And that's why ye think he will bide with the Romany?'

'He speaks English with a very strong accent. And he may well speak the language of the gypsies. We don't know much about him, but we do know he does not blend into a Scottish crowd. He may be less noticeable in a foreign group.'

Rollo looked over at Brown, who was no more than a shadow. With little light in the woods, his dark clothes kept him hidden. Only the silver nimbus of his breath gave away his location.

'But ye feel they are kin to his sort?'

The man had a knack for asking questions.

'No, I don't.'

'Then, sir, why are we on this fool's errand?'

148

Sighing, Rollo stopped and clenched his fists, the iron one as keenly aware of his frustration as his flesh. Originally, Brown was not one of those intended to know of the threat, but Buchan had convinced Rollo the man had a need to know. He had the Queen's ear and confidence, and if Her Majesty's safety was at stake, he was their best hope of preserving it. So he would give Brown as much information as he dared and hope to God it would shut him up.

'We have little to no knowledge of how, or even if, he made his way from Edinburgh to Balmoral. We don't know his target, where he might be hiding, or anything else about his plans. We only know that wherever he goes men die.'

Brown looked over at him, impassive. 'Ye could ha' just said so in tha first place. I'd ha' been looking further around than the castle, ye ken. Noo I'll ha' to waste time searchin' the hunting lodges an al.'

'Hunting lodges?'

'Oh aye. Three o' them. And a few caverns. I'd bide there if I were he. But haps the Romany know something.'

***

Having wriggled her way into her lawn petticoat, Marian smoothed her hands over the ridges where thin bands of watch spring, yards and yards of it, formed hoops. Stiff, yet pliable, it stood out from her body in the shape of a church bell. Next, her maid helped her into a net petticoat trimmed with a hand's-breadth of lace around the bottom.

'I'll just get ye gown, ma'am.'

Marian smiled at Beatrice as she scuttled off. It was bothersome to be helped into her clothes like a toddler, but this was the *beau monde*.

Quickly, Marian opened the bottom drawer of her jewel box and pulled out both the pistol and tiny dagger Doyle had given her. She lifted the brown leather waistcoat from the chair and slipped the weapons into the secret pockets sewn into the front points of the waist. She traced a finger over the faint bulges.

'The pistol can fire three shots, not one like its predecessor,' Doyle had said. 'It's small, compact and loaded.'

Before Marian had done more than replace the waistcoat, Beatrice returned. She'd appeared bright and early, had pulled back the curtains so vigorously, she'd caused Marian to jerk awake and grab for her dagger.

After she'd recovered from the rude awakening, Marian had been stunned to find herself draped over Rollo's side of the bed. But she'd taken consolation from the fact his pillow had been ice-cold. He would have been long gone, surely, before she'd rolled into his space.

The bath had been a pleasure like she'd never encountered—her tin bath at home was scarcely big enough to kneel in. She usually just dampened her skin, lathered up, and poured a large jug of water over her body to rinse. Here, the steam powering the dynamic lights, which the late Prince Consort had installed, was redirected towards the bathrooms, resulting in the tub being filled with water hot enough to make her wilt. And she'd had yet more with which to rinse!

Beatrice dropped the navy linen day dress over Marian's head and quickly buttoned it. Marian then slipped her arms into the dark leather waistcoat and fastened the brass buttons while Beatrice tugged on the buckled straps at the waist and shoulders. As Beatrice turned away to find a hat pin, Marian attached her dove gizmo to her lapel and coiled her snake over her ear. It hid deceptively in plain sight, a mere ornament.

Mrs Doyle had told her ladies dressed for the occasion, not the day, and that she would have to change if she were to go riding or hunting, as well as for dinner. It seemed absurd, not to mention frustrating. She'd have to disarm and then rearm herself, repeatedly each day, for the sake of fashion!

Lastly, she slipped her own dagger, larger than the one Doyle had given her, into its holstered band and slid it up her forearm. Good. Now she was ready.

Once Beatrice had inspected her and smiled her approval, Marian turned to the stairs and the breakfast room, where other members of the party would be gathering.

***

Rising from the breakfast table, Marian nodded a polite farewell to the other ladies. She had been careful to stay within the proscriptions of their cover this time and had taken the opportunity to learn more about her fellow guests. The Empress was not at breakfast, of course, and most of the men had long departed.

Slipping past a footman bringing more coffee, Marian almost collided with a rotund figure approaching the door.

'Oh, goodness!' Marian put a hand on Mr Brunel's arm, both to steady herself and to preserve a decorous distance. 'Good morning, sir. What a pleasant surprise! I thought you would be out hunting with the other guests.'

'Good morning, my dear Mrs Titus.' The old gentleman beamed and, swapping the long-necked silver cog pipe into his left hand, held out his right, caught hers and bowed briefly over it. 'I was wondering if you would care for a mid-morning stroll. We could continue our interesting conversation.'

'Why, yes, I would. Thank you.'

Mr Brunel turned and fell into step beside her, his gaze going to her ear. 'I see you are wearing another of your interesting devices.'

'You miss nothing, sir.' She wondered what else he had noticed.

They strolled around the edge of a substantial garden attached to the castle. Although many plants had slowed with the season and a handful of gold leaves covered the path, the prospect was stunning. Mr Brunel led Marian to a small stone seat set in a curve of hawthorn laden with red berries. He dusted it with his handkerchief and bade her sit.

'I do admire your intricate little turtle dove. May I ask, what does she do?'

By way of response, Marian unclipped the gizmo from her lapel and laid it in Mr Brunel's hand.

'Oh my, this is very fine work.' He looked at the bird from all angles, peering through his goggles at the gossamer wings and the mechanism in the throat and chest. 'What artistry! How does the inner mechanism work?'

Marian leaned closer. 'As you can see, I made the body primarily out of hammered copper. The wings, of course, are silk, and the eyes are bottle glass. The inner membrane is specially dried-and-treated cow intestine.' She pointed to the open beak. 'It's fitted at the back of the dove's mouth, and just behind it, I placed a miniature phonograph.'

'A phonograph? But, my dear, how clever! Where did you acquire it?'

Marian demurred. 'I designed it, sir. It took me several months and more than one attempt, for it is very small. The internal device is designed to listen, while the sounds would be conveyed to this.' She slipped the serpent from her ear and laid it in her palm.

'Good heavens!' He tipped and turned the dove in his hands, studying it carefully as if trying to learn all her secrets. He looked rather like a boy who had received his very first train set for Christmas.

With a sigh and a degree of reluctance, he passed the dove back to her. 'It is remarkable work. Does it also fly?'

She shook her head. 'That's what I intended, but so far, I have not been successful. It flutters, and I think it would fly, but there is no way to steer it.'

Mr Brunel considered for a moment; it seemed as if his mind took out and examined his thoughts before filing them away. Thirty seconds later, his eyes lit up like a firework over Castle Rock, and he offered her his arm.

'My dear, I have an idea.'

Chapter 16

'Ready?'

Marian's heart fluttered frantically behind her firmly boned, fancy corset. She opened her palm and lifted her turtle dove gizmo up to eye level.

'Ready, Mr Br—' She stopped when he shook his head, though his eyes were twinkling with amusement. 'Sorry. Ready, Isambard.'

They sat on a low bench seat under a shady oak overlooking the pond. It was a lush green swathe of land, flanked on two sides by palace wings, and on the other two by long stretches of walls and hedges. From where she sat, Marian could see through a gap in the wall to the thick forest beyond and, to her right, the arch that led to the stable courtyard. But it was on the technological wizardry that sat between her and Isambard that she now fixed her gaze.

He lifted what, an hour ago, had simply been Marian's mirror messenger. He'd sacrificed his own device to incorporate parts of its information transfer and signal elements into the body of the dove. Then he'd jury-rigged her messenger with a dial and lever. Now, he pointed the messenger to their right in the direction of the garden wall a hundred yards away. He pushed the lever gently and turned the dial. Marian stifled a gasp as the dove spread her silk wings and rose from her palm. It soared into the clear blue sky, heading for the corner of the distant roof.

Isambard chortled. 'Brilliant work, my dear.'

He was generous, but it had been his brainwave to use messenger tek to transform her dove, and her snake, into what she had only been able to imagine.

'Can you still see it?' he asked.

'Only just.' She was watching carefully, but the dove was very small.

'Right, then. We shall set her down and test her, shall we?' Isambard beamed down at her like a benevolent gnome, and it was all Marian could do to keep from dancing with delight.

'Oh, yes, please.'

He pointed the front of the mirror messenger at the top of the high stone wall that peeked over a hedge to their left. It was wide enough for the dove to land on and would keep it within view. He pushed the lever down.

With a sigh of relief as the dove folded her wings, Marian adjusted the copper snake over her right ear, aiming the creature's tiny mouth towards her ear canal. It had been designed to act as a receiver, but she would never have dreamed of using messenger tek to link the two devices.

She heard something, a muffled sound in her ear. It wasn't the anticipated sound of birds, however, but a dull harsh murmur. She stood on tiptoe, peering as far as she could, but whoever was speaking must be on the other side of the wall. For a moment, she considered the politeness of listening to another person's conversation. Manners lost. Science won.

She glanced at Isambard. 'I can hear a voice, but it is very distorted.'

'Hmm.' He picked up his tiny jeweller's screwdriver and applied it to the messenger. 'Tell me when it's intelligible.'

It took maybe twenty seconds, during which time she caught only single words. Then she held up her hand and grinned. 'People. Two voices, I think. One deep, one soft.'

But then she heard a word that sent a chill right through her. With wide eyes, she turned to Isambard, and he moved towards her, clearly sensing her alarm. Holding up one hand to stop him, she laid the other over the snake to block out ambient noise.

'I want no part in the murder of a child,' came the softer voice.

'You have no say in the target,' said the other. 'You will take the message now or the next house he visits will be yours.' At the pause, Marian held her breath, fearing the connection was lost. 'If he misses this target and contract because of your squeamishness, he will be angry. You're married, aren't you? I hear he likes to take his time with the ladies ... before he slits their throats.'

Oh God. Marian's stomach lurched at the remembered horror. But it wasn't over yet.

'Aye.' The soft voice was back. Sullen. Cowed. 'Aye, Mr Grey. I'll take ye message fer ye. The bridle path. The French prince is the lad in the peacock-blue coat, on the bay cob.'

'Now, go. We've wasted enough time.'

Marian ripped the snake from her ear and spun, lead in her belly, bile in her throat.

'What is it, my dear?'

'Isambard,' she pushed her next words out, 'I need your help to stop a killer.'

***

Grim-faced, Rollo followed Brown out of the first hunting lodge, his mind already on the next possibility. The walk to the gypsy camp had been interminable, as well as a singularly fruitless endeavour. After a score of monosyllabic replies, they had struck out along the ridge.

'Nae a single person's been heer in months.' Brown was matter-of-fact as he turned the key in the door.

'I gathered as much.'

'Ye shoulda let me ask the questions o that wee scunner. I'd ha' got more oota him.'

'It wouldn't have helped, Brown.' Rollo could understand, indeed shared, the man's frustration. 'You know as well as I do, the Roma never give up a person they believe they're protecting from the law. In any case, I think he left them as soon as they arrived. He wouldn't want witnesses to his comings and goings.'

'Aye. Mayhap.'

Rollo heard the soft ting of an incoming message and, slipping his hand into his breast pocket, pulled the device free. He flipped up the lid.

'*Jævla faen!*' He read the message again, carefully.

'I dinnae ken ye Sassenach words, but I can heer a curse when it is uttered.' Brown seized him by the shoulder. 'What's happened? The Queen?'

'He's not after the Queen.' Rollo spun on his heel, his sense of direction telling him the palace was behind them and to the right, but …

'The bridle path, which way?'

***

Marian gripped Isambard's wrist and squeezed. 'Tell the Queen or Lady Claire. Anyone who can send every available man out after him. Send a message to my husband and tell him everything. And secure Mr Grey.'

'And you, Marian?' Mr Brunel snatched up her device.

She was already ten yards away. 'I will stop him. I must.'

Running across the soft lawn towards the stables, she cursed the dictates of fashion. She was not laced as tightly as some ladies, but the leather corset and heavy skirts were a burden, nonetheless.

It seemed, though, as if the fates were on her side. A stableboy was tightening the girth on a side saddle. Mrs Buchan and another lady, young and well dressed, were chatting as he worked.

'No time for questions. I am commandeering that horse.' She pointed to the grey in question.

'I say, that is my horse!' The brunette waved an imperious hand. 'We were just—'

'Hush, Charlotte.' Mrs Buchan put a hand on her friend's arm as her eyes sought Marian's. 'You've identified the threat?'

'Aye.' She tensed. Though she trusted Mrs Buchan, she would say no more in front of the other woman.

'Do as she says, Pip.' Mrs Buchan turned from the stable lad to Marian. 'How well do you ride?'

Marian bit her lip. It would take too long to explain. She could not permit her inexperience to slow her down. 'I'll manage.'

'Ride behind me, ma'am.' It was the boy who'd spoken, his voice cracking with youth and excitement. 'I'll take you wherever you need to go.'

He leapt into the side saddle, then steadying himself with hand and stirrup, he reached down for her.

Marian put a foot on the mounting block and her hand in his, then looked up into his shining eyes. 'The bridle path, Pip.'

'Right, ma'am.'

In seconds, she was precariously perched on the horse's rump and clinging to the stripling in front of her. The horse shot forward and she could do little more than pray.

They sped across the gravel and onto the grass, heading for the forest's edge. Marian hung on for dear life. Pip leaned forward over the horse's neck, calm as a centaur, and they forged ahead. A low hedge, no more than three feet high, rushed up to meet them. Pip set the mare at it; horse and rider leapt effortlessly. Marian, her heart in her mouth, curled her fingers into Pip's livery jacket.

They were in open land now, the shimmering lake at a short distance, the forest ahead. And there they were—four children on ponies, several women and a couple of grooms in a long string. Marian heard a child laugh. Prince Louis Napoleon was riding behind Her Majesty's youngest daughter, the one closest to him in age.

Marian extended her arm past Pip and pointed at the middle of the line. Pip nodded and swung the horse's head around. One by one, those in the group looked up as they noticed her and Pip riding hell for leather at them. Another movement at the edge of the forest caught Marian's eye. Rollo and the Queen's gillie were running through the waist-high brush, heading towards the clearing. To the right of them, half-hidden behind a tree, she glimpsed a figure from her nightmares—and a long barrel.

'Get down!' Her voice streamed behind her, lost.

The royal party halted and looked at them in confusion. Marian tapped Pip's shoulder and shouted in his ear. 'Get me close to the prince, then go to the head of the column. Take the children into the safety of the trees.'

Pip nodded and, twisting, gave her a swift grin. Then, with a piercing whistle and a signal to the grooms, he swung wide. He surged forward, the danger at their backs now with the prince directly in front of them. At the last moment, Pip swerved, then came in parallel to the group. In a second, they would be beside the prince. Marian judged her moment carefully. She would only get one.

More on instinct than anything, she let go of Pip and hurled herself at the prince. She grappled with her target with one outstretched arm, dragging him from his pony just as an almighty crack sounded somewhere off to her right. Someone screamed, then came a babble of voices and the sound of a woman shrieking.

Her arms now tight around the child's thin body, Marian hit the ground. She had the foresight to turn and took the impact on her shoulder and back, her head bouncing on the ground at the force of her fall. She couldn't breathe, and the boy, the little prince, remained utterly still in her arms.

***

Rollo's heart was in his mouth, every muscle tensed. The blast had come from fifty yards to his left. Both riders had plummeted from their steed, and when he saw Marian had the child in her arms, both of them lying still on the ground, his vision blurred.

In the next moment, however, instinct kicked in. Scanning the area, he glimpsed the figure on the edge of the woods. Half-hidden by a tree, the assassin lowered his rifle. Rollo dropped to one knee and raised his left arm in one seamless movement.

Brown skidded to a halt beside him. 'God!'

But whether it was the sight of Rollo's left hand or the events that had just unfolded that shocked the Scotsman, Rollo had no idea.

He ignored the man and focused on the assassin. His heavy black cape was half-covered under shredded green sacking, but there was no mistaking the man's height or his copper mask.

With icy precision, the likes of which he'd not managed since the prosthesis had been fitted, Rollo curled his fingers into his palm and the crossbow rose smoothly from the vambrace.

He took a slow breath and closed his right eye. 'Dracos!'

The fiend turned on instinct but didn't see Rollo immediately, camouflaged as he was in the bracken. Rollo flexed his wrist and a bolt thudded into the monster's metallic cloak. He flexed again, sending a second bolt after the first. A cry, bitten off, rang out before Dracos threw the rifle into the thick bushes and fled.

Rollo sprang up, intending to follow, but the assassin was nowhere to be seen. He'd been hit though. Might be wounded, which would slow him, but that was not the most important thing right now. Without a second thought, Rollo forced a path through the last few yards of brush and pelted across the clearing towards Marian. She was struggling to sit when he reached her.

'Marian!' He helped her to her feet. 'Thank heaven, you're alive.' For the merest second, he held her to his heart and felt the ice inside melt. Then he turned to the child. 'Your Highness, let me help you? Are you injured?'

'*Non, monsieur.*' He bowed, his eyes wide and shadowed. 'Madame, was that a rifle?'

'Yes, Your Highness. I—'

Rollo's head snapped in Marian's direction when she gasped and stiffened beside him. She'd pressed her fist against her mouth and her eyes were brimming with tears. He followed her gaze.

Brown held the body of the stableboy in his arms. Blood dripped from his sodden jacket.

'He was so gallant. So brave.' She pressed against Rollo's side and together they watched Brown, stone-faced, lay the lad gently over the back of his mare and gather up the reins.

'Did that monster escape?' Her words seemed forced.

'I'm afraid so.'

She looked up at him, her reddened eyes blazing with emerald fire. 'Then we go after him. I want to help you find him, Rollo. He has Pip's blood on his hands, and that of the two boys he murdered in Edinburgh. I won't stop until I find him.'

He stared at her, trying to gauge the depth of her guilt and grief. 'And then?'

'And then I'm going to kill him.'

Chapter 17

Once the party had made its way back to Balmoral, the children were whisked upstairs. Brunel was waiting for Marian, and after sharing a few brief words with her, Rollo sent her with him. Now, half an hour after the gunshot had rung out, he stood in front of Thomas Grey. The man was chained, both hands bound in front of him, to an ancient oak beam in the centre of the stable. Rollo took off his coat and handed it to Moody. In the lee of the wall, Brown stood glowering. Buchan sat on an upturned bucket.

Grey twisted against the chain. 'Do you know who I am?' Clearly, he'd forgotten the punishment for conspiracy to murder.

'I know precisely who you are, Mr Thomas Grey.' Anger gnawed at Rollo's gut, but he kept his demeanour as placid as lake water. 'You are a wolf in sheep's clothing, a liar and a traitor to the British Crown. You're going to tell me the names of your accomplices and the reason the French prince was targeted.'

'You have no reason to suspect I had any part in the attack on the prince!' Grey was pallid. Beads of sweat had begun to prickle along his hairline. His pale green eyes darted from Rollo to Brown and back again.

'Oh, there's not a soul that will save you now … or one that would want to.' Rollo stretched a hand to Moody, and without a word, his man laid the small turtle dove in it.

'You plan to stab me with your wife's brooch?' Grey sneered, though his voice held a slight quaver.

Rollo flicked the switch in the tail and the bird opened its mouth. For a moment, there was only silence, but then Grey's voice spoke from the bird. 'Take a message to the Bulgarian. The target is the French prince.'

Grey's face turned ashen. 'How is that possi … it cannot be.'

Pulling the glove from his left hand, Rollo revealed his iron digits. He clenched his fist, then flexed before finally raising the tips of his metal fingers to Grey's throat.

'You will tell me everything. And you will tell me now.'

***

Rollo's only concern during the interrogation was for where he might find the assassin, and once he had what little Grey knew, Brown made arrangements for him to wait on the Queen. Her Majesty sat at her desk, the Empress on a second chair to the side. Rollo stood facing them, in the centre of a semicircle, with Palmerstone and Buchan on his left, Marian at his right and Brown beside her. As Rollo bowed deep, the Queen leaned forward slightly.

'Mr … Titus, I understand you have been questioning the traitor, Grey.'

'I have, Your Majesty.' The monarch was clearly aware of his fictitious identity but seemed willing to tolerate it for now.

'With respect, Your Majesty,' Palmerstone bowed earnestly, 'it might be for the best if I spoke to Mr Titus privately.'

Rollo opened his mouth, but the Queen waved him to silence and addressed Palmerstone. 'We wish to hear how a royal guest was endangered by the traitor who was travelling in your entourage.' She turned, having reduced the Prime Minister to red-faced speechlessness. 'Continue, Mr Titus.'

Rollo pulled a wad of paper from his pocket—the printed copies of a dozen mirror messages from Doyle. Rollo even knew where the traitor shopped.

'Mr Grey is an Irishman, Your Majesty, one Thomas O'Leary. However, he grew up on the continent and was educated in Paris. His father was a friend of the Young Irelander, Davis.'

'The revolutionary?' Palmerstone was truly shocked.

'Yes, sir. Davis died shortly before the blight hit Ireland, and O'Leary senior went to the continent. Young Thomas was but ten when his family emigrated, although even then he had a facility for the study of languages.' He turned slightly to Palmerstone. 'The very skills that made him an excellent secretary, my lord, are the ones which made him a useful tool of the anarchists.'

'Why is an Irish rebel in league with a Bulgarian assassin?' Her Majesty was in no mood for a long tale.

'O'Leary came into contact, through his association with other volatile men from well-to-do families, with those who seek to reshape their respective countries. They are not foolish enough to use wholesale slaughter. The excesses of the French Revolution and the difficulties in Ireland showed them the folly of that path.'

Buchan spoke. 'They are making a strategic use of violence, Your Majesty.'

The Queen focused on Palmerstone. 'They seek a lever with which to topple governments, or precipitate conflicts that further their ends?'

Rollo nodded. 'We believe so, Your Majesty. Grey is under guard as we speak, and these gentlemen will see he is questioned further. His personal goal was to free Ireland from English rule, but it was only when he became His Lordship's secretary that he was sufficiently valuable to the cabal of conspirators, and they determined to use him in their plans.'

'Who are these conspirators?' Her Majesty's manner was cool and implacable.

Rollo stepped forward and laid a folded slip of paper on the blotter, then stepped back. 'That is the list, Your Majesty. My chief concern is with Grand Duke Gregor of Russia and the Polish rebel, Mazec Drapotnek.'

The Queen reached one plump hand forward and scanned the list briefly before refolding it. 'You have our leave to depart. What assistance or information do you require?'

Rollo kept his gaze level. 'Firstly, may I ask after the health of the Prince Imperial? Was His Highness injured at all?'

The Empress spoke then, her voice quavering a little. 'His Highness is uninjured and very well. He was even bragging a little to the royal physician when he was examined. There may well be bad dreams, but there is no serious injury. And for that, you and your wife have my undying gratitude, and that of France.'

Rollo breathed easier and glanced at Marian. 'We think the assassin is sailing to America, Your Majesty, but for what purpose, we cannot say.'

Marian curtsied and stepped forward. 'If I may speak, Your Majesty?'

'Mrs Titus, proceed.'

'While my husband was questioning Grey, I was in communication with my husband's superior in Edinburgh. There have been sightings of a man fitting the assassin's description travelling south and west of here.'

Rollo nodded reflectively. 'That fits with the information Grey divulged. I imagine he will be heading to the closest western port.' He stopped there. Not for anything would he reveal the last horror Grey had imparted. But it did not affect Britain, at least not directly, and though Brown and Buchan had been present, they had agreed to remain silent. This was his fight.

He stepped forward. 'I am sure you will receive a comprehensive explanation for what has happened, Your Majesty, just as soon as my superiors have all the information. But, right now, we have an assassin to stop.'

Her Majesty folded her hands on the desktop and glanced to the Empress, then turned back to Rollo. 'You and your wife may approach, Mr Titus.'

Rollo glanced at Marian and held out a hand. She was pale and bit her lip, but she put her hand in his and they stepped forward together. Marian dipped in her best curtsey. Rollo bowed. He didn't have time for this.

'You will take this as a surety of our favour.' The Queen passed a small visiting card across the table. On one side, embossed in gold, was the royal cipher. On the other, printed neatly, was a mirror messenger designation code. 'It will open doors for you anywhere in our realm. And if you require assistance, which is in our power to give, use this address to contact us.'

Rollo looked up sharply. This was a signal honour.

'I, too, wish to give you something.' The Empress pulled a sapphire ring from her right hand and passed it to Marian. 'You saved my son's life. This is merely a token of my favour. There is nothing you cannot ask of me.'

Marian took the ring, glanced at it, and curtseyed to the Empress. 'Thank you, Your Majesty.' She turned to the Queen. 'Your Majesty is very kind. At the moment, we have but one request. A fast unicarriage.'

The Queen did not smile, but her expression was one of satisfaction. 'Mr Brown will assist you. You may leave with our grateful thanks.'

Another bow, another curtsey, and Rollo offered Marian his arm. Brown trod heavily behind them.

Putting the Queen's card in his pocket, Rollo swung around to face Marian as soon as they were clear of the drawing room. 'What else did Doyle say?'

'The waystation attendant in Pitlochry was struck down and badly injured. He said the culprit was an injured Sassenach with bad teeth and a thick accent. McIntyre is heading to Oban, and we're to meet him there. Doyle will go to Glasgow, as there's a faint possibility Dracos isn't going to the coast. We have to leave at once, so I've asked Beatrice to pack for us.'

Rollo took in her pale milky skin, the turmoil in her eyes. He shouldn't ask her to come, yet he needed her badly. 'We can't afford to wait.'

Brown took his pipe out of his pocket. 'Take naught but the necessities. I'll send yon heavy luggage on and it weel catch ye up in Oban. I will ha' the Duke's racing unicarriage ready for ye in the porte-cochere in ten minutes.'

Marian pressed Rollo's hand, then flew up the stair. Rollo slipped, as unobtrusively as possible, towards the main entrance of the castle, but he could not avoid Lord Palmerstone, who had inserted himself into a doorway and now drew himself up to his full height.

'Titus, I would appreciate being kept apprised of events. The man used me to do his evil work. That gives me an interest in seeing him, and all his co-conspirators, brought to justice.'

'You know all that I can tell you, my lord.' Rollo could have said more, but Palmerstone had not impressed him with his acumen, to say nothing of having a spy and traitor in his employ.

Marian descended the stair and hurried towards him, Beatrice and Moody at her heels. Moody carried a large valise, Beatrice two thick coats. Marian carried his box containing the crossbow bolts for his arm. As she reached the bottom stair, Isambard Brunel waved from a doorway and padded across the floor towards them.

Brown took the servants outside, and Isambard thrust out a hand. 'Thank God you were in time, Mr Titus.'

'Thank God and thank you, sir, for everything you did to assist my wife, but we must go if we are to prevent further evil.' Rollo put an arm around Marian to hurry her along, but she slipped around it and, stretching up, kissed the old man on the cheek.

'Thank you, Isambard. I hope to see you again one day.'

'I have your mirror messenger.' He placed it in her hand and clasped his over it.

Brown slipped back inside. 'Yon bag is loaded, sir. Yer driver, Bruce McDay, kens the vehicle and the roads. He will see ye to Oban in four hours, or little more.'

'Oban!' Brunel looked to Rollo in surprise, then fumbled in his pocket. 'My pride and joy is docked there, awaiting sea trials. I will send a mirror message this instant. Only give this card to her master and she is at your disposal.'

Rollo stretched out his hand and took the card, then shook the old man's hand warmly. 'Thank you, Mr Brunel. If we need to, we will avail ourselves of your kind offer. I only ask that you keep our confidence for now.'

Brown handed Marian into the Duke's racing unicarriage, which was more streamlined than most, and Rollo climbed in after her. With a slap on the cab's exterior, Brown waved them away. The acceleration was smooth, and the castle was lost to view in just minutes.

Rollo pressed his back into the plush upholstery. He would like nothing more than to tell Marian just how proud he was of her.

Terrified and frustrated by her actions but awed by her bravery and composure. She had saved the prince, while he had been looking in the wrong place entirely. He made a vow never to underestimate her again.

Chapter 18

'Why the west coast?' Marian swayed against him as they rounded the second bend.

'Because Dracos has another target, one last act of political mayhem before he vanishes. His masters will then orchestrate the chaos set to follow.'

'One more target?' She laid a hand on his thigh. 'Who? Why?'

Rollo sighed and stretched his shoulders and spine in an attempt to ease the aches. His body had taken a hammering. Eight hours ago, he had been tramping through the woods towards the gypsy camp. Now he was hurtling through the same forest on the same mission, a quest to find the Romanian butcher before someone died. Though he'd rejoiced in their success in saving the French prince, what came next boggled the imagination. He was unutterably weary, had barely had time to wash his hands after Grey's interrogation or even have a glass of water. What he really needed, though, was a dram of fine single malt.

He let his body rest against Marian's—shoulder, hip and knee. It was all the comfort he would get. And yet, he scowled. His thoughts were awry. There were still too many things they didn't understand.

'From the start,' he said, 'this assassination didn't make sense.'

'How do you mean?'

'Dracos had no reason to kill Palmerstone or the Queen. No reason we could see. The last time a British prime minister was assassinated, a personal grudge and a great deal of resentment had been the cause. Your country had been at war twenty years.'

'There is no motive, is that what you're saying?'

He shook his head. 'There is always a motive, but it isn't apparent to us because we don't know what the conspirators are trying to achieve.'

'And we are not mind readers.' She squeezed his hand.

'We have pieces to a puzzle, but no idea of its size or shape, or where the pieces fit.'

She nodded. 'Very well. What are the pieces?'

Letting go of her hand, he held up his fingers. 'One, a Russian grand duke who is disgruntled with his Tsar for shutting him out of power. Two, a Polish revolutionary set on gaining independence from Russia. Three, a Catholic Irishman who is determined to bring down the Protestant monarchy.'

Marian looked at him and frowned. 'You're right. There's no rhyme or reason.'

'Then there are the ongoing tensions left over from the war in the Crimea, and the game of chess the European leaders are playing—'

Marian turned suddenly, putting her hand on his thigh once more. 'What would have happened if the prince had been killed?'

Rollo shook his head. 'Who can say? Certainly, the Emperor would not have taken the death of his only son lightly. Unfortunately, we don't know who's giving Dracos his orders.'

'So it could precipitate war?'

'Almost certainly.'

'Are there any among your puzzle pieces who might want France to go to war?'

He considered. 'A war against England, perhaps, but not a war against Russia. In any case, the last French war against Russia did not end well.'

Marian was quiet for a moment. 'And yet, Russia keeps being mentioned.'

He nodded. 'Yes. And that's what's troubling me. I wonder why Dracos is going to America. Is it perhaps because the Tsar's younger brother and admiral of the Russian Fleet, Grand Duke Konstantin Nikolayevich, is currently in New York?'

Thoughts whirled in the depths of Marian's sea-green eyes before she spoke. 'Do you think the grand duke is his next target? He's not the Russian noble Grey named, is he?'

'No, he's his brother. And while I don't know what their ultimate goal is, I do know my country is already at war. England and France are surreptitiously backing the Confederacy. Russia refuses to give overt support to the Union States, but she is presumed to be on their side. Who else could the target be? Our President, though I don't think it feasible. His wife?' He felt anger burn his throat. 'Heaven knows! If he was willing to kill the French prince, nothing would be beyond him.'

'No. He doesn't give a damn for the pain he causes and the lives he destroys.'

They jolted over a bump and it threw her into his arms. Grateful for the excuse, he closed them around her.

'Doyle will send all the information we have, and the picture. I only hope it's enough. And that we have a chance to stop Dracos before any of it's needed.'

She nodded, snuggled closer and sighed against him. It was cool in the unicarriage, its light racing construction doing little to keep out the chill. Before them, the sun had long sunk behind the trees and its glow was at last fading to grey in the western sky. Marian sniffed once, twice. A tear fell on his hand, the one that held hers.

'Marian, sweetheart …' He kissed her temple.

'Poor Pip. I should never have let him ride with me. It's all my fault.'

'No. Blame Grey. He and his collaborators are culpable. Not you.' Rollo wrapped her in his embrace, his iron hand resting lightly on her back.

'Why is it always the innocent who suffer?' She pressed her face into his jacket.

'The quest for ultimate power is an evil thing.'

Rollo looked down at her bright copper curls. He, too, regretted the lives lost, but he would be forever grateful the assassin's bullet had found the stablehand and not the woman he cradled to his chest in the growing darkness.

***

Blinking hard, Marian lethargically pushed a snarl of hair out of her face. Rollo shot her a glance, then went back to writing on his mirror messenger. It flashed briefly, leaving behind an acrid smell as he closed it.

She peeped over his arm and he smiled back, but his mouth was hard, his eyes bleak. Exhaustion? Perhaps.

'Did I fall asleep? What's happened?'

'Dracos made it to Oban. McIntyre confronted him at the docks.' He scowled. 'It seems the bolt I put into him was not enough to weaken him.'

Marian's stomach twisted sharply. 'McIntyre? How is he?'

'Badly injured but alive. Dracos held a knife on a local sailor, who rowed him out to a waiting ship.'

Marian sat up straighter, ran her hands over her face and wayward curls. Rollo reached forward and unhooked the speaking tube.

'Mr McDay, how much longer to Oban?'

The driver's voice came back thin and reedy. 'Better than forty minutes, sir.'

'Is there any way you can cut that in half and take us straight to the hospital?'

There was a long pause as Marian watched the dark trees fly past. They were already travelling much faster than they had in Her Majesty's train.

'I'll no promise ye half, but I can mebbe shave a bit off. Ye and the missus best hold on tight.'

A strange winding sound made Marian's heart freeze in her chest. The carriage seemed to sink and the roof above them nudged closer. A high-pitched hiss came from beneath their feet. They'd only just managed to tighten the sashes over their laps when the unicarriage jolted, leaping forward like a deer fleeing a hunter, and it was as if a giant's fist pressed them back against their seat.

'Are you sure the unicarriage was built for such speeds?' Marian kept her voice even despite the sudden stab of excitement.

'If we make it to Oban in one piece, then, yes, I suppose it is.' Rollo gave her a glimmer of a smile, but his lips had paled. Sweat trickled down his forehead.

In no time at all, Marian could feel the carriage begin to slow, and it emitted a series of hisses. The curve of the waterfront and the rows of houses lining it were shadowed. Only a few old-fashioned lamps spilled pools of light on the cobbles.

After pulling up at a low-slung building of grey stone, McDay opened Rollo's door. 'I've brought ye to the infirmary as requested, sir.'

Rollo helped Marian out, then turned to McDay and slipped him a rectangle of card from his pocket. 'Thank you. Could you take this card to the docks, find Mr Brunel's ship and let the Captain know we will need to board as soon as possible. He should've had a message from Brunel already. We must catch the tide, so please return for us within the hour.'

Marian hurried to the heavy door, rapping lightly rather than lifting the heavy knocker. By the time Rollo stood beside her, a female form could be seen approaching through the glass. Marian clutched at Rollo's arm as the door opened, her patience too thin for delay.

The young woman who answered wore a drab olive skirt and blouse, both partially covered by a white wrap-around apron. Only the starched veil covering her hair betrayed her medical calling.

'Good evening, Sister,' said Rollo. 'We are here to see Detective McIntyre.'

At the detective's name, the girl clasped her hands and wrung them. 'Excuse me, sir, ma'am. I'll call the matron.' She darted off, far more fleet of foot than she had been in opening the door.

Marian studied a painting on the wall, a watercolour copy of Florence Nightingale receiving the wounded at Scutari. It was captioned, *A Mission of Mercy*.

Rollo came to stand beside her. 'An appropriate painting for a hospital.'

She nodded. 'Dr Somerton once said she was deeply indebted to Miss Nightingale for her theories on fresh air and hygiene.'

A woman, middle-aged and statuesque, opened the door at the far end of the hallway and came towards them. 'If you would come with me.'

When they passed through a door into a tiny room with a single bed in it, Marian caught sight of the detective and gasped. His body was immobile under a grey blanket; his head was swathed in bandages, which, on the left side of his face, weren't white but vivid crimson. Only his lips were exposed, which allowed him to breathe. While the right side of his mouth was swollen, the left was covered in gashes and purple bruising.

The matron shook her head. 'If we did no' have instructions to admit ye, ye would no' be allowed in. The poor man's injuries are the worst I've seen. He lost a quantity of blood, and even if he survives … the doctor says there is little he can do.'

'I see.' Rollo nodded, his attention on the silent figure lying on the bed. 'Perhaps you will give us a moment?'

When the matron closed the door behind her, Marian looked down at the detective once more. He had been such a handsome man—tall, broad, kindly on the one occasion she had met him. It was a tragedy.

A shadow moved in the window alcove and made her jump.

'The monster crushed the left side of his face and pulverised his jaw.' Doyle sounded as tired as he looked. 'It's a miracle he's breathing, but I don't know how much longer he will last.'

'Is there no hope?' Marian strove to keep her voice even.

'Little, they say. And if he does make it, the scarring and loss of bone …'

'What about the rest of him?'

'Broken forearm and ribs, lacerations. He could survive those injuries.' After a pause, Doyle stepped up to the window, cracked it open and muttered, 'Never could stand the stench of blood.' He took a gulp of air before turning back to them. 'According to the young constable, McIntyre cornered the Romanian but underestimated the brute's strength.'

'I can well believe it.' Rollo glanced from Doyle to McIntyre's still body.

Doyle took a flask from an inside pocket and took a swig before offering it to Rollo. 'Our lad was mumbling about the face of a monster, a coat of blades and a hand covered in wee silver balls—that's what did the damage. Who knows how many blows he took?'

Rollo rubbed his hand along his jaw, and Marian knew he was remembering the gash he'd suffered from that lethal coat. 'So it's only a matter of time.'

Marian stepped closer to the bed and took in the detective's unnatural breathing. 'Is he sedated?'

'Of course.' Doyle took his flask from Rollo. 'The doctor has given him as much as he can for the pain. Better for him if his passing is easy.'

She shook her head. 'Maybe these people cannot help him.' She laid a hand on Rollo's arm. 'But the three of us know of a doctor who can achieve what others dare not even hope is possible.'

'Marian, the Somertons are on the other side of Scotland.'

'If anyone can help him, it will be them.' Doyle took another swig from his flask. 'I can send a message.'

Marian beamed at him. 'Do that, Mr Doyle. And tell them the detective will be at their door as soon as may be, travelling in the Duke's racing unicarriage.'

Chapter 19

Marian had insisted on waiting twenty minutes, until Doyle and the unconscious detective were on their way to Edinburgh. As soon as they'd left, Rollo handed Marian into a local unicarriage and had them driven tc the docks, where the wind was whipping up the sea so high it soaked the bollards. Their driver took them along the quay to a smal private shipyard with a single pier.

At the gate, a young lad of twelve or thirteen came out and retrieved their single valise. As the boy shut the heavy door behind them, a voice, sweetly stern and unmistakably female, rang out from high above.

'And not a minute too soon if you were wanting to catch the next tide.'

Rollo spun and looked up. He could see, faintly illuminated, the figure of a woman.

She stepped off the platform halfway up the mast and, with delicate movements, descended through the rigging, dropped to the deck and strode towards them. From underneath her feathered tricorn, bundled braids hung like ropes of liquorice down her back. She wore ivory trousers, which contrasted against her smooth tanned skin and were studded with bronze along the seam. The same buttons adorned the pale, leather-edged cuffs of her frock coat, the tails of which fell to the back of her thighs. She wore tan knee-high boots with bronze tracery on the side, and her black corset was set with small bronze rings. On her shoulders were two gold-encrusted epaulettes.

She stopped at the top of the gangway where two flambeaux burned and stretched out her hand. 'Welcome to the *Calliope Jane*.'

Rollo escorted Marian forward and held out a wary hand. 'To whom am I speaking?'

'Captain Jeanne de Clisson.' The woman removed her tricorn, which Rollo now saw was ringed in snakeskin and had a pair of spyglasses perched on the brim. Her eyes held no smile. 'Pleased to meet you, Mr Titus.'

Marian had been taking in every detail of the ship, her hand on his arm fairly thrumming with excitement, but now, she too reached out.

'It is a pleasure, ma'am.' Her eyes sparked—a look Rollo had seen before. 'What a marvellous ship! You must be an exceptional captain if Mr Brunel has entrusted it to you.'

Her enthusiasm was infectious. The captain's reply was genuinely warm this time. 'You are too kind, Mrs Titus. You will find all in readiness.'

Fate kept throwing extraordinary women in his path, Rollo mused, but despite his surprise, he could find no argument with it. If a female doctor had succeeded in giving him a new hand, and Marian had been his match in both courage and spy craft, surely this woman could captain a fine example of seafaring engineering.

He offered a respectful bow. 'Thank you, Captain. We are in your debt.'

'I will have you shown below shortly.' Captain de Clisson called over a heavyset seaman and gave him a litany of orders, punctuated by gestures towards the rigging and the docks.

Rollo only saw about a dozen men, fewer than he'd expected based on what he knew of the larger clipper ships that plied the world's oceans Most of the crew were around his age, perhaps a little younger, but they worked briskly in the cold and dark. Their bearing reminded him of his former brothers-in-arms.

At his side, Marian craned her neck in every conceivable direction. He smiled down at her; she couldn't have been happier if she'd died and gone to heaven.

'I can see why you and Brunel got on so well.' It was folly to be jealous of her platonic friendship with a man twice his age. But he couldn't help it.

She looked up at him, her eyes ablaze with wonder. 'I knew the Somertons had created something amazing with your hand, but I never dreamed there were others out there who were doing such incredible things. First the train, then the unicarriage, and now ...'

'You never thought there would be others as ambitious and creative?'

'It hadn't crossed my mind.'

Rollo considered her for a moment, then shook his head, hardly believing her modesty. 'One day, Marian Finlay, you will invent something that will change the world, I'm sure of it.' Even now, he was prouder than he had any right to be. 'If not for you and your dove gizmo, France would be in mourning right now, with who knows what kind of war looming.'

When a blush traced up her neck, he had to resist the urge to kiss her. Instead, he put his hands to her shoulders and turned her. 'Look, the sails are extraordinary.'

They disappeared into the inky sky.

'I know.' She glanced over her shoulder at him, her eyes as wide as saucers. 'They have struts like giant folding fans. And look here!' She ran to the side of the deck and pointed over the side.

Following her, he studied the large metal structure lying snugly against the side of the ship. 'What is it?'

'I wish I knew.'

The captain strode towards them, the heels of her boots making surprisingly little noise. 'The wings? They give us stability, without much ballast, and considerable lift.'

'Truly?' Marian's wonder burned in her eyes as if it were a reflection of the nearby flambeaux.

'When we are out to sea, once we can expand the main sail and the tail, I'll demonstrate how they work. Until dawn, we'll make our way out under ordinary steam propulsion, but that won't be necessary once we are underway, with wind for the sail and plenty of sun by day to give us a good head of steam.'

'Does the ship not burn compressed wood brick, like a unicarriage?' As always, Marian was thirsty for knowledge.

'Not usually, Mrs Titus. Mr Brunel intends to test the fins on the stern.' She pointed aft. 'They are deployed to catch the sun's rays. Sea water pumps through them, is heated and provides steam for the engines. We only burn fuel if there is no wind at night.'

As Marian dashed to the stern, Rollo felt the vibrations in the deck as the engines spun up, and as she leaned over the balustrade to get a closer look at the fins, he had terrifying visions of her going overboard. He was behind her within seconds and grabbed the back of her jacket to prevent any such catastrophe.

She put a hand over his and gave him a swift smile, as if for reassurance. 'I won't fall over, Rollo.'

The captain joined them. 'The fins are stowed for night, but they are very large. Over eight feet wide and fifteen feet long. If they were arrayed, you could see the thin copper pipes from here. There's a web of them set into the fabric of the fins, which is how they collect the heat of the sun.'

Marian's eyes glittered. 'That's incredible!'

'From there, the steam goes directly into the main engine and the drive shaft. It's the same principle as in a unicarriage, except that oil or coal is seldom needed.' The captain glanced at her crew and put a hand on the rail, perhaps assessing the vibration.

They turned together and walked back to the railing that separated the main deck from the quarterdeck. Set into it were two wood-and-metal mounts, but they were empty, like outsized inkwells, although the inner surfaces were ridged as though to receive a large screw.

Rollo leaned forward, ran a finger around the rim. 'And these, Captain?'

She frowned. 'Experimental propellers. We could have used another week to finish assembling them, but no matter. We will do the work while we are underway. We can always test them on the return journey.'

'This is the most incredible ship.' Marian ran her hand over the propeller mounts. 'Is there any way we can be of assistance?'

'You are our guest, Mrs Titus.' The captain smiled. 'If you'll excuse me, I have things to attend to. I'll have Tom show you to your cabin. I dare say you are exhausted after the day you've had. There will be plenty of time to show you around once we have cleared the harbour.'

Rollo frowned at the captain's back as she departed. 'I would dearly love to know how much Brunel has told her about us.'

'Perhaps that it's of grave importance we get to New York in record time.' Marian squeezed his hand. 'And in this ship, we will!'

As young Tom led Marian to their cabin, high in the stern, Rollo stayed on deck. Grasping the starboard railing, he took a lungful of crisp salt air and contemplated the toll it would take on him to share a cabin with her for the duration of the journey. He had survived the night they'd spent sharing a bed at Balmoral, but it was becoming increasingly difficult to resist her, with her guileless enthusiasm, her beauty, the wonders of her agile mind. He only had to glance at her to find his desire rising. Little things caught his attention—the deepening green of her eyes as she drank in every detail of the ship, the feel of her hand on his during their short carriage ride. It was all he could do not to pull her into his arms and plunder her mouth.

But that would never do.

'Mr Titus.' The captain's voice at his shoulder startled him.

Damn it! To be taken unawares in his profession could be fatal—further proof that Marian Finlay was a dangerous distraction.

'Can't say it's every day I see a man looking at his wife with such longing.' Captain de Clisson lifted the spyglass from the curled brim of her tricorn and scanned the retreating shoreline. 'I take it you are recently married?'

'Quite recently.' Rollo frowned as he glanced at the small wake forming in the moonlight. If a new acquaintance could read him so easily, he had no business being a spy. Chagrined, he spoke as if only mildly interested. 'How long do you expect the voyage to last, Captain?'

She considered. 'Our fastest route would be west-northwest, as far as the Labrador Sea, then south. It's winter, so the bergs shouldn't be a problem, not as much as they would be in spring.' She reached into the breast pocket of her jacket and pulled out a flat device, larger than a messenger and fitted in the centre with a compass rose. Turning to face northwest, she nodded. 'Yes, fifty-five degrees north and thirty west, give or take, would be a good moderate course.'

'Give or take?' Rollo pressed.

'Yes, Mr Titus.' Her accent was clipped. She was clearly unaccustomed to explaining herself. 'It is the start of winter and we should be mindful of uncertainties. We've not taken her far out as yet, certainly not across the Atlantic at speed.'

Her tone did nothing for Rollo's anxiety. Uncertainties meant storms and this ship was both small and untested.

'Will we be able to catch the clipper that left dock earlier?'

'If you can tell me what route she is taking, then certainly.'

'She is heading for New York.'

The captain met his eye and waited. 'We are not travelling on land where there are only a few roads. On the sea a ship may go wherever she pleases. Even if the clipper is heading directly to New York, there are a score of headings she could take. And a good-sized trading ship with full sail and some steam will make good time. What else can you tell me?'

'Very little, ma'am, I'm afraid.'

'Well, then. We can sail south with plans to overtake and board her, but we could easily miss her. And in any case, this ship is not armed. By going north, we can shave a few days off the trip.'

Rollo curbed his tongue. He'd been so close to the Romanian, so very close. Now he was faced with weeks at sea and an entire legion of frustrations.

'So if we take your northerly route, when will we get to New York?'

'We will dock in Halifax ...'

'Captain, my quarry is going to New York.'

De Clisson crossed her arms over her chest, her tone scraping like steel across his will. 'But this ship will go no further than Boston. I don't know if you are aware, Mr Titus, but half the Russian Navy has dropped anchor in Flushing Bay. My orders are to keep this lady out of sight, of both the Americans and the Russians. Mr Brunel isn't ready to share his technology with nations who are at war.'

'The Russians aren't at war.'

'Yet.'

Rollo took a deep breath. They could take a dirigible from Halifax or Boston. Dracos wouldn't be expecting that.

'Please tell me how long you expect this voyage to last, Captain.'

'A clipper will take anything from sixty to one hundred days, but one of the new steam vessels will only take about eighteen days. Do you know which he is taking, sir?'

God forbid Dracos was on one of the newer ships that would take less than three weeks! But, to be fair, those rarely left from Oban. Still …

He gestured to the side wings and the stowed fin assembly in the stern. 'And Brunel's ship?'

The captain pursed her lips, calculating. 'If the weather is on our side, four weeks. If not, perhaps six.'

So they'd finish their journey with either two weeks in hand or possibly a week behind. Rollo looked down at the pale grey wake behind them. It was about time Lady Luck smiled on him. If all went well, they'd reach New York before the assassin and have time to spare. If not, God help them all.

Chapter 20

Rollo stuck his head into the engine room and immediately regretted it. The air was full of the acrid tang of smoke, despite the vents drawing it away. Simons, the apprentice, was stirring red-hot rivets in a small brazier, while Crooks, the engineer, plucked them out with long tongs and hammered them into an engine mount. Marian was nowhere to be seen.

'Yer looking for yer missus?'

Rollo shook his head, though he would love to see what Marian was getting up to down here. 'For you, actually, Mr Crooks. It's almost dark. The captain wishes to know if you can run the engine or if we're limited to the sail?'

Crooks ran a hand over his face. 'Sail for the nonce, I think. There are a few tests we must run. To be safe.'

'And you'll finish the engine welds?'

Much to Rollo's frustration, they'd been unable to run the engines for two nights now. Though they were not becalmed, their lack of engine power was slowing their progress considerably.

'Aye.' Crooks hammered another rivet to an accompaniment of brilliant sparks. 'Simons, leave that. Mr Titus will do it. Go get the sling for the engine support.'

Rollo took over stirring the rivets, focusing on keeping the heat even. 'Why are you supporting the engine?'

'Because when yer wife took a look at the engine innards, she found a host of stress fractures along the top joins, caused by the torque. The collars should be enough. But until we can run a supporting beam under the whole, we're going to sling that section from a hook.'

Crooks hammered another rivet, then knocked on the pipe, a bare yard from where he had been working. He raised his voice a little. 'Marian, are ye done, lass?'

'In a minute.' Her muffled reply came from within the copper pipe that ran through the mount into the engine.

'Good heavens! What is she doing?'

'Checking our latest welds.' He hammered the final rivet and took the crucible off the brick furnace, put the iron cover in place and smothered the fire.

Marian's cotton-turbaned head peeped out from the end of the pipe, followed by her two dainty hands and trousered body. Rollo's mind immediately went back to a deserted dock and a small firelit apartment.

She stood, pulled the safety wool from her ears and beamed at him. Rollo suddenly felt as though his heart was in that glowing crucible behind him. For better or for worse, he was riveted to Marian Finlay with a bond forged in fire. Now, what was he to do about it?

***

Marian tied off her braid and twisted it up, pinning the coil into place as best she could before checking her reflection in the tiny cabin mirror. A lock of hair escaped, and she adjusted a pin. Dinner with the captain had become something of a respite from the stresses of the voyage.

She glanced over at Rollo. 'We are expected in ten minutes.'

Even she could hear the longing in her voice.

'Thank you.' But he didn't look up from running a dash of blacking over his boots.

Turning to the mirror once more, she stared at the melange of emotions reflected in her eyes. Disappointment, frustration, sorrow. Hope had all but withered away. Yet it was not that Rollo was unkind, discourteous or harsh. He'd just been distant. They had been growing so close, both in Edinburgh and at Balmoral, that the sudden chill in their relationship left her grieved and puzzled.

These past two weeks he'd spent each day on deck with the crew, acting as a willing pair of hands for anything that needed to be done. When they were alone, he'd ask her how she'd spent the day, listening attentively as she described the improvements she'd made to her gizmos since the captain had given her a free hand in the tek workshop. The evenings were the worst, though. She would retire to bed, and following much later, he would slip under the blanket but never the sheet and turn his back to her. He was always gone by the time she awoke.

She watched him in the mirror, tying on a clean collar and pulling on his good waistcoat. He used both hands, she noted, so dexterous now with his left that it was hard to believe the glove covered metal rather than flesh. She had done that, had given him a semblance of normalcy, and she took pride in her efforts. She could return to work for Mr Somerton, head held high, and know that she'd be helping people. She could do that for the rest of her life, which should be an exhilarating thought. But it wasn't.

Her thoughts returned to the private discussion she'd had with Doyle before he'd left the hospital in Oban to return to Edinburgh with the detective. The more she thought about her options, the more alluring the alternative became.

'If the offer suited you,' he'd asked her, 'would you consider remaining in the service of the Queen once this matter is settled? You seem to have quite the talent for this sort of work, and we could always use a mind such as yours.'

Would she? Could she? The offer was there. She had the chance to lead an exciting life, which had been a dream for so long now. Did she have the courage to cast aside security for a life lived in secrecy and shadows? Or perhaps Mr Brunel would give her a place in his workshop. The challenge might distract her from what she couldn't have. It would be a decent second best.

She sighed.

'Penny for your thoughts.' Rollo's voice jolted her out of her reverie.

Marian looked up at him dourly. 'I was just considering what I will do when all this is over.'

'I'll be pleased to escort you back to Edinburgh, or someone from the agency will see you safely home.' His eyes weren't shadowed as they had been of late, but his voice was diffident. 'Somerton told you that your job would be waiting for you.'

She ran a hand over her temple, pushing back an errant lock of hair as she contemplated his offer. 'I don't know that I can simply go back to the way things were. How could anyone return to a normal life after the experiences I've had?' Rising, she turned towards him. 'Could you?'

He came around the bed and stood before her. 'No. I don't expect so. But I've been doing this for a long time. Sometimes, I think normal would be a wonderful thing. This has been something of a holiday for me.'

Despite everything, Marian choked out a laugh. 'You have been working ten hours a day at least.'

He grinned at her. 'It's been honest physical labour. No skulking in alleys, no secret codes, no fights to the death.'

'Thank goodness for that!'

'Indeed.' He paused and the smile went out of his voice. 'So what will you do? Will you stay in America and find work there?'

'I don't know a soul in America.'

'You know me.'

At his offhand comment, her heart sank. She fixed her eyes on his, holding him fast. 'Yes. I know you. But I want more than just another workplace.'

There, she had revealed a piece of her heart.

In the moment that followed, as Rollo studied her mutely, it was as if Marian could see the icebergs of indifference melting away. He smiled softly at her, looped a tendril of hair behind her ear. Then, slowly, he reached for her, took her hand, drew it to his lips and kissed the inside of her wrist where her pulse kept double time.

'Do you know what I feel for you, Marian?'

A slow bubble of joy warmed her; a pang of desire made her quiver. 'I hope it's what I feel for you.'

The warmth in his blue eyes burned for her, but when he raised his left hand, it hovered near her cheek.

Immediately, she knew the cause of his hesitation.

'You can't hurt me, Rollo. You won't.'

Lifting her free hand, she caught his, brought it to her lips as he had done with hers, and kissed his iron palm.

Rollo hauled her into his arms with a suddenness that drove the air from her lungs, then kissed her with a ferocity that was scarcely short of madness. Marian instinctively pressed her body to his, eager to receive the passion she had been craving.

'Do you know how hard it's been, denying what I feel for you, Marian Finlay? I never thought I would meet anyone so brilliant, so daring, so perfect.'

He pressed his mouth to hers and wrapped his arms around her. They were steel bands, holding her to him, and she could feel the hard planes of his chest, belly and thighs against her body. She opened her lips and welcomed him into her mouth. The wave of passion crashing over them broke the accumulated tension and she sagged against him.

'Tell me this is what you want.' His voice was harsh. Husky.

'It's everything I've ever wanted.'

He slid his hands down her body and, clasping her at the waist, put some distance between them so he could look at her. On the other side of their bedroom door, someone sounded the watch. Rollo closed his eyes on an expression of pain.

'We are expected at dinner.' Marian heard her own regret.

'I know.'

Stretching an arm around his neck, she pulled him closer. 'We can continue this conversation at a more convenient time.'

He smiled, then kissed her lips. 'I'll look forward to it.'

***

Rollo held Marian's chair as she and the captain both took their seats. The first time they'd come to dinner, he'd attempted to act the gentleman and do the same for the captain. De Clisson had been polite, but it was clear she desired no assistance.

Now, Tom brought in the soup, fragrant chicken, creamy with vegetables, and set it on the table. The captain's cabin was in many respects a mirror of their own. A bed in a frame sat against the wall, a small dressing chest beside it. Opposite it was the table at which they now sat. But while their cabin had a small sofa and worktable under the multi-paned windows, the captain had a massive oak desk and a set of shelves, neatly made to keep books, charts and maps.

The captain ladled soup into three bowls. 'Marian, Rollo, thank you for your company.'

Rollo nodded. 'It's our pleasure.'

Usually, it was no hardship to dine with the captain. Rollo had been impressed by her breadth of engineering and seafaring knowledge. No doubt it was the reason Brunel had chosen her. To-night, however, his desire for privacy with Marian was at odds with his sociable nature.

De Clisson turned to Marian. 'Have you had any success with your beetle gizmo? You had high hopes, I believe.'

'I have.' Marian fixed her eyes on the captain and smiled. 'I was able to use the mechanism from the old gyroscope I found in the workshop. I had to reduce the size somewhat, but that and the messenger tek Mr Brunel used when he modified my dove have allowed me to make a prototype.'

'That's excellent.' The captain nodded at her and Rollo felt a surge of pride. 'And I have to thank you for the help you gave Mr Crooks.'

'I was happy to be of service.' Marian took a mouthful of soup.

'He was not keen at first to let you near his precious engines.' The captain gave a low chuckle. 'He was not convinced a mere lassie could do the work, but I think you surprised him.'

Marian shook her head. 'Fixing the broken join wasn't difficult, but the real issue was identifying the strain on the weld. If we hadn't fixed it, the pipes would have leaked again. Mr Crooks won't need me any longer.'

'And the experimental propellers?' Rollo asked, determined to make a contribution to the conversation. 'How close are they to being installed?'

'Simons has been testing the cables inside them,' said Marian. 'Thank you for sending him below, Captain. It has been much easier with a second pair of hands.'

'Thank your husband.' De Clisson smiled. 'He's taken over several of the jobs topside, and that alone has meant Simons was free to assist you.'

Marian glanced at him, a small smile playing on her lips, then she turned back to the captain. 'I do thank him.'

Rollo ate his soup, though his head was full of Marian. She had been in her element down in the engine room, dressed in an old pair of the captain's trousers and one of Tom's shirts. She had all the skills of an engineer and the mind of an inventor. No wonder she was unconvinced about returning to work for Somerton. She needed more of a challenge.

'And I thank you, too, Rollo,' said De Clisson, 'for all the work you've been doing up on deck. Mr Pinter was telling me your help with mending the bowside inlet pipe was vital. He was very grateful for your support. It was a tricky manoeuvre and he had no wish to go into the sea.'

'It was my pleasure, Captain.' Rollo picked up his bread roll and broke off a chunk. 'When I came across the Atlantic a month ago, I worked my passage on a clipper and learned a few new skills along the way. This voyage has been a wonderful opportunity to refresh them.'

'Well, you may both sail with me whenever you please. I appreciate your willingness to offer your talents.'

Rollo laid his napkin on the table and nodded politely at de Clisson. 'We appreciate the chance to assist, Captain.'

'I only ask that you don't send me to the galley again.' Marian grinned. 'I'm far happier in the engine room, as you can see.'

De Clisson laughed. 'Certainly. The next time you tell me you are terrible at something, I won't assume you are being modest.'

Tom came to clear the table. Pinter was at his heels.

'Mr Pinter?'

'Begging your pardon, Captain'—he wrung his hat in his hands—'but the watch has just sighted a ship. Low slung, twin masts and funnels.'

De Clisson was on her feet in an instant.

Rollo rose and extended a hand to Marian. 'Please allow us to accompany you, Captain.'

They followed her into the darkness and up to the bow. Though the moon was high, the outline of the ship was little more than a break in the horizon on the port side. The captain pulled her spyglass from the brim of her hat and trained it on the newcomer.

'What can you tell me, Mr Masters?'

The officer at watch kept his eye fixed firmly on the ship. 'I saw her about five minutes ago. With that profile I'd expect speed, but there is no way of making out anything else unless she gets closer.'

'Well done, Mr Masters. Keep your eye on her.' She turned. 'Mr Pinter, no sense in running risks. Run the ship as dark as is practicable. Call me at the change of watch, if you will.'

'Aye, aye, Captain.'

Pinter gestured and one of the men turned down the dynamic lights until they were a mere flicker. With a final glance into the distance, the captain led Rollo and Marian back to her cabin. Tom brought in the main course, thick fillets of Atlantic salmon, freshly caught. Then he went to the windows and drew the curtains tightly, trapping the light within.

'I take it you are concerned, Captain?'

De Clisson was more than competent, Rollo knew, but the vessel was both precious and untried. Was her concern valid, or an over-reaction?

De Clisson speared a forkful of fish. 'I am wary, that is all. The ocean is large and busy, but we've been fortunate so far.'

'Might they simply sail past?' he asked. 'They are very far away after all.'

'Yes, that's true.' Her voice was uneasy, contemplative. 'Marian, how much more is there to do in the engine room before we're able to use full power?'

'Half a day's work, perhaps a little more. We dare not risk running full pressure through the pipes until we've checked all the welds. If it blows, we'll be in worse shape than before. But Mr Crooks has it under control.'

Rollo tapped one finger lightly on the table. 'It's regrettable that we don't yet have the experimental propellers running. Would they make a difference, Captain?'

She nodded. 'Perhaps only by two or three knots, but it would help.'

Marian steepled her hands together and pressed them to her lips. 'I can assist. We can work through the night if necessary. No one will see the light from below deck.'

'I would appreciate that, Marian,' said the captain. 'Once we've dined, would you see what Mr Crooks wishes to do? Our first priority is to get the engine to full power. And Rollo, if I may, I will ask you to stand the middle watch tonight.'

'Of course, Captain.' He picked up his fork, though he had little appetite. 'May I ask what concerns you?'

De Clisson rested her fist against her chin, deep in thought. 'The other ship is light, fast. Its configuration is much like those used by the blockade runners who come from your southern states, Rollo. I've heard reports, probably untrue, about attacks on ships like ours. The Confederates need small, light ships to engage in trade, and not everyone is fussy about where they find them. It's a risk we cannot take.'

Her words chilled Rollo to his soul. No. Risk was not something he could countenance, and not only because of the mission to New York. He was willing to hazard his own life, but Marian's was something else. They had unfinished business, the two of them. He would see there was time to resolve it.

Chapter 21

Marian came up through the hatch, into the dull light of dawn. Being this far north, it was half past nine and the sun was not yet fully up. In spite of that, she could see that the foreign ship was much closer.

She shivered a little, the wind chilling her after so long spent in the close confines of the engine room, then spotted the captain standing on the quarterdeck. Rollo was on her left, Pinter on her right. Marian made her way to them.

When Rollo caught sight of her, his strained expression lifted for a moment. 'Good morning, my dear. You look as though you have been enjoying yourself.'

Marian glanced down. Her shirt—well, Tom's—would never be clean again, and she had grease and smuts all over her hands. Heaven only knew what her face and hair looked like. She grinned and held her arms out to him.

'Good morning, dearest. Shall I kiss you?'

He laughed and fended her off. 'I'm a little busy now. Perhaps later?'

Turning to the captain, Marian sobered. 'Captain, Mr Crooks says you can run the test now.'

Captain de Clisson looked her over critically. 'Excellent work. Mr Pinter, bring the speed up by degrees, but as quickly as possible.' Pinter nodded and hurried across the deck. The captain turned once again to Rollo. 'I appreciate your assistance. You must be exhausted.' It was a polite dismissal.

Marian shielded her eyes with her hand. She could see the other ship, plain as day; it was no longer a speck on the horizon.

Rollo raised a hand. 'A moment, Captain.'

De Clisson paused.

'What defences does this ship have?'

Marian was glad he'd asked. It seemed apparent they'd need something.

But the captain scowled. 'We have no cannon, if that is what you mean. The crew have training with rifles, and we've an armoury.'

'And how confident are you that we can outrun this ship?' Rollo glanced at it, and Marian guessed he was measuring time and distance.

'If we can get up to full speed soon, our engines have an excellent chance. But'—the captain gestured to the approaching ship—'she has more sail area.'

'Why is she trying to intercept us?' Marian asked. 'What will happen if they catch us?'

'They will seek to take us as a prize.'

Marian frowned. 'But why?' None of this made sense to her. 'We are not at war with the Confederacy.'

'That won't matter to them. Ultimately, prize law is on our side, but that won't stop them trying. After all, they can claim we're flying a false flag. And Rollo is an American citizen.'

Rollo put a hand on Marian's forearm. 'Their reason doesn't matter. We can't let them take us. We might be able to talk our way out of it, but this ship is filled with new technologies, which we can't allow to fall into their hands. And, of course, we must consider our mission. We have to get to New York on time.'

Marian leaned against the railing and studied the other ship. Smoke was now visible above her funnels. Her aspect was changing too—she was no longer parallel but heading directly towards them.

'How can we defend ourselves? We don't have cannons.'

Rollo surveyed the deck. 'What do we have?'

The answer lit up Marian's mind like the noon sun. 'Hot water!'

Rollo straightened, considering. 'It would be a powerful deterrent.'

'But only if we can employ it at a distance.' The captain looked from Rollo to Marian. 'What are you contemplating?'

Marian stared out over the port railing and across the sea, but her thoughts weren't occupied by the ship that was slowly but surely encroaching on them. Thanks to her recent sojourn below decks, she now knew the engine room as well as her Edinburgh flat. Images and diagrams flashed through her mind as she formulated a plan. She glanced at Rollo, who nodded, then she spun around.

'Captain, will you give us permission to make some changes to the engine system? I believe we can cobble together something that will give us a fighting chance.'

Captain de Clisson didn't hesitate. 'Go. Take whatever stores you need. Use whatever manpower you require.'

Twenty minutes later, Marian had Tom and a young midshipman sewing canvas and slathering it in pitch while she dangled from a rope over the bow. She was widening the intake pipe through which water ran. It passed under the engine room and into the rear fins where it was heated by the sun, and from there, it was forced into a holding tank where it gained pressure, allowing it to turn the turbines.

'There. All done. You can pull me up.'

Mr Pinter, who doubled as the ship's carpenter, went down next to caulk up the rough edges left by her surgery.

Rollo gripped her arm and brought his face close. 'Take care, damn it! You have no business dangling from a rope over open sea.'

'You do it.'

'I've done it before, but never at these speeds! The captain has us up at twelve knots and we're still gaining.' He kissed her, hard. 'By God, I don't scare easily, Marian, but watching you ...'

She held up a hand. 'Spank me later, if you must. Did you make the nozzle?'

He laughed. 'I certainly will. And yes, I did.'

'Good. Come down to the engine room.'

It was hotter than the bowels of hell below decks after dangling above the freezing ocean, but Crooks had followed her instructions to the letter. He had fitted a brass collar on a second outlet before the turbines and had connected the long canvas snake to it. At the far end, he had attached a copper nozzle, with a long leather loop at the top, and a hefty trigger.

'Is this how ye wanted it, missus?'

Marian beamed. 'Yes, Mr Crooks. It's wonderful.'

Rollo shook the engineer's hand, then wrapped his arm around Marian, grease and all. 'You are a genius. Now we are ready.'

She grinned up at him. 'There's just one more thing.'

***

A cannon ball whistled towards them, then splashed into the sea, about fifty yards to port, sending up a great gout of water.

Rollo winced.

'Damn.' The captain lowered her spyglass. 'Mr Pinter, what do you make of their speed and heading?'

'They will intercept us in twenty minutes, Captain, give or take.'

Rollo gripped the spare binoculars he'd taken from his cabin. 'I thought you said blockade runners don't have cannon.'

'They don't, generally. And I don't imagine she has many, but it explains why she's coming after us so aggressively. Well, we shall call her bluff.'

Silence, as taut as the main sail over their heads, settled over the deck crew. All the preparations were complete; the low wings that swept down the sides were stowed. It would've been better to fully extend them as it would give them the stability they desperately needed, but they couldn't afford to have them damaged.

Marian came up through the hatch, having taken over from Simons, and hurriedly connected the experimental propellers to the turbines in the engine. On deck, the tall multi-bladed propellers were being screwed into their mounts. She smiled wearily and nodded.

Rollo turned to face the captain. 'What's your intention? Do we flee or fight?'

'We fight. We either need to stop her or slow her enough to put some distance between us. We're travelling at fourteen knots and might gain one or two more.' The captain eyed her crew. 'Issue arms to all hands. Mr Simons'—she addressed the lanky midshipman who stood next to Marian and a tub of pitch—'are you ready?'

'Aye, Captain.' He patted his modified rifle.

'And Marian, are you ready?'

'Aye, Captain.'

'Mr Pinter. Take her to port.'

'Aye, Captain.'

The ship shuddered as she began her turn. At this speed, she would be broadside to the enemy in ten minutes. It was a calculated risk, but at least it took her out of range of the mounted cannon.

Rollo picked up the nozzle of the hot water snake and looped the leather bandolier-style over his shoulder and chest. He had a thick towel strapped to his chest to protect him from the heat and a leather glove on his right hand.

'Prime it,' he called over his shoulder.

Tom waved down the hatch to Crooks in the engine room, and within seconds, the snake grew thick and hot.

The enemy ship charged ahead, as though it meant to ram them. Half a dozen men stood on the forecastle. Rollo pulled his goggles down over his eyes, put a finger to the trigger and waited. A man stepped forward and lifted a large speaking trumpet, such as fire-fighters used.

'This is the Confederate ship, *Falcon*. Prepare to be boarded.'

'This is the *Calliope Jane*,' de Clisson shouted back. 'Go to hell!' And she gave a downward sweep of her hand.

Four of their crewmen stood and fired, then Rollo took aim with the nozzle and let fly with a thick stream of hot water. Steam slapped his face as the water arched over the strip of ocean between the two ships. His goggles fogged instantly, making it impossible to aim; he pushed them off.

Screams came from the other ship. Men who had ducked down at the first volley of rifle fire had nowhere to run from the boiling liquid.

Rollo eased his hold on the trigger, rubbed his sleeve over his face and let the pressure build again. The crew of the *Calliope Jane* fired once more, and this time, at least one of the opposing men fell. The enemy returned fire. Mr Pinter staggered back, a low rose blooming on his white shirt. Tom rushed forward with the emergency satchel.

'Rollo, look!' The captain pointed.

The enemy's cannon, far from being out of range, was being wheeled to the bow by two sailors. The *Calliope Jane* was now fully abreast of the *Falcon* and moving fast. Rollo again turned the hissing snake on the enemy. They fell back but still managed to bring the cannon forward.

The hot water slowed to a trickle, so Rollo threw off the leather loop from around his chest. 'Now! Fire now!'

Five feet away, Simons dipped the thick head of the arrow shaft sticking out of his rifle into the pitch. Marian scooped her dragon gizmo out of her pocket and opened the tiny jaws.

Whoosh! Flame burst to life at the end of the rifle barrel.

Simons took careful aim and fired. On the *Falcon*, the mainsail went up in a blazing sheet of orange. The enemy crew threw down their rifles and ran for their firefighting gear.

The entire crew of the *Calliope Jane* cheered.

'Now, Marian!' Captain de Clisson called as she hauled down the wheel to bring them about. 'Engage the propellers! Get us out of here!'

Simons threw down his modified rifle. He and Marian wrenched on the heavy levers controlling the masts of the tall propellers. Slowly, the curved blades began to move, forcing more wind into the sails. The *Calliope Jane* gathered speed.

Rollo eyed the *Falcon*. One man on board did not run. The captain walked calmly across the deck to the cannon, bent down and pulled the heavy iron gun around.

'*Jævla helvete!*' Rollo breathed.

At this range the cannon could not miss, and though the *Calliope Jane*'s speed was increasing, they weren't moving fast enough to evade a direct hit. Without a second's hesitation, Rollo pointed his left hand and flexed his wrist. The tiny crossbow lifted. A bolt slid into place. He pressed his fingers into his palm as he'd practised a hundred times and felt the smooth release.

On the *Falcon*, the captain clutched at his chest and sank to the deck.

Chapter 22

Marian crunched one of Dr Somerton's special herbal lozenges between her teeth, then set the inlaid box back on the shelf. Rollo staggered into their cabin, a full bucket of water in each hand. He dumped the contents of both into the hip-high tub.

'At least we have plenty of hot water for bathing.' Stepping back, he set the buckets down. 'You first.'

'Thank you.' She rose and stretched, rolling the kinks out of her weary spine. 'How is Mr Pinter?'

'Holding his own. Still, I've offered your services as nurse. I know just how capable you are. But the captain wants you to sleep first. You were up all night.'

'We both were.'

Glancing at the steaming bath, now half full, Marian unbuttoned the side of the trousers she wore, pushed them over her hips and down her calves. Her grimy shirt hung to mid-thigh. She looked up, caught Rollo's eye and held it.

'Marian ...'

Crossing her hands over her midriff, she bunched the shirt in them ... and then it was on the floor.

In front of her, Rollo sucked in a breath. 'Lady, you are a tease.'

'Will you give me a hand?'

'Depends. What are you going to do with it?'

She still wore the lightly boned linen corset and was itching to take it off, but she was enjoying the dazed look in his eyes far too much. 'It clasps in the front.'

'I can see that.'

He unsnapped the little bronze buckles and the tiny teeth relaxed. The corset gaped, and Marian sucked in a lungful of air. The boned linen dropped to the floor; all that remained was her lawn chemise.

Rollo edged closer to the door. 'I'll come back in half an hour.'

'I thought we were going to talk.' She kept her voice low.

'And are you planning to bathe in your undershirt?'

'No. But you don't have to look if you don't want to.' She shrugged and, turning her back on him, pulled the chemise over her head.

'Hell, but you are lovely.'

'Thank you.'

She stepped into the bath and told herself it was the heat of the water, not Rollo's words, that made her face, her whole body, flush. She sat down, but though the water rose, it didn't quite cover her breasts. They bobbed on the surface like apples.

Rollo stood looking at her, arms crossed, a broad smile on his face. 'Have you forgotten something?'

Oh bother. 'Would you mind bringing the soap? There's a bar on the washbasin.'

He picked up the soap, then came and stood by the bath. He held the bar out to her, but she made no move to take it from his hand.

'Would you mind?'

'What did your last servant die of?'

She stuck out her tongue. 'Oh well. If I must, I can do it myself.'

He bent forward and kissed her lips. 'Never say I wasn't willing to give my all for my duty.'

Dipping the soap into the water, he ran it over her body. His touch, when it came, was a jolt of lightning. His hand was calloused, the skin roughened by weeks of working as a sailor, but he was so very gentle. It was slow going, as he used only one hand, but he was delightfully thorough. He lathered her neck, arms, shoulders, then he filled a cup with water and used it to rinse the suds from her body.

'I should wash my hair.'

He kissed her again, more leisurely this time. 'You should indeed. You look like you've been wiping the engine with it. I'll go collect another bucket of water to rinse it.'

Once he'd slipped out, Marian lathered her hair and relaxed in the heat of the bath, warm water and lassitude melting her bones. She was weary, but the admiration she'd seen in Rollo's eyes and the delight she found in his attentions were delicious. She had no intention of going to sleep just yet.

He came back quickly, two buckets in hand. 'Here, this one isn't too hot.' Holding it high, he used both hands to pour it over her head and body, then he picked up the towel and held it open. 'Ready?'

She stood, and he wrapped it around her, steadying her as she climbed out.

'Your turn.' She folded the towel at her breasts and wrapped a second around her wet hair.

'What if I'm shy?'

'Would you rather I didn't peek?'

He shook his head. 'I'd hate to deprive you.'

He was quicker than she. His shirt was off and his falls undone in a trice. She drew in a breath when he bared long pale flanks, but when he climbed into the bath, the most interesting sight was hidden from her view.

Rollo glanced at her. 'Would you care to return the favour?'

She bent and picked up the soap. 'I'd be delighted.'

His muscles were hard and smooth, reminding her of the marble statue of a naked man she'd once seen. She dipped her hand into the water and ran the soap over his belly.

'Thanks.' His voice was gruff. 'I'll take it from here.'

'Shall I do your hair?'

'Please.'

She foamed her hands, and when she ran her fingers through his hair and massaged his scalp, he closed his eyes and sighed. 'That is bliss.'

'I'm going to rinse it now.' The bucket was quite heavy, but she let the water run over him in a slow stream.

He rose, flicked the water from his eyes and stepped from the bath. Marian tried not to stare as he ran the towel over his arms and torso, the thick linen sucking up most of the water.

She moved closer.

He wrapped an arm around her and tilted her chin up. 'You remember that talk we were going to have?'

She nodded.

'Well, I think we've left it a bit late.' And then, he kissed her.

Raising both arms, Marian wrapped them around his neck and pressed her body close to his. He lifted her, took three steps and placed her lightly on the bed. Lying beside her, he trailed two fingertips down her neck and traced the swell of her breasts.

'I've wanted this since you nursed me in your flat the night we met.'

She felt rather flattered. 'Is that why you left?'

He shrugged. 'One of the reasons.' Bending his head, he bussed his lips over her skin, laying a trail of kisses, like breadcrumbs, up to her mouth. Then he pulled back and studied her. 'You know there's no going back, Marian. You have to be sure.'

She slid a hand along his chest. 'I'm sure.' There was no way she would let this moment pass. That was the road to regret.

'Have you done this before?' he asked.

'No. But I'm a quick learner.'

He kissed her lips, then under her ear. 'There's no hurry.'

Deftly, he loosened the towel from around her body until it lay open. His lips made a slow passage over her skin, and she quivered as his hand ran down her thigh and back again, ranging over her body, learning its way.

Resting his chin low on her belly, he stared up at her. 'Earlier, when we were on deck, I was looking at you in those damned trousers. And I wanted this.' He placed a kiss an inch south of her navel.

She shivered. 'You should be careful what you wish for.'

'I'll be very careful.'

His kisses, his fingers, trailed lower. But then he was back, lying on his side and facing her. He'd tucked his left arm under his body, and his hand, gloveless, lay passive on the bed between them. As he pulled her close with his right arm, she reached down, eased open the fingers of his iron hand and wriggled closer.

'Marian.' His voice held a note of warning.

'I want all of you.'

She pressed his hands to her breasts, and he curled his fingers around them. Pulling his mouth to hers, she opened herself to the taste of him. He groaned and kissed her with greater urgency as she slid his hands down his body and squeezed his flanks.

'Don't be in such a rush, woman.'

'I was afraid this would never happen.'

'I was afraid you were going to get yourself killed. I've been in a dozen battles but only ever had myself to worry about. Today ...'

She leaned up and stopped his words with her lips. He moved his body over hers and she gloried in the sensation of his weight, the feel of his hips between her legs. Yet he didn't move to possess her, just plied her with kisses until her head swam and she was panting. He pulled the damp towel from her hair and slowly caressed her scalp, then he cast spells down the length of her body, stroking casually over her skin. He tilted his hips, then paused.

'Look at me, Marian.'

She opened her eyes and met his gaze, his face only inches above her. He was tense, the sinews of his throat tightly corded. Sliding her fingers into his hair, she pulled his face down to hers.

'Love me.' Lust made her voice husky.

'With pleasure.'

She gasped when he joined his body fully to hers. He took her mouth as well, kissing her deeply. The rough tenderness of the moment overwhelmed her, but this was the completion she'd wanted for weeks now; the perfect act of intimacy—raw and unbearably sweet.

He moved slowly, rhythmically, and his breath was hot against her throat. 'Darling … *kjære, så søt.*'

His trembling urgency increased. She lifted her hips against his, and the tempo of his movements quickened further. A flame roared to life deep inside her, and she forgot everything in the grandeur of the moment.

Her limbs were made of lead, but she came slowly back to languid awareness to find Rollo sprawled beside her, his hand still lying lightly over her breast. He opened his eyes and kissed her unhurriedly.

'Go to sleep, sweetheart. You must be exhausted.' He pulled her into a loose embrace. 'You've nothing to worry about. We'll talk in the morning.'

She lay against his chest. The excitement of the last twenty-four hours, particularly the last hour, was at war with the battalion of thoughts that suddenly marched over the horizon. But the sound of his breathing and the creak of the bed and the ship lulled her. She had nothing to worry about. They would talk in the morning.

Chapter 23

Rollo took Marian's hand and she stepped lightly off the cutter and onto the gloomy deck in Halifax. Far out in the bay, the *Calliope Jane* swung at anchor, somewhere between McNab Island and Point Pleasant Park. The harbour was quiet with only a few ships in dock, and no one paid any particular heed to the small, unarmed cutter. Rollo waited until Marian got her balance, then reached down and collected their single valise.

'Godspeed, Tom, Mr Simons.' He touched the brim of his hat.

'Thank Captain de Clisson for us again,' Marian called softly.

After a nod, a grin and a whispered 'Good luck', Tom and Simons cast off from alongside the dock.

'Where now?' Marian misstepped and stumbled backwards.

Rollo shot out a hand to help her and pulled her close. 'Are you all right?'

She was abnormally pale, and it clearly wasn't only the weak moonlight and the single wavering lamp making her appear so.

She swallowed and put a hand to her belly. 'I'm fine. What do we do now?'

'I'll send a message.' Cautiously, he let her go.

Though she stood firmly on her feet, she kept her head bowed. No wonder. It was late, they'd had a long day and the icy wind was cutting them both to the quick. He led her out of the worst of the wind and wrote a short message with his stylus before closing the messenger's lid. Tapping the burned flash paper onto the cobbles, he ground it underfoot, then kept an arm around Marian's shoulders as they waited for the reply. She stood still, shivering slightly, and pressed against him. At the flash from his messenger, he opened the cover and memorised the address.

He tucked a hand under Marian's arm. 'Shall we go?'

'Where, exactly?'

'To see a friend.'

'You are as close as an oyster.'

'Thank you. I do my best.'

She shook her head at him. 'It wasn't a compliment.'

'I gathered that.'

He studied her carefully and wondered whether she felt as well as she claimed. She was more pallid than she had been on the ship, though her eyes sparkled with adventure.

She glanced over her shoulder as they left the dock. 'Does it bring back memories?'

After a moment, he caught her meaning. 'Yes, this is how it all started, isn't it? You and I, meeting on a dock at midnight.'

'It's barely after ten. And that was a different life.'

'Very different.'

They walked briskly as they made their way down a winding alley and turned left onto a wider road, muddy and lined with houses and shopfronts. Several had dynamic lights over their doors, but most had old-fashioned gas lamps. A door opened; rowdy music and a few casual profanities rang out. The third door down was dirty, had obviously once been white, and over it was a large copperplate sign that read: *The Stone and Hammer*.

'We're here.'

But as Rollo reached for the knocker, the door slammed open. Marian reacted first, pushing Rollo aside as a burly, smelly man flew backwards through the doorway.

'No cheaters here!' A balding gent punctuated his statement with a jab of his pipe.

Behind him, two enormous shadows with arms the size of a cannon's chase glowered down.

Rollo straightened as the fellow looked him and Marian over. They were ridiculously overdressed for an evening in a low tavern. Under his coat, Rollo had on the outfit he'd last worn in the Queen of England's study, and Marian wore her elegant navy day dress. Their fabric and tailoring, even in this light, were much too fine for the Halifax docks. The tavern keeper obviously thought them an easy mark.

'Sir, ma'am, please do enter. Don't mind him, sir. We was just dealin' with the riffraff.'

When Marian shivered, Rollo frowned. 'My wife is cold.'

The barkeep led them to a table at the back of the establishment, close to the fire, and wiped a cloth hastily over the table. It was a shabby place. The coils running around the rim of the bar were more verdigris than brass, and on the wall opposite, the dynamic light waned and flickered.

When Marian rocked on her feet, Rollo guided her into a chair. The other patrons, what few there were, looked at them oddly before returning to their own business.

'Can I bring you anything, sir?'

Rollo glanced at Marian. Her pallor was accentuated by the firelight, and she was pulling nervously at her skirt. Perhaps food would help. And something to warm her.

'A plate of bread and cheese, plus two warm ciders.'

'At once, sir.'

When they were alone, Marian turned her chair and stretched her booted feet towards the hissing flames. 'Is someone meeting us here?'

'Yes.' But Rollo was listening with only half an ear. Concern twisted his gut. Was she sickening for something? He couldn't leave her here.

The barmaid sauntered over with two pewter tankards and a plate, grimy around the rim, on which sat several thick doorsteps of old bread and a wedge of crumbly yellow cheese. It had been trimmed, but there were still traces of mould.

Marian, caution written on her face, lifted her mug and took a sip. 'It's not bad.' She took another sip, and another.

'Best you eat something. That cider is strong.' He slipped his knife from its scabbard, sliced off some bread, topped it with cheese and held it out.

She shook her head and closed her eyes, looking more than a little green. 'I'm fine, thank you.'

She took off her bonnet and rubbed a hand at the nape of her neck. Her hairpins were fighting a losing battle with her autumn curls, which glowed like a nimbus. Then, pressing her lip between her teeth, she looked up at him. She might be exhausted, sick or at the end of her tether, but her eyes were bright emeralds, lit from within.

'So,' she said, 'what happens now?'

Rollo gave her a tight smile. 'We wait.'

***

Marian took another sip of cider. The warm bubbles soothed her churning stomach, though she still felt dizzy. It could be from the alcohol, she mused … but from the second she'd set foot on land again, her world had been tossed on its head.

When the room swayed again, a strange sensation prickled within her—a fear she'd been loath to name. She'd felt so well, then suddenly …

She glanced over at Rollo as he downed the contents of his mug. His mind was clearly on the mission, and she could not distract him from that, or from their impending meeting with the person who might meet them, might help them.

During the last few weeks, she and Rollo had been reckless in their passion. Must she now pay the piper? It had been so easy on the ship. The crew thought them man and wife, so there'd been no need to be cautious. It had been a time out of time. But babes and spying did not make for a marriage made in heaven.

A shadow fell across their table.

'Good evening. I see you are new to our fair city.' The newcomer nodded to the valise on the floor and, to her surprise, held out his left hand to Rollo.

Perhaps they had a different etiquette in the colonies.

Clearly unperturbed, Rollo stood and shook the man's hand. A flicker of surprise crossed the newcomer's face, and Marian wondered if he could tell Rollo's hand was not flesh.

He glanced between them. 'Are you visiting from the States?'

'Not exactly.' Rollo smiled urbanely. 'We have been abroad on business.'

The other fellow nodded gravely. He was tall, well dressed, and had unremarkable hair and eyes, though the latter had a sharpness to their expression. He carried a polished bamboo cane, and on his ring finger he wore a gold signet.

'Ah, then you have missed the worst of the recent fighting. The tragedy of Gettysburg is not one I will soon forget.' He shook his head mournfully. 'Meade crushed Lee with an iron fist.'

Marian watched the exchange carefully.

Rollo met the stranger's eyes, reached down and pushed the edge of his left glove down, showing a glint of metal. 'It would be a terrible thing to see.'

'Indeed.' The newcomer nodded, though Marian sensed nervous indecision when he glimpsed what lay beneath Rollo's glove. 'It seems there is no stopping Lee or the south.'

226

Rollo stepped back, sat down and gestured for the other man to do the same. 'Quite true. The man has the cunning of a ginger fox.'

Yet another nod came from the stranger, and Marian noted some of the tension leave both men.

'We clearly see eye to eye.'

'It is always a pleasure to make a new acquaintance.' Rollo leaned back in his chair. 'May I introduce my wife?'

'It is a pleasure, ma'am.' When Marian nodded politely, he turned back to Rollo. 'Are you staying in Halifax long?'

'We have an urgent appointment, but once our business is carried out, we shall not tarry.'

'Of course. With Christmas so close you will undoubtedly wish to be with family. He stood and handed Rollo a white slip of pasteboard. 'Do feel free to call. It has been a pleasure to meet you.' With a nod and a tip of his hat, he was gone.

Rollo looked intently at the calling card, then held it to the fire and watched it until it turned to ash.

'What do we do now? Do we have to meet someone else? Who is the ginger fox?'

Rollo's voice held a hint of amusement. 'You are. It's what Melville dubbed you.'

'Was that Melville?'

'No. Melville's my superior and doesn't travel, so he's still in New York. That man is his local contact and our liaison. Come.' He held out his hand and pulled her to her feet, then dropped a small pile of coins beside the uneaten bread.

'We are not staying here for the night?' Weariness, and her nameless malaise, made her tetchy.

'He has arranged our accommodation for tonight and transport for the morning.'

'Perhaps if you had told me more than our destination ...' Marian grumbled.

But Rollo didn't answer, just picked up their luggage, nodded to the innkeeper, then led her out to the dark and frigid street once again.

She shuddered. 'There is no end to the games you men play, is there? You meet face to face, but that isn't enough. Trust is a foreign concept to you.' She turned away, unwilling to say more. She understood the need for secrecy, even duplicity. But she was too tired, too ill and too damn cold to care.

Rollo put a hand on her waist and pulled her close. 'Sweetheart—'

'Rollo, I don't give two ... frigates ... for spy games right now. I want a hot bath, a soft bed and your arms around me.'

'And you shall have them, my lovely vixen.' Putting two fingers to his mouth, he whistled, and a passing public unicarriage halted. 'Come. Your chariot awaits.'

Chapter 24

The clip-clopping of the dozen rubber-shod hooves of the central unicarriage wheel ceased when the vehicle halted, and a moment later, Rollo handed Marian down. Their breath turned opaque in the freezing air, blending with the steam billowing from the bronze nostrils of the equine cab.

Once Rollo had tipped the driver, he turned to Marian and read frustration in the stiffness of her posture. Reticence was more than habit with him, but it was no excuse; she deserved his trust. Except, when she shivered, concern for her wellbeing overrode his good intentions to reveal something of his plans.

'Are you still unwell?' he asked as the vehicle steamed quietly into the night.

She gave him a blank stare. 'Simply disoriented. What do we do now?'

Still worried, he slipped her arm through his and surveyed their surroundings. Around them, houses slept. This was an affluent neighbourhood and dynamic lights graced the streets as well as the homes and porches. The road behind them was a pattern of gleaming islands of light in a shadowy sea. Apart from the tall maples standing sentinel, they were alone.

'This way.' Rollo turned due east, back the way they'd come. There must be a fault, for half the light poles were in darkness.

'So we walk in circles while you and your puppetmaster make certain we were not followed?'

He frowned. Couldn't she see he was trying to keep her safe? 'If that's what it takes.'

'Look around you, Rollo. We are alone.' She gestured to the street, empty but for a handful of vehicles. 'Everyone with a brain is in a warm bed tonight.'

'And you know this how?'

She had colour in her cheeks now, like warning flares. 'Rollo Rahgstadt, what is it you doubt? My powers of perception? My vigilance? I am not helpless or brainless.'

He put his arm around her and kissed the top of her head. 'I do not doubt you, wife.'

She twitched in his embrace but remained silent as they reached a corner.

He looked up at the pole, then tapped it. An acorn, caught in the crook of the pole's arm above the name plaque, fell into his palm. 'We go left here.'

She glanced down the silent road, took in the pattern of lights, one lit, one unlit. 'Rather obvious, isn't it?'

'Not if you camouflage it.' He nodded to the street opposite where the same pattern occurred.

The dotted path led to the hardwood door of 2507 Brunswick Street. Three lamps running past the house were dead, wrapping everything, himself and Marian included, in a deep charcoal blanket. He wrapped an arm around Marian, who was beginning to shiver in earnest, and raised his fist to the door. Three knocks and a pause, then twice more, and finally, a single knock.

An endless moment of silence stretched out before he heard the bolts slide back. When the door opened, the man from the tavern stood before them, backlit by the warm glow of the foyer lights. He popped his head out, glanced left and right, then stepped back with a beaming smile.

'Iron Fist, Ginger Fox. Welcome.'

After a fifteen-minute sojourn with a roaring fire and a steaming cup of tea, Rollo led Marian into Jonathan McCuddy's guest room and turned the key in the lock. He was grateful. With McCuddy at his back, he would not have to be on watch all night.

He turned from the door to find Marian unbuckling the leather clasps on her corset. That done, she loosed her skirt and shrugged off her blouse. Her camisole was next—she had never been shy.

She folded her skirt, keeping her back to him. 'We leave at dawn?'

'We need to be aboard by then, yes. Melville has chartered a dirigible, which will take us directly to Flushing Meadow.'

'Mr McCuddy has been very helpful.'

Rollo slid an arm around her, under her breasts, and pulled her close. He laid his lips under her ear. 'We're working towards a mutual goal. And we've been known to help the Canadians when it suited our interests.'

'It's good to know there's some benefit to your spy games and one-upmanship.'

He chuckled. 'Don't hold back, darling. Tell me what you think!' As he held her, his breeches immediately shrank and every nerve in his body burst to life. Her effect on him only grew with every passing day.

She turned in his arms and looked up at him, but there was no pithy barb on her lips. She looked tired and pale as the moon.

Gently, he ran a hand down her back. 'Marian, are you unwell? You haven't been yourself all day. Even McCuddy remarked on it. Should I call a physician?'

'No. I don't need a doctor.' She pulled out of his embrace and plonked herself down on the low velvet fainting couch, then covered her face with her hands. Her delicate shoulders trembled.

Panic and a nameless unease surged through his veins. 'Marian, for goodness sake, tell me what's wrong!'

'We were foolish on the ship. I was foolish.'

He crouched in front of her and took her hands in his. 'Sweetheart, talk to me.'

'This life is not meant for a family. And it's not as if we're truly married.'

Realisation dawned on him. This was an eventuality he'd briefly considered on the boat, and to him, it was logical what the next step in their relationship would be, once this mission was over. He'd assumed she felt the same.

Now, she took a deep breath and looked up at him, her emerald eyes swimming. When she spoke, her voice shook. 'I've not felt myself since we made landfall. And I'm overdue, just a day or so. Dr Somerton gave me some herbal lozenges, which I've been taking, but she said there'd still be a risk. Oh, Rollo, what shall I do?'

That she believed herself alone was a greater surprise to him than a suspected pregnancy. He stood, lifted her in his arms and carried her to the bed Setting her down, he turned back the coverlet and ushered her onto the warmed sheet. He took up his position beside her, boots and all, and pressed close.

'You need not worry, my dear.' He ran a light hand over her middle. 'We'll work everything out together.'

Marian turned towards him, and his breath froze in his lungs at her loveliness.

'What is there to work out? This world was not made for babes and unwed trollops—'

He placed a finger on her lips. 'You should not call yourself that. You're my wife.'

She caught up his hand. 'In this story only, Rollo. But in the real world, I'm nothing.'

'Our marital status is nothing more than a technicality, and one I will be delighted to address. And I promise you this, if you are with child, I will be the happiest spy on earth.' He leaned in and placed a gentle kiss at her left temple, then her right, and on the tip of her nose. Then he kissed her mouth, slow and sweet.

She sighed and shook her head. 'I don't want you to have to marry me.'

'On the contrary, it will be my greatest pleasure to marry you.'

It was true. His words were not intended to merely comfort and soothe. If he was granted just one wish today, it would be to wed her.

'You and the babe will have my name, my protection and my love, lifelong. But consider, Marian, whether you might simply be feeling the disorientation common after so many weeks at sea.'

'Do you think so?'

He shrugged. 'Either is possible. But whether you are suffering from land sickness or expecting a visit from the stork, it doesn't change how I feel. I love you, Marian, and I know you love me. In this world, that's the greatest blessing one can hope to receive. I would be a fool to neglect it.'

When she coiled a hand around his neck and pulled him down, he went willingly, kissed her passionately. And when she fiddled with the buckles on his breeches, he stood and dealt with his boots and clothing while she watched with languorous eyes. He returned to the bed and she reached for him, her kisses rich with desire.

Later, when she lay curled against his side, he brushed his lips against her fiery brow. How had he lived until now on loneliness and shadows? When had he reached the point where life without this special woman had no meaning?

***

Marian stepped from the hired unicarriage, her hand on Rollo's arm. Tilting her head up, she took in the dozen or so dirigibles swinging at anchor, their colours bright against the pale dawn sky. It was excitement, not the cold, that made her shiver now.

One was lower than the others, its car connected with thick chains to the keel-girder links of the ballonet; a narrow portable ladder was pushed against its side.

'This way, my dear.' Rollo offered his arm, and she took it.

She was much less nauseated today, had been able to consume a boiled egg and some tea, but the ground still seemed unaccountably uneven. She was glad of his arm and even gladder to know he would not discard her if she was with child.

They climbed the ladder, and the pilot met them at the top. He was a taciturn fellow, who shook Rollo's hand, nodded to Marian, then disappeared into his tiny cabin after giving them their flight instructions and showing them the amenities in the cabin—two padded chairs with a table, a tiny sink and the wherewithal to make tea.

Soon after, the crewman cast off. The rotors in the four corners of the airship whirred, and the craft rose smoothly before the bladed fans pivoted, pushing them south and west. Rollo led Marian to the stern, where they watched Halifax grow smaller and smaller under their feet.

'You have more colour in your cheeks this morning.' He ran his hand down her back and gently squeezed her derrière.

'I'm surprised, given my sleepless night.' She grinned up at him.

'Not entirely sleepless.'

She simply leaned against him, closed her eyes briefly with a sigh and let the icy breeze play against her cheeks.

He kissed her lightly. 'We can go inside if you wish to get out of the wind.'

She shook her head. 'I'm fine. This coat is beautifully warm.' She snuggled into the fur-lined garment McCuddy had given her. 'Besides, this view is incredible. I've never stood on a cloud and looked down at the earth.' The golden sky was turning blue, though the sun was still very low.

'*You* are incredible. This is your first time on an airship, and you aren't nervous?'

She laughed. 'I feel marvellous. And the higher we rise, the better I feel. The swaying motion is soothing.'

'Melville will be waiting when we land in Flushing.'

'That won't be for a while, though.'

'Another three hours, so the pilot says.' He laid a hand over hers—the left, she noted idly, as dexterous and as gentle as the right.

She couldn't help smiling as she looked up at him. 'Then let's not borrow trouble. Melville can wait. Up here, it's just us.' She slid her arms around his neck as the unfettered joy in his eyes warmed her to the core.

Chapter 25

The seat creaked as Rollo sat beside her. 'We're nearing New York.'

'Oh, good.' Marian tucked the new fairy light she'd built into her pocket, rolled up her small collection of tools and fastened the buckle securely. Slipping the pack into her other coat pocket, she stood and arched her back. 'Shall we go out?'

They stepped onto the open deck and saw the islands and bays of New York glinting far below. A forest of white sails, on brass and wooden vessels, dotted the harbour. Marian eyed the largest frigate, which sported two massive turbines and a plethora of copper-sheathed fittings.

'Oh my. She is gorgeous. Are those American ships?'

'No. That, my dear, is the Imperial Russian Navy.' Rollo leaned on the rail. 'Their presence, according to Melville, may have a far-reaching influence on the current state of the Civil War.' He pointed out the ship Marian had first noticed. 'That beastly beauty is called the *Alexander Nevsky* and was sailed by none other than the Tsar's brother, Grand Duke Konstantin.'

His body seemed at ease, but the strained edge in his voice betrayed him.

Marian's heart raced as she turned to face him. 'So why are they here? And what does Dracos want with them?'

'Our government has implied the visit is in support of our long war with the South. But intelligence suggests the Tsar and the admiral are concerned that if hostilities are renewed in the Crimea, the Russian Fleet will find herself trapped in her own harbours. Of course, it could be a cover for something else.' His face grew grim. 'As for Dracos, we need to find out why the Russian presence has drawn him here. Is someone within their ranks his next target? Or an ally?'

Again, Marian ran her eyes over the seven frigates and the five smaller clippers.

'I can hear your mind ticking over, Marian. What are you thinking?'

'England and France are not hostile to your country?'

'Not openly, no. But it's well known they're happy to see us at our brothers' throats and both have fought on this continent before. Russia on the other hand has no love for them but no argument with us. We're natural allies.' He snaked an arm around her waist. 'The enemy of my enemy ...'

She looked up at him. 'Well, I can't believe my Queen and the French Emperor are best pleased, but how will this impact our problem?' Her voice sobered. 'I imagine Dracos will find it easier to blend in here, with so many men of similar appearance and accent.'

'Yes, that's the problem. And let's not forget the dozens of Confederate spies. It's quite a challenge.'

'We will succeed.'

'We don't have a choice.'

They both turned back to the vista before them. The sky was bright. Flashes of reflected light glinted between the billowing sails. The large war ships were particularly spectacular, each with multiple masts and impressive armoury, all polished and on display. A chill ran down Marian's spine as she remembered the cannon on the *Falcon* and considered the damage this fleet could do.

They heard the cabin door click open, then closed; it was nearly time for the crewman to reposition the turbines to bring the dirigible down. They were almost to port and had begun a gentle turn inland when Marian spotted something.

'I wonder?' She leaned closer to the balustrade.

Rollo gripped her arm and tugged her back. 'Careful! What do you see?'

Thinking hard, she rubbed a knuckle against her lower lip. 'Captain De Clisson said something once about Mr Brunel having an Eastern European correspondent. Look over there'—she pointed— 'see the clippers and their similarities to the *Calliope Jane*?'

Rollo pulled out his small expanding telescope—she had made it for him out of some oddments on the voyage—and focused it carefully. 'You're right! Do you think he sold his design to the Russians?'

Soft footfalls came from several feet away, and as Marian reached for the spyglass, she glanced at the approaching crewman. There was something about his stance. He had one hand at his belt as if he intended to—

'Rollo, look out!'

Rollo pivoted instantly, swinging his arm up and twisting his body away from the crewman's blade, which stabbed upwards, towards his heart. With a firm grip on the metal spyglass, Rollo struck downward and clipped both the crewman's hand and knife. The weapon rang like a bell as it fell to the deck.

Keeping one eye on the villain, Marian sprinted towards the cabin door. She had to find a weapon, something she could use ...

Just as she threw the door back, a muffled thud came from the end of the walkway. Hurrying, she scanned the room, but it was almost bare. She quickly discounted the china tea service. There must be something in the storage locker. She turned and her eye caught the most obvious weapon—a boathook mounted on a long pole and resting on two hooks above the door.

She jumped and grasped the end of the six-foot-long pike, then raced back to Rollo. He and the crewman were circling each other in the tiny space. Rollo had managed to free the stiletto stowed in his vambrace, which was marginally longer than the wicked dagger the crewman held. As Rollo stabbed his weapon towards his attacker, the crewman made a long, sweeping slash and struck Rollo's outstretched left hand. A loud clang rang out, but, undeterred, he aimed for Rollo's undefended right arm and his chest. Rollo had a streak of scarlet on his sleeve but was holding his own. The crewman was marked on his hand and cheek.

Marian gripped her weapon with sweaty hands, hoping to knock the knife from the villain's hands, but the angle was wrong. Rollo stepped back—onto the discarded spyglass! His foot shot from under him, and he went down heavily on his side. He lifted his arm and the vambrace took the brunt of the crewman's next blow.

Marian couldn't wait any longer. She thrust the boathook forward and caught their assailant under his ribs. She felt resistance as blade met flesh, but the momentum carried her forward. Appalled, she pulled back and dropped the boathook. A spurt of blood soaked the villain's white shirt as he fell against the rail and dropped his knife. Rollo kicked it, sending it spinning over the side of the walkway. Panting, he pulled himself to his feet and kept his eye on their attacker. The man was bent over, one hand pressed against his wound, though a steady stream of blood dribbled between his fingers.

Rollo turned to Marian. 'Are you all right?'

She could only nod. Her stomach heaved at what she'd done. Their enemy looked up, his face blank and paling rapidly. Then, without a word, he hauled himself upright and leaned, too far, over the railing.

Rollo rushed forward, but he was too late. The man had already toppled backwards and out of sight.

Marian shuddered. 'Why?'

Rollo clenched the rail tightly, avoiding the bloody handprints, and scowled down at the city. 'He was dying, and he knew it. This way, he avoided awkward questions.'

The pilot opened the door and popped his head out. 'It's time to descend. Can you let Peters know?'

Rollo wiped his hands on his trousers. 'I'll see to it.'

The pilot nodded and stepped back inside.

'Come, my dear.' Rollo took her hand in his. 'You should take your seat.'

Back inside, her stomach shuddered, but it had nothing to do with their loss of altitude. Though she'd carried a knife for years, she'd never used a blade on a man—until now. She felt sick. Did this make her a murderer?

'Who was he?' Marian curled against Rollo's shoulder.

'I've no idea. We'll see what Melville has to say.'

Melville. She was beginning to hate the name of Rollo's mysterious chieftain. He'd organised their flight and they'd almost died. What would New York bring?

'You saved my life, you know.' Rollo turned to her as the treetops came into view. 'You were incredibly brave.'

'I didn't feel brave.' She shook her head. 'I was terrified and didn't know what to do. But I couldn't let him hurt you.'

Rollo lifted her hand to his lips. 'That's exactly what bravery feels like.'

***

Rollo scanned the landing field at Flushing Meadow. The space was large and open, the grass brown and still dusted with grey frost. To the west, bare trees lined the field. Their gnarled branches reached for the sun, trying to scavenge a morsel of warmth. Beside him, Marian shivered.

On the road to the east, three chrome-and-bronze unicarriages stood wreathed in steam, half-hidden. As soon as the anchor of the dirigible hit the frozen soil, Rollo moved forward.

Marian stood gazing at the tall masts that were visible over the trees and buildings. She appeared to have recovered from her shock; she had colour in her cheeks, and her lips were like cherries.

Rollo took her arm. 'Come.'

Their pilot waved down, and a young lad ran the passenger ladder up to the dirigible. Rollo hooked the steps to the aircraft, opened the passenger gate and ushered Marian forward. But as soon as his feet touched the ground, just seconds after hers, Rollo sensed her tension. She was coiled tighter than a spring.

They were surrounded by a phalanx of tall broad-shouldered men in thick woollen coats and bowler hats. One, he recognised.

'Smithers.'

He received a nod in return.

'Rahgstadt. This is Booth. And Carter.'

Carter had skin like cauliflower soup, and Booth's lumpy face was set in a perpetual glower. The men looked him and Marian up and down, their faces expressionless, and each kept one hand in a coat pocket. They turned and nodded. Melville, nattily dressed in a pinstripe suit and a sapphire-blue cravat, sauntered over and came to a stop in front of Rollo.

'Melville.' Rollo kept his voice tapioca bland, absent of any note of welcome or loathing. At his touch, Marian's intensity reduced to a mere simmer.

Melville rocked on his heels, scrutinised Rollo and then Marian. 'Ah, Iron Fist. Well turned out as always, I see.'

The name on his lips carried a whiff of disdain. Heaven only knew the man could be pompous.

'And this must be Vicky's Ginger Fox.'

Marian threw Rollo a questioning glance.

He kept this face calm and lowered his eyes.

She didn't take the hint. Instead, she curtsied. 'I have the honour of being Her Majesty's most loyal servant, sir.' She looked up and met Melville's gaze with a distinct air of challenge. 'You are Mr Melville, I presume?'

Despite himself, Rollo smiled. She had the right attitude. Show no fear was the first lesson he had learned in his early training.

Melville removed his hat, revealing snowy hair, and bowed over her glove. 'You presume correctly, ma'am.' He turned to Rollo. 'It's good to see you again, Rahgstadt. And all in one piece despite the bloodstains?'

Rollo nodded. 'Thanks to Marian. Have them anchor the dirigible and ask the pilot to come down. I'd like to find out as much as he knows about the crewman on the flight. He tried to kill us not twenty minutes ago.'

Melville's eyes darkened and he nodded. 'Smithers.' He turned back to Rollo. 'Who knew you'd be on the flight?'

'Only your courier and whoever you told here. We didn't even tell McCuddy.'

'We'll look into it.' He offered Rollo, not his right hand to shake, but his left. A test.

Rollo took the hand and shook it, then squeezed until he read discomfort in Melville's eyes.

Melville pulled his hand free and stretched his fingers. 'So, it seems this new appendage of yours is worth the small fortune the President paid for it.' He turned and headed for the warmth of the waiting vehicles.

Rollo offered Marian his arm. She didn't need it despite their recent experience—and the glint in her eye suggested she didn't want it—but Melville needed a lesson in courtesy. They followed after him. He was gentleman enough at least to permit Marian to enter the unicarriage first and take her seat. Booth got in last and closed the door before they rumbled forward.

Melville glanced at Rollo from across the carriage. 'You made good time. I'll give you that.'

'We were fortunate.' Rollo didn't plan to give Melville any more information than he needed, and he didn't need to know about the *Calliope Jane*. 'And just as well. If our information is correct, the Romanian is headed here.'

Melville sobered abruptly. 'Yes, we heard. Your Scottish contact got word out by official channels, even before you left. Sent a mirror message to London and into the diplomatic bag. It arrived on one of those new steam vessels two days ago.'

Rollo was undeterred. 'You've heard no rumours of a man who wears a bladed cape and mask? Nothing from the dockers or steve-dores?'

'We've made generous offers for information, but there's no sign he's here. While several ships have come in, there are no strangers among the crews, and no one fitting Dracos's profile in the passenger manifests. Of course, he might have landed further along the coast.'

'Just as we did.'

'Indeed. We've had men on the docks every day since Doyle's message came, but it contained precious little detail, just a bare description. Since then we've had nothing but false leads and mistaken identities.'

'We suspect he'll try to blend in with the Russian sailors and the local dock workers.' Rollo looked out at the passing slum. 'Easy enough for him to do so. Only a person who has an ear for dialects would be able to pick him out, and even then …'

'Ah, but Doyle tells me you've seen him.'

Marian stiffened beside him.

Rollo shook his head at his boss. 'Not I.'

'It's not a face one simply forgets.'

Marian might not have noticed Rollo's warning glare, but he wouldn't bet on it. Her voice was smooth and as cold as a shard of glass, the soft burr of her accent subsumed under a manner to suit Her Majesty's court ladies. Everything about her body language trumpeted her dislike of Melville, and it wasn't hard to guess why. Doyle, though sometimes curt in his dealing with her, had at least treated her with respect.

Melville only glanced at her briefly before his gaze shifted back to Rollo. 'We have the description Doyle sent.'

'Only a description?'

Melville nodded. 'He mentioned there was a likeness made, but he didn't have it on him when he sent the message from Oban. My guess is it'll arrive any day now.'

Marian spoke once more. 'It might be too late by then. You should send an artist to our accommodation posthaste and I will see to it that you get a detailed sketch. It's the least I can do.'

'That would be most gratifying … Mrs Rahgstadt.' He turned back to Rollo, a smirk on his lips. 'Four weeks aboard ship as husband and wife. My, my, it must have been tedious. How did you pass the time?'

'I don't appreciate your tone, Melville.' Rollo glared at his superior.

Marian crossed her arms and put her chin in the air. 'For a start, we fought off a marauding frigate full of Confederate rebels.'

Melville ignored her. 'Just because you're a Culper golden boy, Iron Fist, don't think to chastise me. I merely want to ensure your behaviour remains … professional. You are back in the States now, and unlike dear Queen Vicky, we do not rely on women to get the job done.'

'Oh goodness, that would never do.' Marian's eyes glittered. 'Better forget, then, that a woman surgically attached your agent's iron fist, and another made it into a weapon *and* saved your golden boy's arse … *sir*.'

Chapter 26

'I like it.' Marian looked around the snug apartment. It wasn't anything fancy, but it had two bedrooms, a small kitchenette and dining table, and a parlour with a fireplace and a surprisingly comfortable sofa. She pulled back the striped velvet drapes and frowned; the window faced a blank brick wall.

Rollo glanced around, unimpressed. 'Your Edinburgh flat was smaller, but at least it had character. This one feels impersonal.'

'The bed looks comfortable. That's important.'

He pulled her close, kissed her lips. 'Get your mind out of the bedroom, Mrs Rahgstadt. We have reconnaissance to do, not to mention shopping. Cinderella requires a gown for the ball.'

She shook her head and grimaced. 'I never wanted to be a princess in a fairy tale.'

'It's only for a night.' He handed her the bronze jacket McCuddy had given her. 'Besides, we need to blend in. I'll order some clothes so we can make do until our trunks arrive. The dressmaker's and tailor's shops aren't far. We can walk.'

'Do you know this area well?'

Rollo shrugged, his face cool and grim. 'I've never lived here. I grew up in an area even poorer than this. But I've been here often enough.'

She put a hand on his arm. 'There's something bothering you.'

'Not at all.' His shook his head, dismissing her concern. 'Come on. Let's familiarise ourselves with the neighbourhood, shall we?' He opened the door. 'After you, ma'am.'

They had walked for several minutes before they spoke again. Marian could orient herself as long as she kept the bay on her left.

'Melville called you Rahgstadt. What name will we be using here?'

'I think Mr and Mrs Rahgstadt has a pleasant ring to it, don't you?'

'If you think it best.' Marian struggled to understand him. He'd sounded matter-of-fact, almost businesslike.

'I think you should get used to it.' He put a hand over hers, the gesture at odds with his demeanour. 'You will be using it for a long time.'

'Weeks?'

'Decades.'

'Oh.'

He gave her a brusque glance as they turned a corner. 'Why are you surprised? You know I want to marry you.'

'I don't think Melville will approve.'

'Then I'll be sure not to ask his opinion.'

When she laughed, he gave a distant smile, then glanced over his shoulder. 'This is the dressmaker's shop. I'll be back for you soon.'

From inside, as Marian watched Rollo head down the street towards the doorway with the tailor's sign swinging in the breeze, she noticed a shadow pass across the window. The joyless Booth from Melville's carriage followed at a distance. Well, that was one reason for Rollo's stiff demeanour, and it was far easier to stomach than the one she had feared.

'Mrs Rahgstadt. Madame?'

Marian spun around. 'Oh, I'm sorry.' Then she blurted the first reason she could think of for her distraction. 'I'm new to town and a little nervous.'

The woman smiled. 'Ah, *oui*. I am Corinne St Gervais. How can I assist you, madame?'

This was … complicated. 'I need a plain, respectable day dress I can wear anywhere in the city without standing out or attracting comment, and a ball gown for an event three nights from now.'

The woman looked her over. 'The Winter Ball?'

'You know it?'

'Of course. It will be huge. Even bigger than the ball they held for the foreign officers last month. But three days? Goodness!'

'I'm sorry for the short notice.' Marian straightened and looked her in the eye. She couldn't be timid. This was urgent. 'I will, of course, pay extra for your trouble.'

The woman put her hands on her broad hips, where her black leather corset met crimson wool. 'You're not a difficult size or shape to fit, and I've one or two gowns returned for bad debt. I can fit one of them for you. And as for the day dress … I can work something out. Like what you're wearing?'

Marian passed her hands over the bottle-green fabric and elegant frogging. 'No. Something dull and unremarkable, so even my husband could pass me in the street.'

'I see.' Her expression was one of polite surprise. 'I have a plain navy gown I can adjust and a tan cloak. Wear the hood up and you will be as invisible as you please.'

'Thank you. That will be ideal. And the ball gown?'

The woman clicked her fingers and a second woman stepped forward. 'Lucille will take your measurements. If you leave your direction, we will deliver the plain gown and cloak this evening and the ball gown in two days.'

When Rollo returned, he paid the account without batting an eyelid. Marian made her farewell to the ladies, then she and Rollo went out into the chilly street.

She took his offered arm. 'I have so much to tell you.'

'Such as?'

'The Winter Ball will be enormous, as big as the ball given in November for the Russian officers, and the cream of society will be there. Corinne and Lucille have made a dozen gowns for those attending. Envoys' daughters, political wives …'

'The First Lady?'

'We have made several gowns for her, but not for this event, no.'

'I did not pick you for a social butterfly.' Rollo was tracking their surroundings, not really looking at her, although he kept their shadow well in view.

Marian sped up. 'I am not, but I assume Melville wants us at this ball for a reason.'

'Melville does nothing without good reason.'

***

'Oh, it smells wonderful!' Marian had seemed wary as they approached, but now she was practically salivating as she took a seat at the counter.

Rollo stifled a laugh. 'This is Rafaele. He makes a wonderful traditional Italian pie. We have the best of every continent here in New York. Curries from India, Chinese foods … and these delicacies.' He placed a broad triangular slice before her. 'Try it.'

She lifted it to her mouth and took a bite. 'Oh, it's so good.' She made short work of it, savouring each pepperoni-topped mouthful.

At her pleasure, intense delight rippled through him. 'Your appetite has improved.'

'Yes.' She glanced up at him, her eyes brighter but unsure still.

After a few moments, the proprietor turned from the customer he'd been serving and came over, beaming. '*Buon pomeriggio*, Rollo.'

'Good afternoon to you, too, my friend.' Rollo offered him a grin.

'I have not seen you in many months.'

'I've been away.' He nodded to Marian, and she laid down her serviette. 'I'd like you to meet my wife.'

Rafaele took Marian's hand and bowed over it. 'The pleasure, it is mine, *bella donna*. My friend here is a good man, and a fortunate one.'

'Thank you for the vote of confidence.' Rollo leaned closer. 'Have you seen or heard anything out of the ordinary? Anyone who … stands out?'

Rafaele laughed. 'Rollo, this is Flushing. We have people from all corners of the world here every day of the year, and now with the Russians …'

'Do you see much of them?'

'Not in here. They flirt with our women but turn their noses up at our food.'

'The man I am looking for may sound like a Russian, but he isn't. Still, I think he will try to blend in with them.'

'And he will stick out, no?' Rafaele slapped his chest. 'Like a Siciliano who tries to pass for a Napoletano.'

'Yes and no. He is tall, taller than I. He has a livid scar down the right side of his face and death in his eyes. He has murdered more men than anyone knows for sure.'

Rafaele's expression sobered. 'I will have the boys look out for him. They go everywhere, see everything.'

'Be careful. He won't hesitate to kill.'

'*Mio Dio.* I will tell the boys to stay well clear.' He bent closer. 'I need not tell you that you are being followed?'

Rollo smiled slightly. 'By a lumpy man in a grey wool coat and a bowler?'

'You spotted him.' Rafaele grinned. 'You are awake to their tricks, *si*?'

'Either he is spectacularly bad at his job, or Melville wants us to know we are being tailed.' Rollo couldn't decide which was more likely.

'Melville. He does not change, that one.' Rafaele grimaced, then smiled. 'But let us think on happier things. Come tomorrow. I am making lasagne.'

Rollo shook his hand. 'Thank you, Rafaele.'

'It is a pleasure.' He kissed Marian's hand. 'And to meet you, *bella volpe*.'

'I like him,' Marian told Rollo as they made their way down the street.

'Everyone likes him. His good nature is his stock-in-trade. But he is careful about sharing information and with whom.'

'What did he call me?'

Rollo smiled grimly. 'He called you beautiful fox. He knows who you are, which makes me wonder who else does.'

They headed down the hill, towards the famous slips. Markets and taverns lined the street, and directly before them, a forest of masts rose up.

'Are these the Russian ships?'

He shook his head. 'No, they're further along. We'll head in their direction, but I want to see if there are any vantage points that will allow us to observe the area. We have the spyglass you made and your gizmos, so there is no need to be obvious.'

They skirted a busy waterfront tavern serving dockers, and a polyglot babel enveloped them. He could hear Russian, but the pair of sailors speaking it were discussing the attributes of the barmaid. Marian paused at the haberdashery next door and admired a delicate lace collar while he listened to the voices around him. Nothing.

'This is useless,' Marian said pointedly. 'We don't even know if he's here yet.'

'If we waited until we knew he was here, he might find his victim before we find him.' Rollo put his hand on her sleeve, and they kept moving. 'He has only to make his hit and leave.'

'All right.' Her green eyes flashed. 'We should do what we did in Edinburgh.'

'Smoke him out? Because that was so successful.'

'And this is working better? We need to visit taverns. He won't change his ways just because he's in a new country. Besides,' she waved a hand, gesturing to the scenery, 'the New York docks are endless compared to Edinburgh's. It was sheer good fortune we ran into him there, and we can't expect the same luck again.'

'He did try to kill us.'

She shrugged. 'Do you have a better plan?'

'No.' He paused and led her to the entrance of a seedy establishment. 'I see what you mean. We could do everything right and miss him entirely. We can't be everywhere, so we need more eyes and ears on the ground. You're right.'

She looked up, a spark of eagerness in her expression. 'Should we start now?'

'Not quite. We go back to the apartment and get an image down for Melville's artist, then we sleep. We'll see who's abroad tonight.'

She nodded and took his arm.

'Rollo!'

He stopped short and looked down into an unwelcome, though familiar and beloved, face. 'Marte. You look well.'

'*Lillebror?* God in heaven, it is you!' She flung back her red wool cloak, stretched out her arms and hugged him fiercely. 'I do not believe.' Then she stepped back and gave him a stern look. 'I have not seen you for months!'

'I've been away.' Resigned, he turned to Marian. 'My dear, I should like you to meet my sister, Marte McFadden. Marte, this is my wife, Marian.'

At the introduction, Marte's face took on a beaming maternal smile. 'Ach. I have a new sister? And so beautiful.'

'I'm pleased to meet you, Marte.' Marian smiled a greeting.

Marte's eyes widened. 'That is not an American voice.' She gripped Marian's hands and kissed both her cheeks. 'You must come and meet Niall.'

'Marte …' But Rollo held his tongue. He'd have better luck trying to stop a runaway unicarriage as his sister.

Marte put one hand on her hip. 'So, no wonder you were so long away on your business trip. Come to dinner tonight.'

Unfortunately, they had a monster to track down. Rollo deliberately drew Marian and his sister to a small table outside the tavern, pulled a chair out for each of them and ordered three ales from the passing serving girl. 'Marte, we—'

Marian slipped her hand over Rollo's and squeezed. 'We would be delighted.'

Marte nodded placidly. 'Everyone will want to meet the girl who snared the heart of Rollo the rogue.'

Rollo shook his head. 'Just Niall and the children, Marte, please. We have work to complete before we're at liberty.'

He caught a stinging glance from Marian before she turned to Marte. 'I didn't know Rollo's family lived so near.'

'Ach. I am surprised you know his name, he is so miserly with his information. We grew up near here, after our parents come to America. We were both born in the old country, but he was too young to remember it.' She reached out and patted Rollo's hand.

The girl brought three foaming tankards, and Rollo slipped her a quarter and a dime. 'Another for my friend over there in the bowler hat. With my compliments.'

When Rollo finally nodded to Marian and made their excuses, he sensed she was reluctant to leave.

Marte clasped Marian in a fierce hug, then took his hands and kissed his cheek before he could stop her. 'I shall see you at dinner, Rollo. And you, sister.'

As soon as Marte had bustled away, he turned to Marian. 'We must go. We still have to meet Melville's artist and plan for this evening.'

Marian pulled out her pocket watch. 'It's still early. We have plenty of time.'

Rollo sensed that something had changed in Marian. She had been focused on the mission but now seemed ... less so. It could only be due to meeting Marte, but for the life of him, he couldn't see why. Sure, family was important but ...

Ah. Yes, to him family was important but not always convenient. A distraction. Marian, though, had just glimpsed something she'd thought lost to her. He understood, but she had to realise that even those you loved could not interfere with the task at hand. Not when so much was riding on it.

He pulled her arm through his. 'Come, we have work to do.'

Chapter 27

Marian smiled as she handed her gift to Marte and received a hug in return. She hadn't realised how much she missed the uncomplicated affection of Judith and Will—they were the closest thing she had to a family. Beside her, Rollo accepted a hug from his sister too, but Marian sensed his slight resistance.

'And a wee gift for Niall.' Rollo handed over a square bottle wrapped in brown paper to his brother-in-law, who gave a shout of laughter and poured two drams immediately. Two boys broke from the fireside and ran to greet Rollo.

Marte took Marian by the arm. 'Come with me, sister.' She led Marian into the narrow kitchen, where she began stirring a thick stew and nodded to a cob loaf sitting on a wooden board. 'Would you mind slicing that?'

'I'd love to.'

The women worked side by side for a few moments in the warm kitchen.

'Has Rollo told you much about his family?' Marte asked eventually.

'A little.' But with as much willingness as a man on the rack. 'We had been married scarcely a week when we were obliged to come to New York.'

'And how did you meet?'

'I worked for the man who made Rollo's new hand. Since we met, we've seldom been apart.' That much, at least, was true. Marian smiled at the recollection of Doyle, bidding her to keep to the truth when crafting a lie.

Marte caught the smile. 'Ah, you are true newlyweds. I can see it in your face. Rollo is a good man.'

'The very best.' Marian felt an unwelcome cramp and grimaced.

'Are you well, sister?'

'Oh, yes.' She pasted on a smile. 'I had hoped … but I found out just before we left home tonight that … it was not to be.'

'Ah, dearie.' Marte laid a comforting hand over hers. 'You have time enough and, for all that I love mine, babes are a mixed blessing. Enjoy the few months you have to yourselves. Parenthood is forever.'

'I know. Thank you.' Except, Marian thought, not if it never happened. Had she missed her only chance?

Marte opened a cupboard and pulled down a brown bottle, then measured half a teaspoonful into some water. 'It will ease the pain better than whisky.

'Thank you.'

After adding some seasoning to the stew, which was rich with shreds of boiled beef, potatoes and other root vegetables, Marte ladled it into a large tureen and sent Marian to the dresser for plates. They carried everything to the table and called the men to dinner.

'Congratulations are in order, Niall. How is the new job?'

'I like it well enough. It is easier on my back than porterage, and the extra money is welcome.'

'Not too many problems then?'

'No.' Niall McFadden wiped a chunk of bread across his dish and laughed. 'My section is easy enough, thank the Lord.'

'No problems with the Russians? Sailors with not enough to do can be the devil.'

'Ah, those are fine ships. There are fights from time to time, but when are there not? The Russian officers are stern with their men, though. No, it's not the Russians who are the problem.'

'Is something the matter?'

'Ach, a terrible thing happened down by the coffee slips this morning. A dinghy was found, half-sunk, and the lad in it …' He shook his head. 'Not fit for our ladies to hear.'

'No, indeed.' Marian felt the heat of Rollo's glance.

Marte reached across the table and touched Rollo's sleeve. 'Marian says you have a new hand and that it's more comfortable than the old one.'

'It is.'

Marian looked up at him and winked, then smiled at her hostess. 'I'll never forget the moment he walked in. It was like I couldn't breathe.'

Rollo stared at her for a moment, then nodded. 'They might have fitted me with an anvil for all I noticed. I only knew I had to see her again.'

Marte clasped her hands against her heart and beamed. 'Oh, my. I couldn't be happier for you, my dears.'

When, an hour later, Rollo kissed his sister's cheek, shook his brother-in-law's hand and bade the boys goodnight, Marian was exhausted. The tissue of half-truths and oblique lies clung to her like a spider's web. And her situation had changed, though she had not yet found the opportunity to tell Rollo. He would not need to marry her now; there was no longer a compelling reason. She would not be part of this family or have that sense of belonging that she craved so much. It was likely that she'd never see Marte McFadden again, and for that her heart ached.

Rollo offered her his arm. 'I can summon a unicarriage.'

'No. Let's walk.' She didn't take his arm but fell into step beside him. 'Were you ever going to tell me you had a sister?'

It wasn't Rollo's fault she yearned for family.

'Of course,' he said. 'I'd even planned to take you to see her, once our mission here was over.'

That warmed her heart a little. 'Were you always close?'

'She is almost ten years older than I, and it has been years since she left home to wed Niall.' His eyes were cool, his voice sharp. 'I haven't written to her recently. I've been busy.'

'Too busy to write to your only kin?'

'I write to her every year for her birthday. More often than that would be foolish, perhaps dangerous.'

'Because to love is to give a hostage to fate?' And she guessed that was the last thing Rollo wanted. She was beginning to understand him. He'd kept his distance from her on the ship, at least in the beginning, and from his family here in New York—it was behaviour designed to protect both his heart and the people he cared about.

Rollo nodded. 'Something like that.'

***

On their third evening in the city, Rollo stood in the sitting room of their apartment, listening to the women's soft voices coming from the bedroom. Two hours ago, the dressmaker's assistant had arrived with Marian's gown.

He'd scarcely seen Marian in the last forty-eight hours. After they'd left Marte's, he'd gone straight to Melville and repeated Niall's story about the lad in the half-sunk dinghy down by the docks. The following morning, he'd set out to seek witnesses; the little he learned only confirmed his suspicions. And while he and Marian had walked abroad by day, he'd led his dour tail Booth, or the equally gregarious Carter, to the taverns each night, and Marian had been asleep when he'd crawled into bed.

Now, the bedroom door swung open. Marian stepped forward and her emerald eyes glowed.

'Sweetheart, you are utterly breathtaking.' He took one of her gloved hands in his and lifted it to his lips.

263

In that moment, the look of cool apprehension she'd worn like armour the past few days was stripped away. For just a moment, she was simply a stunning girl, flushed with the delight of wearing a beautiful gown and anticipating a ball.

Lucille twitched Marian's skirt and smoothed the edge of her glove. *'Elle est magnifique.'*

Marian's rebellious locks had been tamed, braided beneath a slim gold tiara, and a single ostrich feather curled demurely over her head. The bodice of her dress was white silk, but her velvet corset was old gold. It flared a little at her hips and was embellished with ostrich plumes where it met the skirt. From there, the dress frothed with layers of silk, satin and velvet in all the colours of a flame. Her beetle gizmo sat high on her shoulder and the small dove was pinned to the other in a tumult of tiny bronze cogs and fine gold chain. Her dragon gizmo clung to her wrist with its teeth clenched around its tail. Ingeniously, her best weapons were within reach if she should need them, and yet were hidden in plain sight.

Rollo's gaze travelled higher until he encountered her strawberry sweet lips, and a wave of desire rocked him.

She lifted her dreamy eyes to his, then turned. 'Thank you, Lucille. You have worked a miracle.'

'The pleasure is mine, madame. The gown looks very well.' Lucille curtseyed, then left, closing the door quietly behind her.

Rollo picked up Marian's thick cloak, but she held up a hand.

'Before we go, there's something I want to give you.' She uncurled her fingers, revealing her small silver snake gizmo. 'I think you should wear this. I have my dove, and this way, we have a means to communicate if we're separated at the ball. I spent some time working on it today while you were out.' She draped it over his right ear, then drew a few strands of his hair over it. 'You look handsome.'

He wore black, though his cravat was white, as was the silk scarf wrapped around his top hat, which had a large silver cog affixed to it. The other silver about his person were his ornate boot buckles and his watch chain.

'Thank you. But you, my dear, are going to set hearts aflame.' He caught her hand, tasting the delicate scent of her perfume in the air, then leaned forward and kissed her lips tenderly.

She nodded at his ear. 'It might feel odd, but you will still be able to hear normally. And if I do this—' She tapped the dove's head with one finger, cupped her hand over it and whispered. Her voice spoke clearly into his ear.

'I can hear you. Marian, that is brilliant!'

'It works well enough here, but we'll be in a ballroom with five hundred other people. Still, it's better than nothing. We shall see.'

'We shall, indeed. Come, our unicarriage will be here by now.'

He offered his arm and she took it, as elegantly as any lady. She had changed so much since the beginning of this adventure, from a fiery, feisty ragamuffin, sneaking out in disguise to play cards. Yet while she now seemed to be soft and delicate, like other women who wore such gowns and danced at balls, she was not that, either. She had a sharp intellect, steely determination and as much raw courage as any man he'd worked alongside. She had slipped into his world of secrets and shadows like a hand into a glove. He was proud of her. But given that she held his heart in her dainty palm, he was also a little terrified.

They stepped out of the elevator and he looked carefully at the driver. Yes, it was the same man he'd hired.

Though he'd hoped to sit beside her, Marian spread the skirts of her gown deliberately over the seat, then looked out the window. It was confirmation to Rollo that something was amiss.

He took the seat opposite. 'What is bothering you, my dear?'

She turned to glance at him. 'Nothing. Only … do you really think he will make an attempt tonight? And who is his target?'

Rollo reached over and lifted her gloved hand in his. He rubbed his thumb over her knuckles. 'Yes, I do think he will strike tonight. And because of that, I don't want any misunderstanding between us.'

She looked down. 'I don't know what you mean.'

'Yes, you do.' He swept her skirts aside and moved across the cabin to sit beside her, hip to hip, thigh to thigh. 'You know how I feel about you. You've known since our time on the *Calliope Jane*. I haven't wanted to act on those feelings with Melville breathing down our necks, but nothing—*nothing*—has changed.'

'You've been feigning indifference to fool Melville?' She sounded sad, but her voice held a thread of hope. 'Would your job be in danger if he suspects our relationship?'

'Not necessarily. But he believes an emotional connection will muddy the waters, that it might even jeopardise the mission.'

'So it's me he doesn't trust?'

He shrugged. 'He serves the United States. To him, nothing else matters.'

Her eyes sharpened and a little of the hurt he sensed there receded. 'And what of England? And France?'

He curled his hand around hers. 'England and France have been secretly supporting the Confederates. At the moment, while they aren't officially our enemy, he certainly suspects their intentions. And you did say you were Her Majesty's loyal servant.'

'Wonderful. If you ask me to dance tonight, he will probably arrest me for stealing state secrets.' Marian glanced briefly out the windows, then she squeezed his hand and met his eyes once more. 'Then we had better find this damned assassin, once and for all.'

Chapter 28

Marian was quixotically grateful that she'd experienced life at Balmoral before being pitchforked into this social purgatory. The ballroom was enormous, ornate chandeliers dripped with illuminated crystals, and silk-panelled walls were adorned with massive paintings in sumptuous gold frames—but it was the people who took her breath away. The women were gorgeous, dressed in gowns of every colour of the rainbow, plus some she'd never imagined. Many wore elaborate tiaras or exquisite parures. And alongside these flowers were a host of men, some dressed in formal black like Rollo, but perhaps half wore one kind of uniform or another.

Marian grew dizzy looking at the different uniforms. Some were of the Union, blue wool trousers and frock coats with breasts full of medals. Others bore scarlet sashes and glittering honours across the wool worsted. Sleeves and shoulders were heavy with gold braid. She and Rollo passed down the receiving line, exchanging innocuous pleasantries, but that didn't mean Marian couldn't detect the sharp intellect behind President Lincoln's eyes when she was introduced to him.

Once they'd taken their leave, Rollo held her arm. 'Come. I see Melville.'

'Wonderful.' She followed Rollo through the laughing, chattering throng until they reached the far side of the room. 'Mr Melville, how pleasant to see you again so soon.'

Melville's glance barely grazed her before he turned to the man at his side. 'Your Highness, I would like to introduce our employee, Rollo Rahgstadt, who has recently returned from the United Kingdom. Rahgstadt, this is His Highness The Grand Duke Konstantin Nikolayevich, Admiral of the Imperial Fleet and brother to our friend and ally, Tsar Alexander.'

'It is an honour, Your Highness. May I introduce my wife?'

Marian lowered her gaze and sank into the curtsey taught to her by Mrs Doyle. The grand duke had the most resplendent uniform she had seen; three diamond-encrusted stars of noble orders were emblazoned on the left-hand side of his chest. His handsome, hawkish face was bronzed from a life at sea.

'The pleasure is all mine.' The grand duke turned to Rollo. 'Mr Rahgstadt, no doubt Melville has much to discuss with you. I should like to dance with your lovely wife.'

When Rollo spoke, his voice was cool. 'My wife is free to dance with whomever she chooses, Your Highness.'

'Excellent.' The grand duke held his arm out and Marian took it, smiling carefully. Dancing was not one of her talents but dance she must. At least it would afford her the chance to reconnoitre the ballroom. The sooner she spotted Dracos, the better for them all.

His Highness led her to the set now forming and took her hand. 'It is a pleasure to make the acquaintance of so many American ladies.' His eyes roved over her. 'So amiable, all of them.'

Marian shook her head and smiled. 'I am even newer to this country than you are, Your Highness, for I have not been here above a week. I am from Scotland.'

'So, you are a Caledonian lass. Your fiery hair tells me so. This is why I have not seen you here, at the parties.' He gave her a broad smile. 'Be sure, I would have noticed.'

When the music started, Marian watched the other ladies in her set and followed their lead with only a second's delay. Once she'd mastered the pattern, she took every opportunity to scan the room. After a while, she felt someone's gaze on her, following her as she moved over the dance floor.

She glanced up. It could be the grand duke, whose admiration of her was unnerving. Or it might be Rollo; she could see him, when the crowd parted, standing some feet away.

The grand duke stepped close, then spun her away to her next partner, and she remembered to smile at him.

But then she saw something that pierced her heart.

Rollo's crisp blue gaze was on her and the grand duke, his expression not of anger but of forlorn regret. She could read the naked longing on his face, could hear his thoughts as though he'd spoken in her ear. *He* wanted to be the one twirling her on the dance floor, the one to receive her smile. The dance turned again, and she lost sight of him—the man who had given her this new life. He'd bravely stepped beyond the shadows and murmurs, in a world filled with lies, spies and deceit, to love her with all his heart. As she loved him.

The set ended and the grand duke escorted her to where Rollo and Melville stood, but the prickly feeling of being watched did not diminish.

'Thank you for the dance, Your Highness.'

The grand duke lifted her hand to his lips and kissed her gloved palm. 'Thank you, madame. Perhaps we can dance again later in the evening. If your husband can spare you.'

Marian decided that breaking an ankle was not too great a price to pay if it kept her from the duke's gallantries. Besides, if Rollo killed him, it would cause exactly the kind of problems they were trying to avoid.

Melville and Rollo were standing with President Lincoln—a tall, cadaverous and dark-haired man—and the First Lady—a short, plump and elegantly gowned woman. Marian recognised them from earlier, and she curtseyed again.

President Lincoln took her hand and bowed over it. 'I have read the reports of your intrepid action at Balmoral. Mrs Rahgstadt, it is an honour to have you here with us.'

'Why, thank you, Mr President.'

Melville looked sour, but Mrs Lincoln reached out. 'Mrs Rahgstadt, perhaps you could tell me about the time you spent at Balmoral.'

Marian glanced warily at Melville, who, with a slight shake of his head, weighed in on the conversation. 'Mrs Lincoln would like to know who you met there and what the ladies were wearing. Is that not so, ma'am?'

'Oh yes. And I'd love to hear a description of the furnishings of the house, for I am trying to furbish up the executive mansion.'

Marian didn't know whether to be angry or exasperated. Melville was forcing her to engage in social chatter when there was a job to do and a monster to stop. Besides, what did she know about folderal?

She plastered on a smile. 'It would be my pleasure, ma'am.'

She and Mrs Lincoln stepped away, giving the men the impression of privacy in their conversation.

'Is this the first time you have been to the States, Mrs Rahgstadt?'

'It is, ma'am.'

'How exciting!' Mrs Lincoln slipped a friendly arm through hers and they moved further away. 'And when you went to Balmoral, were you presented to Her Majesty?'

'I was, indeed. And to the Empress of France.'

Mrs Lincoln gave a gleeful squeal. 'Oh, that is just too exciting. I have seen portraits of both ladies, and I believe the Empress is very beautiful. Do tell me all about it.'

They walked the room slowly, though one of Melville's men, Marian noted, stayed a few paces away. She shared with Mrs Lincoln details of Balmoral and her short stay there, though she was careful not to mention the attack on the Prince Imperial. Mary Lincoln was the mother of sons, including one she still mourned.

Another set of dancers began forming, and Marian glanced wistfully towards it. She had joked with Rollo earlier about dancing together, but it would be a dream come true to dance with him here.

She and Mrs Lincoln stopped to observe the dance, and their conversation turned to the great parlour at Balmoral. The unease Marian had felt earlier returned tenfold, but Melville's man did not come any closer. He was not watching her, she realised; he was there to protect Mrs Lincoln. She let her eyes roam over the dancers in their lines when a uniformed man on the far side of the assembly caught her attention.

She bent close to her companion. 'Mrs Lincoln, there is a man in uniform on the far side of the ballroom, just behind the pillar bearing the holly wreath. Please, what uniform is that?'

To Marian's relief, the lady was discrete.

'Oh, that is the uniform of the British admiralty. The envoy, Lord Thompsett, is here with some of his staff.'

A shiver ran down Marian's spine. What better way to hide in plain sight? And yet, here she was, standing in the open with a tempting target for a political assassin. When his eye turned her way, her skin crawled and she was certain it was him.

'Ma'am, I believe that man is our villain. Behind us is a man wearing a black suit. Please ask him to take you to the President, then let my husband and Mr Melville know I'm following the suspect.'

Across the room, a slight change in Dracos's manner meant he was no longer standing at ease, and Mrs Lincoln moved away with a swoosh of her skirts.

Marian raised her hand to her shoulder, tapped her dove, then covered it and spoke into it. 'Rollo, I've seen Dracos. He's dressed in a British uniform. I'm about to follow him.'

Dracos moved his head from side to side, then turned and walked briskly towards the swinging doors behind him. A waiter carrying a tray of glasses emerged and Dracos slipped through the doors.

Hell!

She spoke again to her dove. 'The kitchens.' She flicked a glance behind her. Mrs Lincoln and Melville's man had disappeared. 'Damn it!'

With a lot of ground to make up, she held her skirts and scuttled towards the kitchen doors, muttering apologies. Breaking into a run, she avoided people as best she could but knocked into several figures and kept running. When she reached the door, she pushed a waiter out of the way and his tray of drinks crashed to the ground. The kitchen was long and busy, but a clear path led to a door, fifty feet away. She ran, glancing down at a young kitchenhand on the ground as she passed, blood pooling under a gash to his arm. It confirmed what she suspected. Dracos had come this way.

She opened the door to the freezing December night and ran out of the bright kitchen into the gloom of the courtyard. A hand snaked out and caught her fast. She was pulled into a deadly embrace and a sharp point was pressed under her chin. A huge, scarred hand slid up her bodice to her dove. As the foul stench of Dracos's breath hovered over her shoulder, he crooned two foreign words into the dove's beak.

'What did you say?' Marian gasped.

He ripped the dove off her gown, jerking her sideways. 'I tell your lover it is time to play.' Then he crushed the dove in his fist.

Rollo had left the President mid-sentence when Marian's voice came through her snake gizmo. He'd turned in the direction she'd gone, but the crowd had swallowed her up. When Melville's man appeared with the President's wife at his side, Marian's sweet voice had spoken in his ear again.

'The kitchens.'

He looked towards the disguised doorway in the far wall and thought he saw Marian's flaming head bob through. He shouldered forward, his iron fist clenched and every muscle in his body shouting at him to run Damn her! Why did she have to do this? Why did she head towards danger? She was killing him.

As he skirted the dance floor, two soft words sent a sick chill right through him.

He dodged past knots of officers and ladies, heard a crash of glass and a few shrieks. Seconds later, he reached the door and barged into the kitchen. Several wait staff were kneeling beside a bleeding boy. Rollo sped past.

He reached the far door, but as he put a shoulder to it, had his hand on the door handle, a choked scream came from outside. Marian's voice followed, breathless, furious.

'Let go of me, you bastard!'

Her words were answered by a hollow laugh.

Icy dread gripped Rollo, but he ignored the clamour in his gut urging him into the darkness to rescue his love. That's what Rebeniuc wanted, what he was counting on. Instead, Rollo ripped the glove from his left hand and pulled the stiletto from its scabbard in the underside of the vambrace as the crossbow loaded.

In the last second before he opened the door, he shot a bolt into the base of the dynamic light hanging from the kitchen ceiling. The room plunged into blackness. At least he would not be silhouetted in an open doorway.

He emerged into the courtyard, and fifteen yards away, the fiend held Marian as a shield, one arm pressed diagonally across her chest, the other held the tip of a knife at her jugular. She twisted in his arms, stretching her head away from the point of the blade.

'Let her go, Dracos, and I might let you live.' He did not dare look at Marian, could not risk being witness to her terror. It might make him do something foolish.

The monster laughed. 'No, Iron Fist, it is you who will die. First I play with your pretty *păpușă*.' He kissed Marian's cheek, though his gaze was locked on Rollo. 'When I tire of her screams, I finish you both, and then I leave knife in my enemy's heart.'

Rollo glared at the monster. Though the freak's British uniform was pristine, his façade different from the black-caped nightmare of weeks ago, his eyes remained cold and evil.

'Rot in hell.' Rollo raised his left hand, flexed, and was about to let fly when he saw Marian's gesture—she raised her hand, her palm open. He stopped, nodded.

Rebeniuc laughed. 'You see, Iron Fist? You are too afraid of hurting her, so I will.'

Marian twisted again, and this time, Rollo saw she'd taken her dragon gizmo from her wrist. In a move that was as fluid as a Bolshoi ballerina, she slumped, wrenching away from the hand and knife at her throat, and pressed the tiny dragon against Dracos's jaw. A tongue of flame ran up his oiled beard and into his hair.

It took only a second for him to react, but in that time, Rollo had fired. The bolt caught Dracos high in the chest. He gave a hoarse cry, slashed at Marian and thrust her from him in one motion before slapping at the fire licking at his face.

Rollo leapt forward and pressed his stiletto at the monster's sternum. But before he could ram it home, Dracos chopped his hand downwards and knocked the knife to the ground.

Without conscious thought, Rollo clenched his iron fist and slammed it into the bastard's chin. Dracos fell to the ground.

Rollo resisted the urge to run to Marian. He had to end this. They could not give Dracos another chance. 'Marian?'

'Aye. I'm well enough.'

The kitchen door burst open and two of Melville's men surged into the courtyard. Rollo didn't care. Marian was safe and he had the butchering demon in his hands at last.

He locked his left hand around Dracos's neck. 'I should play with you, Dracos the Destroyer, but you aren't worth it.'

He tightened his grip and Dracos's eyes bulged. His mouth opened in what might have been a scream, only his neck snapped. The light went out of his eyes and his body slumped. Rollo dropped it like a rotten fish and dove to where Marian lay curled.

He cradled her in his arms. 'Sweetheart, you were incredible! Are you all right?'

She nodded and gave a crooked smile. 'Just bruises.' Her voice was rough. 'And I think the tip of his blade caught me.' She lifted the hand pressing against the back of her head—it was red with gore.

Booth knelt beside the body, ripped the coat open and felt for a pulse. He shook his head. The other hulking brute turned. 'You killed him, sir.'

'Bring Melville. And a doctor.' Rollo waved the second man away, then turned to Marian and kissed her brow. 'It's over. We're safe now.'

Chapter 29

'I cannot trust your judgement, Rahgstadt.' Melville paced the wooden floorboards before the fireplace, brushing carelessly against Marian.

She'd felt sick after the attack, but a doctor at the ball had treated her head wound with basilicum powder and a bandage. He'd also prescribed laudanum for the shock, but she needed her wits about her still. Now, she was no longer sick, only seething.

Rollo stood in the doorway that led to the room where Dracos's body lay under a sheet. Sounds of revelry could still be heard from the President's ball, but here, in a small, bare office, it seemed a world away.

'I stopped a ruthless assassin,' he said. 'I did precisely what you ordered me to do when you sent me to Scotland.'

'You killed the one lead we had! Or are you fool enough to think that Dracos was acting on his own?'

Rollo pushed his hand deep into his pocket and his face hardened. 'Of course not.'

'So why kill him?' Melville turned towards Marian and flung an angry hand in her direction. 'Was it because he threatened your lovebird? You've fallen under the spell of an enemy snare!'

At that Marian threw off the blanket and stepped straight into Melville's path. He was a good head taller than she, and broad too, but she would cheerfully rip out his heart and feed it to him. She and Rollo had survived the beast who'd stalked and threatened them, more than once. The rage in her heart, the fear still curdling her blood after being in the monster's hands again, roiled up.

'Enemy? How dare you, sir! I have given up my job, left my home and my country to chase this monster. You are incapable of respecting me because I am a woman and therefore useless, but now I am some kind of Jezebel, a siren who lures good men to their doom?'

Melville cast a fulminating glance at her. 'If it weren't for you, Rahgstadt would have been thinking with his head instead of—'

Rollo slammed Melville into the sitting room wall, his left fist clutched at his collar. 'You will not speak to my wife like that.'

Marian felt a brief, savage joy as Melville wriggled like a fish on a spear, both his hands trying to break Rollo's hold. Melville's lackey, Booth, who'd been standing by the door, seized Rollo's right arm and twisted it up behind his back. Rollo kicked back but didn't release his grip. He kept the arrogant head of the Pinkertons clamped to the wall like a bug on a pin.

Melville forced his words out. 'As I thought. Compromised.'

Marian touched Rollo's sleeve. 'Put him down. He's playing stupid spy games.'

Rollo let go and Melville straightened, one hand going to his throat. Booth released Rollo's arm and stepped back.

'Thank you, Miss Finlay.' Melville lingered over her name to make his point.

'My pleasure.' Marian linked her arm with Rollo's and pulled it firmly to her side. She wanted to be done with this and get out of here. 'To be brief, Mr Melville, thanks to Rollo, there was not an assassination of a dignitary on American soil tonight.'

'We still don't know who was behind it.'

'That's not my problem.' She smiled sweetly. 'I work for Her Majesty. I'll be glad to tell her that, thanks to Mr Rahgstadt, Britain will not be fighting a war. Because if a man dressed in a British admiralty uniform had killed Mrs Lincoln, your President or the grand duke in front of five hundred witnesses, that's what we would have had.'

Melville ground his teeth and glanced at Rollo. 'I'm not finished with you, Rahgstadt. And as for you,' he said, turning to Marian, 'I shall be speaking with the envoy within the hour. You will answer to him.'

'I will be glad to do so'—she crossed her arms—'because I sure as hell don't answer to you.' She strode to the door and opened it, glared at Booth as he went out, held the door for Melville as he stomped through, then slammed it behind him.

Rollo wrapped his arms around her. 'We should go home.' His voice soothed away some of her hurt, and her rage began to subside.

'I'm just so tired. But I'm glad it's over.'

'I was so proud of you tonight.' He kissed her tenderly, then put his hand under her chin and tilted her face to his. 'Don't misunderstand me. I hate that you chased after him. You should have waited for me.'

She leaned back in the steel of his arms. 'I had to chase him, or we would have lost him for good. Who can say what might have happened then? He recognised me, Rollo. And he called you, Iron Fist.' A tremor roiled through her. 'Do you think someone we trust might have fed him information?'

'I think our organisation is compromised, yes.' Picking up his greatcoat, he pulled a slip of paper from his pocket and showed it to her. 'While you were with the doctor, we searched Dracos's body, and I found this in his pocket.'

'Melville's messenger code? Does this mean you're still in danger?' She clenched his coat in her fists. 'I can't bear it.'

'I understand.' He cupped her cheek. 'You have no idea what it did to me, seeing his knife at your throat. If he'd harmed you, I'm not sure I could have borne the pain. This world is too dangerous for you.'

She looked up at him, lifted a hand and stroked his jaw, then drew him to her. 'I hadn't realised ...' Being in Dracos's grasp had terrified her, but it was nothing compared to the heart-stopping horror of seeing the crewman on the dirigible attack Rollo. 'When I consider the possibility of losing you, of not hearing your laugh again or feeling your touch ... it overwhelms me. I never thought you would feel the same.'

He shook his head, and when he spoke, his voice was softer than down. 'My sweet little vixen, it works both ways. I want to keep you safe.'

'I think I understand.' She looked up at him and briefly considered falling into his arms, playing the damsel to his knight, but she couldn't be that woman. And that wasn't the woman he wanted. She knew that, deep in her core.

'Thank you for holding your fire,' she said, 'when Dracos had me. You understood what I wanted and let me act. You trusted me.'

He remembered her signal, just before she'd turned her dragon gizmo on Dracos and freed herself. He rested his chin on top of her head and pulled her close. 'You were so damned foolhardy to put yourself in that position. And so brave afterwards.'

She shrugged and pressed into the crook of his shoulder. 'Thank you. But we had to stop him.'

'That's true.' He picked up her cloak, helped her on with it and gently fastened it at her throat. He smoothed the velvet down over her shoulders, and she felt the faint trembling of his palms.

'You might have been incredible standing up to Dracos,' he said, 'but you were positively heroic just now, going toe to toe with Melville.'

'What?' She laughed and looked up at him dumbfounded. 'How do the two even compare?'

With a twinkle in his eye, he kissed her witless.

Chapter 30

Marian opened her eyes as morning light crept into the bedroom. Something must have disturbed her. She had been exhausted when she finally fell into bed, and it wasn't only the stress caused by the night's events, either. Instead, it was as if all the tension that had been coursing through her veins since her first terrifying encounter with Dracos on the Edinburgh dock had evaporated. That part of her life was over now, heaven be praised!

The bedroom was warm enough, with the steam tek under the floor hissing nicely, but she rose and went to the sitting room, expecting to see Rollo. He wasn't there, but two travelling trunks were propped by the door. She grinned when she read the note perched on top of them.

Back for breakfast.

After making a cup of tea, she put away the clothes she hadn't seen since Balmoral. How long ago that had been! But when she sat down to enjoy her drink, her heart was still in a tumult. Rollo loved her—she knew that as surely as she knew she loved him—but he was still labouring under a misconception. She had to tell him she didn't need to marry him. Or rather, that he did not need to marry her. She trusted him with her life, and even more than that. She needed him, almost like the air she breathed. But he chose to live as much as possible outside the bonds of love and family. He loved his sister but kept his distance. He would love a wife and would have loved his child, but she didn't know if she could live with that kind of emotional distance. She would hate to hate him.

And yet, she could not deny him the choice. His work was vital; no one knew that better than she did. And if he needed to be free of emotional ties, well, she'd understand. He did not need any hostages to fortune, any shackles around his heart or mind.

By the time she heard him slip through the door, she'd dressed in one of her favourite gowns, given her by Mrs Doyle, and was sitting in front of the mirror, brushing her hair and thinking furiously.

She turned when he entered the room. 'Rollo, you have been such a—Oh, what pretty flowers!'

'They seemed like a good idea under the circumstances.' He kissed her cheek and pressed the posy of peonies into her hand. 'I see you have found the luggage. I've always liked that green on you.'

She shook her head at his grin. 'What's going on?'

'I would explain'—there was a knock at the door—'but I am fairly confident you will work it out.' He left the room quickly and answered the door; Marian followed. The concierge of their building stood there, as did a tall, slender gentleman in a cassock accompanied by a middle-aged lady. The clergyman took off his wide-brimmed hat and beamed at her.

'This must be the lovely Marian you spoke of, Mr Rahgstadt. Pleased to make your acquaintance, Miss Finlay.'

'Marian,' Rollo put his arm around her and pulled her forward, 'this is the Reverend Westwood and Mrs Westwood. The reverend has agreed to marry us without further ado. Mr Sommers and Mrs Westwood will be our witnesses.'

Oh God! Marian slipped her hand into Rollo's. 'Pleased to meet you, Reverend, Mrs Westwood.' She curtseyed and smiled towards Mr Sommers. 'Rollo, may I please have a few minutes conversation with you?'

'Of course, my dear.' The slight upward inflection in his voice told her she'd surprised him. 'If you good people will excuse us for one moment.'

Marian pulled him into the bedroom, then turned to face him, twisting her hands together in front of her. 'I didn't expect this.'

Rollo pulled her towards him. 'Are you saying you don't want this? Or that it's too soon? You wanted a lace veil and a dozen bridesmaids, perhaps?'

She shook her head, the lump in her throat was like a billiard ball. 'I love this. And you. But I cannot marry you until I tell you …'

'Tell me what?' His voice was soft and warm, and she wanted to nestle into it, as if it were an embrace.

She looked down at her hands. 'You are under no obligation to marry me. That is, with all the travel and excitement, my body got a little out of sorts.'

Rollo cupped her face. 'Are you saying there's no baby?'

'Yes.'

'How long have you known?' he asked slowly.

She drew a deep breath, and her lungs shuddered. 'Since just before we went to your sister's house.'

A flash of relief passed over his face and made her heart hurt.

'You are glad?'

'I'm glad your altercation with that bastard last night didn't cause you to lose it I would have had to kill him all over again.'

And just like that, she fell in love with him a little bit more. 'So then, you see—'

'Sweetheart,' his voice was low and slow and as deep as the ocean, 'do you believe I only wanted to marry you because of an obligation?'

She looked into his eyes, saw they were clear and bright and tender. When she remembered how he had held her, she knew she'd misjudged his intentions.

'No, Rollo. I believe you want to marry me because you love me the same way I love you.' She put her hands in his and kissed his lips. 'Shall we go back out?'

He slid his hands to her hips, anchoring her fast. 'Not yet. Marian, I think I know why you were unsure of my motives.' He smiled ruefully. 'I never really asked you, just took your agreement for granted, but every lady deserves to hear a gentleman's offer. This may not be what you imagined for your wedding or for marriage, and we still have hurdles to overcome. Our life is precarious, but I want to spend it with you.' He went down on one knee, looked up and fixed his eyes on hers. 'Marian Finlay, will you do me the very great honour of becoming my wife?'

Her heart melted, and she wiped a knuckle across her eyes. 'Rollo Rahgstadt, I would love to be your wife, to be with you no matter what. We will brave danger together.'

He pushed to his feet. 'Then come along, my darling. We don't want to keep the good reverend waiting.'

They passed through the bedroom door and into the sitting room.

The minister cleared his throat. 'Let's begin, shall we?'

***

'I can think of better things to do on our wedding day than go dress shopping.' Rollo glanced at the dressmaker's shop where he'd brought Marian only days ago. With Dracos out of the picture, some of the urgency had gone out of their mission. But after a good night's sleep and time for reflection, Marian had come up with a plan. And it was a good one. He'd been too concerned about the prospect of a traitor in his organisation to think of another strategy.

'I told you,' Marian said, 'the President's wife loves to shop. She has accounts all over town, and these ladies serve the cream of society.'

'It sounds like a ruse to me.' He bent and nuzzled her neck, then winked at her as they entered the shop. It was a pleasure to use the guise of doting husband. He would never tire of it.

Corinne, the proprietress, hurried out of the back room. 'Mrs Rahgstadt, I hope everything was satisfactory last night, with the gown.'

'It was perfect. Thank you.' Marian clasped her hands in front of her. 'I had the pleasure of speaking with Mrs Lincoln last night, and she mentioned she'd purchased a new gown from you recently. The neckline …' She touched her fingertips to her décolletage.

'The deep vee, madame?' Corinne nodded approvingly. 'That is a very pretty gown, and it looks well with the sloping shoulders.'

Marian beamed. 'Oh, wonderful! Do you have one I could see?'

Corinne shook her head, dismay written all over her face. 'I am afraid not, madame. But if you will let me know where you can be reached, I will contact you in a day or so.'

'Why, thank you, Corinne.' Marian slipped her calling card from her purse. 'Do you have the designation for my mirror messenger?'

Corinne reached under the counter and removed a leather-bound book. 'I shall write it down.'

Marian closed her eyes and swayed a little, then put her hand out to Rollo. 'Oh dear, I don't know what's the matter with me.'

Rollo leapt forward and she tumbled into his arms. 'Marian! My goodness, are you well?' He carried her to a fainting couch a few feet away and laid her down. Patting her hand, he turned to Corinne. 'Madame, could I ask for a glass of water?'

'Of course.' She whisked out of the room.

Instantly, Rollo rushed to the service counter, flipped open the book to the page marked *L*, scanned it and, once he had the information he needed, closed the book once more. He was back at Marian's side in a flash, a full five seconds before Corinne reappeared.

Marian took the glass of water and sipped it gratefully. 'I am so sorry.' She gave Rollo a half smile and raised an eyebrow.

'Nonsense. These things happen, but I think I should take you home now.' Rollo smiled at her, then at the proprietress. 'Madame, please contact my wife when it is convenient for her to see the gown.'

Back on the street, Marian leaned heavily on Rollo's arm. 'Did you get it?'

'I did. And you are a rogue. You will have to buy another dress now.'

'Yes, and you will have to pay for it. All your worldly goods, I think you said?'

'Not all at once, wife. Come.' He took her to a small bench and they both sat down. 'What will you say?'

Marian wound silver charge paper onto her messenger and picked up her black wax stylus. 'Dear Mrs L,' she wrote neatly, 'I enjoyed conversing about Balmoral. Several things you would wish to know. When might we speak? M.R.'

She handed it to Rollo, and he levered in the destination details before closing the lid. Once the message had sent, Rollo tapped out the ash and, as usual, ground it underfoot.

'Now we wait.'

An hour before sunset, a knock sounded on their door. When Rollo answered it, Mr Sommers, the concierge, placed a smooth vellum envelope into his hand and left.

'What is it, my dear?'

Rollo broke the seal and read the missive aloud. 'Mr and Mrs Rollo Rahgstadt are invited to join the President and Mrs Lincoln in their box at the Astor Place Theatre tonight.' He refolded the letter and tucked it into his jacket. 'Well done, my darling.'

He was certain he could trust only one man with the fate of his nation. And clever Marian had managed to engineer a meeting. Events were closing in. Plotting and treachery were afoot. Now, he just needed to root it out—without bringing down everything he loved at the same time.

Chapter 31

Marian entered the Astor Place Theatre on her husband's arm. Her Scottish-made gown was subtly different to the fashion of New York's elite and caused some women to whisper behind their fans. Others hungrily eyed her escort.

An usher led them to the corner box where the President and his wife waited with their son, Mr Robert Todd Lincoln, a young man of much Marian's own age.

'I'm so glad you could join us tonight.' Mary Lincoln came forward, her hand extended to Marian. 'I regret not being able to finish our conversation last evening, but I am so glad you are unharmed.'

'Thank you, Mrs Lincoln. It was fortunate we could deal with the villain in a circumspect way.'

The President shook Rollo's hand. 'Melville tells me there's no longer a threat. I'm glad to hear it.'

Rollo fixed his eyes on Lincoln's. 'I wish that were so, sir, but Dracos was an assassin. He answered to someone else, and we don't know who gave him his orders.'

When the President paused, it was clear to Marian the cogs in his brain were turning.

'I see,' he said. 'Yes, that puts a different perspective on the matter. How, then, do we put a name to this master conspirator?'

Rollo shook his head. 'We are unsure as to both motive and target. It could be you, sir, or a member of your family.'

Mrs Lincoln gripped Marian's arm. 'My boys? You don't think …?'

'No, ma'am.' Marian spoke soothingly. 'We can see no reason he would target them.'

'Mr Robert Lincoln'—Rollo nodded to the young man—'was at the ball last night, but he is a civilian. Your younger son was not present. It is improbable that either is a target. This is not a personal vendetta, sir.'

'Of course.' The President nodded sagely. 'So it must be someone who was present last night. But that could be any of a score. As well as us, the grand duke, various ambassadors, diplomatic persons and three generals were in attendance. My secretary can give you a list.'

'I think you can discount your own generals, Mr President.' Marian spoke softly. 'This is an international plot and the ramifications must be felt beyond your shores. But we suspect the target isn't the British envoy or any member of his staff. Dracos's use of a British uniform suggests he planned to throw suspicion onto the Brits.'

'Yes.' President Lincoln looked grave. 'That makes sense. What was his purpose, Rahgstadt?'

'We can only judge by the probable results of his action, sir. We must assume he wants to start a war. Or to irreparably damage relationships between nations.'

'We are already in a very costly war.' The President's eyes were hooded, brooding. 'To what end?'

Rollo glanced out over the crowd filling the theatre, but after a moment, turned back to the President. 'You are in a civil war, sir. The people behind this seek to change the balance of national power to suit their own ends.'

Lincoln nodded, but before he could speak again, the usher entered. 'Mr President, the Admiral, Grand Duke Konstantin of the Imperial Family.'

The grand duke entered and immediately kissed Mrs Lincoln's hand. 'Madame, thank you for your gracious invitation.' He turned to Marian and paused before he bent to kiss her hand. She felt the pressure of his lips and his scorching breath against her skin. '*Enchantée*, madame. I had hoped to dance with you again last evening.'

Marian gave a small curtsey and kept her thoughts to herself. He must know what had happened last night. No one could keep such a secret from a well-connected diplomat as His Highness.

Rollo slipped his arm through hers. 'You were fortunate, Your Highness, to have had the opportunity to dance with my wife last evening. Now that our time is more our own, it's a pleasure I intend to keep for myself.'

'Ah, that is wise.' The duke pulled on his moustache and considered Rollo with a half-smile. 'Such a beautiful lady deserves the attentions of a man truly worthy of her, don't you think?'

'Of course.'

Rollo escorted her to their seats beside Robert Lincoln, while the duke ushered Mrs Lincoln to the middle seat in the front row and sat beside her. He turned and winked at Marian, but she chose not to notice.

Robert Lincoln turned to her, all earnest bonhomie. 'The entertainment tonight is the Scottish play, Mrs Rahgstadt. I hope it will not make you homesick.'

Marian assured him it would not, but the play was interminable. Gradually, though, she was caught up in the story and the grandeur of the language. Then the plotting started—a play about an assassination, of all things. As Macbeth's wife urged him on, purging herself of womanly compassion, Marian's skin grew clammy. When Macbeth and his wife came out of the king's chamber, their hands red with gore, Marian could not bear to look. This time last evening, she'd had blood on her hands too. She felt sick.

As the curtain fell, there was a knock on the door and a liveried usher entered the box with a note. Mrs Lincoln read it and glanced at Marian.

'Why, Mrs Rahgstadt, you have been invited to call on the box of the British envoy.'

Rollo's mouth turned down. He needed to speak with President Lincoln urgently, Marian knew, and this might be his sole opportunity.

'I will be delighted to escort, Mrs Rahgstadt.' Robert offered his arm punctiliously.

'Thank you, sir.' Marian picked up her purse and slipped her arm into his.

'Yes, go, my dear. See your countryman. I'm sure you have much to discuss.' Rollo nodded at her as Melville shouldered his way into the box.

'As do I,' Melville stated grimly. 'Good evening, Mr President, Your Highness.' He turned and spoke in an undertone to Rollo, but as Marian put a foot over the threshold, she caught every word. 'What do you mean, Rahgstadt, going behind my back to speak with the President?'

Marian turned and glared at Melville. 'His country and his life may be on the line, and your President is entitled to the whole story.'

The old buzzard turned puce as she stepped into the corridor. Young Lincoln stared at her askance. 'Mrs Rahgstadt, forgive me, but was that wise? Mr Melville does not take kindly to plain speaking from those he employs.'

Marian laughed and was still smiling when she curtseyed to the British envoy. Robert left her with him and moved across the box to speak with his pretty daughter. Melville's lackey, Booth, had slipped in behind them and stood against the wall of the box. Marian ignored him. She was inured to his unwelcome presence and Melville's distrust.

She accepted the envoy's outstretched hand. 'Good evening, Your Excellency.'

***

'That insolent—'

'I'll thank you not to insult my wife in my presence, sir.' Rollo stayed calm but his tone clearly gave Melville pause.

'Your wife? Have—'

'My wife, sir, before God and the State of New York.' Rollo nodded at Melville's shocked expression, then returned to the issue at hand. 'Now, you were about to rebuke me for sharing details of the mission with the President, details of which he'd been unaware.'

'I hope not, Melville.' Lincoln paused, hands behind his back. 'This is not a simple assassination attempt. It's a convoluted puzzle and we have but few pieces. Let us not despise what little illumination we possess. Have you yet been able to determine if there are other agents hidden in plain sight?'

Melville scowled and ran a frustrated hand over his thick hair.

'It is a certainty.' Grand Duke Konstantin shook his head. 'You permit that I say this, Mr. Lincoln?'

'Of course, Your Highness.'

'The man who was a traitor in Scotland, the secretary of Palmerstone, he was waiting until called. He was not a new man. He had been employed more than five years, yes?'

'He had indeed, Your Highness.'

The grand duke nodded. 'Then every royal house in the continent must be on its guard. Every nobleman, every politician. It must be assumed there are similar agents in Russia, in Prussia, Austria, France, Spain.'

Lincoln nodded soberly. Around them was a sea of gaiety, but the mood in the box was tense. 'And here, too?'

'Here? Perhaps not.' Grand Duke Konstantin shrugged and pursed his lips in a small moue of displeasure. 'You have greater political change than we. Every four years, yes? To put an agent in place is more difficult. And to what end?'

Melville spoke next. 'Rahgstadt, what did you need to discuss with the President?'

Rollo looked from the President to his employer. In a split second, he weighed up his options, but there really was no choice.

He reached for the note in his inner pocket. 'I removed this from Dracos's jacket when I searched his body. I'll have to admit, it gave me pause. For a while, I didn't know who to trust.' He put the slip of paper into Melville's hand and watched for a reaction as he unfolded it.

Melville turned the colour of ash and went limp for several seconds before roaring back to life. 'Good God, man! My mirror messenger designation?'

'Yes, sir.'

Melville tugged at his cravat, mouth agape. 'Great Caesar's ghost! I would have suspected me too! Only a handful of subordinates and agents have this. Even the President does not know it.'

'Because it's a key point of contact between you and a few trusted eyes?' asked Rollo. Something was bothering him. The glimmer of a thought began to take shape.

'Precisely.' Melville nodded. 'And because tradecraft is ironclad on this. Burn any facsimile of a message to ashes. Never write down a designation. And tell me if your messenger is compromised.'

'Exactly, sir. And that, ultimately, is the reason I'm trusting you now.'

Lincoln shook his head. 'I don't follow.'

The grand duke nodded. 'A true officer in a foreign country memorises such information and disposes of it. He doesn't keep it on his person.'

Rollo smiled grimly. 'Just so. But, if not you, sir, then who?'

The President nodded soberly. 'If there is a traitor in our midst, whoever it is, it will be the person you least suspect.'

Chapter 32

The envoy was a round-faced man with a pink complexion, currently all smiles. He wore no uniform. Instead, he had on a sable velvet evening jacket with a broad spray of cogs applied to the shoulders and lapels, and chains taking the place of frogging. A matching evening cloak was slung over a chair and a bronze-handled walking stick leaned against it.

'Mrs Rahgstadt, I congratulate you. I hear the person who attacked Her Majesty's guest will trouble us no more.'

'You are exceedingly well informed, sir.'

Gesturing to a chair, he shook his head. 'Not so well as I hope to be. But this is an evening of pleasure. May I ask, did you leave Her Majesty well?'

'Very well, sir.' Marian sat and kept her answers brief. It was not for her to tell this man secrets.

He nodded. 'It is a terrible thing to be forced to mistrust those who have, to all appearances, served loyally. The Prime Minister is devastated, of course. His man appeared to have a bright future.'

Marian nodded. What was there to say?

'I regret that England will not have the chance to retain your services. But as the wife of an American citizen …' He looked at her apologetically.

'I am still a loyal Briton, sir.' Marian kept her voice soft, but she made no effort to disguise her fierce tone.

'Your husband is an agent of the Union government, and although we highly desired to retain your services, we cannot ask a wife to work against her husband's nation. Her new nation.'

'But why should I, sir?'

The envoy wrinkled his brow. 'I beg your pardon?'

'Why should I work against America? Or, for that matter, why should Rollo work against Britain?'

'These are uncertain times …'

Marian leaned forward. 'Sir, Britain and America have interests in common, do they not?'

'Well, of course.'

'Then let us help!' All the passion within her, the sheer determination to go out and take hold of life burned within her, and she surged to her feet. 'Do not waste what we have to offer you, sir. I want to serve my queen.'

The envoy stood and inclined his head. 'It is not entirely my decision, but I will recommend we accept your …'

He'd looked over at the President's box, halfway around the curve of the theatre, when his speech petered out, and so Marian followed his gaze. Rollo and Melville were staring at them, open-mouthed.

A pistol shot exploded beside her—and the envoy toppled forward.

***

The theatre erupted in screams as Rollo scanned the chaos. Still in the envoy's box, Booth held a smoking pistol. The envoy's daughter fainted smoothly into Robert Lincoln's arms, leaving only Marian, standing with her back to the crowd, staring at Booth, who now had his pistol pointed straight at her.

No, Rollo thought, he didn't. He was pointing past her, across the theatre, towards the President. He hadn't fired yet, though God knew he had a clear shot. Booth twitched the envoy's cloak off his chair and, with one hand, threw it around his shoulders. Then he stepped to the edge of the box, in full view of the goggling crowd.

Understanding struck Rollo at last. The envoy was known for his foppish dress sense. If a man in the British envoy's cloak assassinated the President, there would be riots in the streets within the hour.

Rollo could take only one course of action. He brought his arm up and flexed his wrist. The crossbow locked into place; the bolt loaded. But then he stopped. Marian stood directly in his path.

A scuffle beside him told him Melville had thrust the President down behind the barrier and the furnishings, yet Booth hadn't moved, his aim still fixed on ...

Grand Duke Konstantin stood tall and straight to Rollo's right. And Marian, damn her courageous heart, was between the assassin and his target. Another second and Booth would surely shoot her. Rollo could not move, or he'd risk putting a bolt into his wife's back.

As though in slow motion, the gun shifted in Booth's grip. Marian remained still. Rollo pressed his fingers into his palm and prayed for forgiveness.

Booth turned suddenly and yelled towards the floor. He shifted his gun, tracking it down in the same direction. Marian plummeted out of Rollo's sight—and it was the moment Rollo needed. In a single movement, he triggered the first bolt, then a second and a third. The first hit Booth in his right shoulder. His arm jerked and the pistol fired. The second entered his side, between the ribs and below his arm. The third pierced his neck.

Rollo leapt over Melville and the President, burst out of the box and ran down the corridor, past shrieking women. Throwing back the door to the envoy's box, he pushed aside the spindly chairs. The President's son was comforting the envoy's daughter, who was covering her eyes and wailing. The envoy had a small wound in his shoulder. On the floor at his side, lay an unsheathed sword stick, its tip red with blood. Marian was on the floor, her left arm holding her right, which was dripping blood. Rollo fell to his knees beside her and checked her over.

'Thank God!'

Booth's bullet had passed through, about two inches above her elbow. Rollo pulled off his silk cravat and wound it tightly around her arm.

Marian winced. 'Damn, that hurts.'

'That's what you get for scaring me half to death.' He knotted the cloth and cradled her face with both hands. 'I was terrified, Marian. For heaven's sake, never do that to me again!'

'I'll think about it.' She turned her head. 'Please, look over Lord Thompsett.'

Rollo put two fingers to the envoy's neck. 'He has a pulse. Is this his only wound?'

'It is.' Marian's voice was a little thready. 'He stabbed Booth in the leg, distracted him.'

Rollo lifted the jacket away from the envoy's shoulder. There was blood on his shirt, but not much, and no exit wound. 'I think the bullet was deflected. See here?' He indicated the decorative cogs. 'These took the initial impact, which lessened the force. The bullet is still in him, but it will have done less damage.'

He pulled Lord Thompsett's cravat free and used it to pad the wound. The envoy groaned. Pale but alert, he tracked Rollo's movements and gave Marian a weak smile, which she returned.

Melville appeared in the doorway, panting. 'The President's doctor is on his way.'

Marian looked up soberly at Melville. 'I'm sorry, sir, that it came to this.'

Staring at Booth's body, Melville clenched his fists. 'Not as sorry as I, Mrs Rahgstadt. And to think I set him to follow you. I should have set you to follow him. Then we might not be in this mess.'

Rollo lifted Marian in his arms and cradled her close, tucking her injured arm against his body. He kissed her lips. 'I didn't want to harm you.'

'I knew you wouldn't.' She lifted her face to his. 'But if I'd moved, he would've shot the President.'

Rollo shook his head. 'He was after the duke.'

She considered that, then nodded. 'He wanted to make it look like an Englishman had shot the Tsar's brother?'

'If they wanted to precipitate a second war in the Crimea, that would do it. The Russians are half-expecting an attack, which is why their navy is here. It would also be why Dracos wore a British uniform last night.'

She rested her head against his chest. 'How long ago that seems.'

Melville crouched beside them. 'Take her to the Astor Hotel, Rahgstadt. Help will be there shortly.'

As Melville offered the envoy his aid, Rollo carried Marian out of the box and through the gawping crowd. No one moved to stop them, or if they did, he didn't notice. Nothing mattered but the woman in his arms. She snuggled against him as they passed into the frigid night. He whistled, and a unicarriage bowled up.

She lifted her uninjured arm and smoothed the back of her fingers over his cheek. Her eyes caught his and held them. 'I'm glad they didn't succeed.'

He pressed his lips to her forehead. 'You are safe. That's the only thing that matters to me.'

He lifted her into the unicarriage, pulled down the blind and blocked out the world.

Epilogue

Marian stepped onto the Edinburgh dock. She hadn't been here since Dracos had tried to destroy her, when she'd found the love of her life. The scene couldn't have been more different. Though the chill wind still whipped off the water, the sun shone and the sky was blue. It was the first day of spring and a new season for her as well. Everything seemed so natural, so normal. Porters arranged baggage and children ran about in orderly happy commotion.

The salty boards heaved under her feet, and she was glad to put her hand on Rollo's arm. She leaned into him and breathed deep.

His gloved hand came up to cover hers. 'Are you glad to be back?'

She smiled up at him. 'I am. To see it like this is like laying a ghost to rest. Do you remember the last time we were here?'

He nodded. 'I do indeed.'

She snuggled closer, taking in the gentle creak of the wooden dock, the slap of seawater, the voices. 'So much has happened since that night. I'm glad we're able to stop here for a few days before we cross to Holland.'

'I wish we could stay longer. Or you could stay here with Somerton.' He frowned. 'I still don't like the idea of taking you with me. A country at war is no place for you.'

'Oh no.' Marian shook her head. 'I won't stay here tamely, while you look for the person who sent Dracos and subverted Grey and Booth.'

'Wife, you will be the death of me.'

'Ha! I will be the one watching your back. We've been over this, Rollo. For better, for worse, remember?'

He gave in. 'We can come back this way, once we have the information Melville wants. Spend a little time with your friends.'

She stretched onto her toes and kissed his cheek; she loved that he was willing to fight his over-protective impulses for her sake. 'We will work together, sweetheart. And I have my own responsibilities.'

'Well, I can at least coddle you for the next few days.'

'Mmm, that would be delightful. Thank you.'

He kissed her slowly. 'It will be my pleasure. I've learned it's important to make time for the people we love.'

She slid a hand over his cheek. 'It is the most important lesson.'

'I had the best teacher.' He smiled and pulled her close. 'From the moment we met, I knew something would happen, but I've realised how much poorer my life would be, if I had not met you here.'

Marian glanced over at the oil drums and fuel logs stacked under a tarpaulin and shivered. 'You saved my live over there.'

It was truer than she'd realised at the time. She had been flirting with danger, looking for an anchor and a purpose. Now she had both, plus a love she hadn't imagined was possible.

Rollo touched his forehead to hers. 'We saved each other.'

'I love you, Rollo Rahgstadt. I don't believe I've mentioned it today.'

A smile lit up his face, then he looped her arm over his and turned to where their trunks were being loaded onto the back of a unicarriage.

'I love you too, sweetheart. Welcome home.'

Author's Note

Melanie Page

When we finished *Iron Heart*, MC and I were giddy with delight. We had finished. Our story was great, and we were ready to move on to other projects. We considered writing a short story involving Marian, the young lady from the Somerton workshop … but before we knew it, the story had morphed into a sequel.

We started reading and researching. MC had an idea about a Russian and an assassination during the American Civil War, which fitted nicely with our timeline. I looked into what the Russians were up to and came upon a fact that, quite frankly, amazed me. In 1863/64, the Russian Navy wintered in New York Harbor and also in San Francisco.

I was astounded, and that event became a must-have feature in the story. Other facts came to light too, like the ironclads being built in a British shipyard for the Confederacy. (Yes, they were real, but no, they didn't sail. Chalk one up to Rollo.) Russia and Britain had, only a decade earlier, fought the Crimean War. But tensions still existed, and Russia was concerned that Britain might blockade their ports and trap them, so they'd left. America, the Union, welcomed them with open arms, seeing it as a show of solidarity against the Confederates. They even held balls for the Russian Officers!

Also, when I discovered that the great Arthur Conan Doyle was alive in Edinburgh at my time of writing, I felt compelled to include him and his father. Many of the facts about Doyle senior, such as his address, are true. I was delirious with joy when, at the prompting of MC's muse (not my decision, I assure you), Marian gave the child, Arthur, her fairy light. It was perfect, given Doyle's later connection with fairies at the bottom of the garden.

At this point, I should apologise to all those who like their history plain and unadorned. I might have tinkered a teeny bit with historical personages, using them in our world where it better suited our story. As a historical purist, I was careful to maintain the appearance of accuracy, but there was one major deviation—Isambard Kingdom Brunel was, in fact, dead at this point in history. In my defence, I would like to point out that steampunk is part of the science fiction and fantasy genre, and the Iron Universe series is set in an alternate timeline. Why shouldn't the great Brunel get another lease on life?

When our hero, Rollo, showed up in Edinburgh, his first act was to rescue Marian. And when he opened his mouth, he was an American. What was a New Yorker doing on the Edinburgh docks? Finding out was great fun. He is also another character who is granted an improved life. When Beauden Somerton replaced the lost prothesis with an arm that is integrated into his very bone and nerves, Rollo sees it as a miracle. And it's a real miracle that is happening today. There is work just as incredible, and not in any way science fiction, going on right now. The name of the professor who made Rollo's arm possible was inspired by a real professor, working in the same field. To all the wonderful doctors out there who do so much good, who take what was once only in the realms of fantasy and use it to improve lives, we humbly salute you.

Naturally, there is a lot of our own interests in people and history in there. MC fell in love with Balmoral. The Empress Eugenie of France made a wonderful character—I have had a lifelong fascination with her—and she would eventually spend her long exile in England. And, of course, we couldn't go to America during the great cataclysm that was the Civil War without meeting Abraham Lincoln. The inclusion of the theatre (though not the same one where he would be shot sixteen months later) and the surname of the final assassin were pure indulgence on my part.

But, as MC was frequently forced to point out during the writing process, 'This isn't a history book, Mel.' It's fiction—a melange of steampunk, espionage, medicine and romance. It's a very different book to *Iron Heart*, the first book in the Iron Universe series, which is a medical romantic suspense.

We began the book with Marian, who had a walk-on part in *Iron Heart*, but one who we felt might have an interesting backstory. And did she ever! She is like a phoenix, disguised as a plain drab wren. But when MC put the first keystrokes down, she threw off her borrowed plumage and revealed herself to be gorgeous. She is an independent Scottish lass, with red hair and green eyes, who not only worked for the Somertons—*Iron Heart*'s main characters—by day but played cards for money (and thrills) by night. How was she going to react to the challenges that would come her way?

One of the issues both Marian and Rollo faced was their openness to love. Rollo cannot afford love; his world is pure peril. Marian lost both parents, and though she loves her workmates, she is essentially alone. She has amazing abilities, too, that she could never acknowledge as a young woman in a restrictive society. Nothing is more natural that she should fall in love with Rollo; and it follows that she should fear the inevitable loss of that love and seek to protect herself from it.

So, what's next in the Iron Universe series? We have another two books in the pipeline. One will follow loyal Will Ayre, who had been at death's door when he first met Beauden Somerton. He is now a skilled limb-maker and an ideal hero, looking for purpose (and for love, though he doesn't know that yet). The other will feature the enigmatic Detective McIntyre who first appeared in *Iron Heart* and is badly injured in *Iron Fist*. Each of these characters demanded stories of their own, and we are excited to have the chance to tell them.

About the Authors

Hi, I'd like to introduce myself. One of my pen names is … tada … you guessed it, MC D'Alton. And I have a passion for telling stories and daydreaming.

I love dark characters and have an oddly macabre soft spot for Frankenstein. I've always been drawn to the darkness in a character. Why are they the way they are? Is there any good inside them? And if so, what do I have to do to find it, love it, and make it shine?

Soon enough, the idea of a romance starring a monster as the love interest began to bloom. Melanie, a dear writing friend, my Iron Universe co-writer and fellow BookBaybZter, asked that special question: 'How could any sane person fall in love with a monster?'

And so, the wheels were set in motion, the story began to unfold and the *Iron Universe* was born!

Hi, I'm Melanie. In a story eerily similar to Clark Kent's, I come from far, far away, but I've lived in the same leafy shire for the last forty-something years. To preserve the secret of my true identity, as a writer of tender and articulate regency romances, I hold down a day job teaching English at a local high school. I am generally considered to be a useful source of irrelevant trivia and obscure words.

I've written and invented stories for my own amusement for a long while. In 2014, I went out on a limb and published *An Affair of Honour*. Little did I know it, but I had opened the lid on a can of awesome, and now there's no putting it back.

Find us at: bookbaybzblog.com.au